End of the Line

Treasure Hernandez

www.urbanbooks.net

Urban Books, LLC
97 N18th Street
Wyandanch, NY 11798

End of the Line Copyright © 2016 Treasure Hernandez

ISBN 13: 978-1-62286-726-4
ISBN 10: 1-62286-726-2

First Trade Paperback Printing October 2016
Printed in the United States of America   .

10 9 8 7 6 5 4 3 2

*This is a work of fiction. Any references or similarities
to actual events, real people, living or dead, or to real
locales are intended to give the novel a sense of reality.
Any similarity in other names, characters, places, and
incidents is entirely coincidental.*

Distributed by Kensington Publishing Corp.
Submit orders to:
Customer Service
400 Hahn Road
Westminster, MD 21157-4627
Phone: 1-800-733-3000
Fax: 1-800-659-2436

End of the Line

by

Treasure Hernandez

CHAPTER ONE

The always ambitious duo thought they could grow up, then blow up being big-time rappers. Maybe owning an NBA team to opening up the city's first drive-through strip club, they were always huddled together scheming about this or that since junior high. Unfortunately, Mike Mike and Jessica were known to dream big and fail hard. For him, those failures were sometimes more than he could stand. His spirit would be broken for days, if not weeks. On the flip side of the coin, Jessica was entirely different. Determined to succeed, she never once looked at anything they'd try or plot up on as a disappointment. If it didn't pan out, the hustle-minded female considered it merely a slight obstacle in the way of getting money or the come up she craved. When the struggling young couple first decided to move in together years ago, they thought it would be all smiles and cotton candy. Jessica was working part-time at the movie theater while taking a night class at the community college. It was minimum wage, but as long as they were together that was all that initially mattered to her. The struggle was real, but it was theirs together.

Mike Mike had dropped out of school in the eleventh-grade; just because. Jessica knew his mild case of dyslexia was holding him back, and he'd given up. Not judgmental, she accepted him as he was. Jessica knew if she did her part and her man did his, no paper diploma mattered; just the bills being paid at their "love nest."

Mike Mike started off good like most young men his age. Not prideful, he was working at Burger King on the day shift. Wanting to stay up all hours of the night, of course he lost his job because he was always late clocking in. Still young in the head, the youth wanted to smoke weed and do whatever whenever he wanted. Even if it meant they starved, the budhead still chose weed.

With bills beyond past due and no other place to lay her head, their situation had become dire. Out here on her own, she had no family to turn to if evicted. It would be the streets or a shelter, neither seeming appealing to the young girl. Jessica was overwhelmed with her life and the way it was going. The clock was ticking on a definite eviction as she cried herself to sleep one late-summer night.

Mike Mike, however, played his new game without a single care in the world. As the hours seemed to drag by, restless, she tossed and turned, worried enough for both of them. With a new attitude in tow, Jessica emerged the next morning as J-Rite; a down-for-that-life bitch, swearing to herself she'd never go hungry or be broke again. Fuck the world and Mike Mike as well if he didn't like it.

"Look, now, I already done told you this more than once. Real talk, if you think a pretty young bitch like me just gonna sit around and not get that money, you dumber than your best friend's brother I just fucked!"

Mike Mike paused his video game. His hands started to tremble. Dumbfounded, he thought he must've been in a dream. He had to be. What else could be the reason for what was happening; what he thought he'd heard. "Hold up! Say what now? I ain't hear you right. Matter of damn fact, I *know* I didn't." He couldn't believe the words he thought were coming out of his supposed woman's mouth.

"Whatever, boy," J-Rite nonchalantly waved her hand. Dismissing him back to the television where his attention always stayed focused on, she kept doing what she was doing.

It was Detroit. And times were tight in their household like everywhere else in the crime-ridden city. The couple struggled and paid bills—well, she did. Mike Mike, uneducated in the books as well as the streets, sat back. He knew Jessica aka J-Rite was worshipping that center stage pole almost every night at the club. And it was no huge secret she'd sell her ass to random motherfuckers every now and then at the end of the month to make ends meet. He'd come to terms with that awhile back. He claimed he didn't like it, but dealt with it just the same. But this right here was some other type of bullshit she'd just casually blurted out. Some type of disrespectful on another level type of shit. Some shit that was gonna get her head knocked clear off her perfectly framed body. "Yo, I'm sorry," he hissed, tossing the X-Box controller onto the coffee table and standing up. "But what the fuck did you just say? See, I know I must be buzzing off these trees and whatnot."

"You heard me, crazy!" Jessica was more than fed up with the mini-interrogation on what she did with "her pussy" the night before. Caught heavy in her emotions, she posted up standing her ground.

"No, the fuck I didn't! Repeat yourself!"

"Yes, the fuck you did, so don't play with me. I ain't got time for it!"

"Well, guess what? You better make time," he demanded, staring at her from across the room with malice. Knowing he wasn't hearing things, his night had taken a drastic turn. Seconds ago, he was on the sixth level of his game and feeling high as two kites. Now he had heard his girl say the unimaginable. Now he had to get her all the way together.

"Mike Mike," she cruelly smirked going in for the kill, "your sorry ass sits around this raggedy motherfucker all goddamn day waiting for me to bring Christmas home, then get mad when I do. Where they do that at? Oh yeah, in *my* house where *I* pay *all* the bills and make shit all good." Jessica sucked her teeth with a fierce attitude showing no remorse or shame in her scandalous actions. "You got the game all twisted. Well, at least with me you do—so beat it. I ain't trying to go there with you!"

"Fuck all that you talking about, Jessica! Did you just say you hit Buzzy wannabe kingpin ass off last night, or what? Is *that* what you said? I swear to God is *that* what the fuck you just said or naw?"

"Yeah, and so what? Damn," she rolled her neck while giving Mike Mike the serious side eye.

"Yeah, and so what this, you ho." Wasting no more time with the back-and-forth word game, Mike Mike was beside himself. With ease, he leaped over the coffee table ready to go berserk. Knocking the controller, his beer, a dirty plate, and some weed onto the floor, Jessica wasn't ready. Running up on the feisty-mouthed female, the fact she didn't flinch made him even madder.

"Ain't nobody scared of you, boy. You ain't gonna do jack shit to me so you best fall all the way back with that drama."

Raising his hand high, Mike Mike brought it slamming down. After two or three smacks across her face, he strong-armed and yanked Jessica up against the wall. Defiant, she was a trooper refusing to shed a tear. In the midst of his physical tirade, he couldn't cope with what she'd said. "Damn, girl, for real, though? How you gonna play me with my fam outta all the tricks in Detroit? You's one straight foul bitch! I should kill your ass right here. I swear, I should choke the dog shit outta you!"

Despite his visible wrath, she coldly dismissed his overly dramatic threats of murder and obvious hurt feelings. "Boy, bye. That's *all* you got? You slap a bitch just like you fuck—weak as hell! And if you kill me, how you gonna survive? You ain't got no hustle in you. Your whack ass ain't got no game whatsoever." Used to putting dudes in their place at the club when need be, she gave Mike Mike a few more swift back-to-back blows to his already-bruised ego. "And let's not forget, Negro, I put food on the table. My pretty ass pay that electric bill that game my cash paid for is plugged into, so—"

"What the fuck ever, Jessica." His voice got louder as his grip tightened, and he overlooked the last statement she'd made. "So is that where ya' stankin' ass was when I kept calling you last night to bring me some food—was it? Tell me, bitch—tell me! Was it?"

"Boy, get on with that, calling me on some damn Obama minute phone you got for free off the corner. And got the nerve to be asking for food. Noncontract-having Negro. Boss ya' life up, Mike Mike. Damn, do something other than play that game and smoke weed."

"What, Jessica? Who in the fuck you think you talking to?" His manhood, already in question, had suffered yet another serious blow, to say the least. Using all the brute force he had, Mike Mike shoved her small frame into the wall. As tiny pieces of paint chips dropped to the floor, Jessica was unmoved in spirit. Repeating the rough tactic a few more times, he saw he had yet to make her cower. "You talking to me?"

"Yes, Mike Mike. You nigga, you! Now get your damn hands off me and pray to God you ain't put no marks on my face. I gotta work later, and it's supposed to be a lot of money in the building tonight! And if you make me miss out on one damn penny because my face ain't looking right, then . . ." Even though she was small for her age, Jessica could take a punch better than most men. Abandoned by her mentally deranged mother when only six, Jessica was hard as steel. She had to be. Raised in foster home after foster home, she'd been abused, not only sexually, but physically, as well. When it came down to it, she trusted no one in the world; sometimes, not even herself. J-Rite did have one brother named Hutch, short for Hutchinson, she used to hang with from time to time growing up, but he got brutally killed by the police. After his untimely death, she, or her attitude toward life, was never quite the same. Knowing another day was never promised, Jessica was definitely cutthroat, the way Detroit raised most of its kids to be.

Infuriated in his feelings, Mike Mike was not ready to let what Jessica claimed to have jumped off go that easily. A bruised ego Mike Mike went in even harder. His wrath intensified. Squeezing his girl's neck, his voice grew louder. "Fuck your face, bitch, and matter of fact, fuck your life! Ain't jack shit sweet around this way. Me and Buzzy's brother is best friends, and you gonna just say y'all did it? And I'm supposed to be like, so what? I'm good with it? You gonna mess around and make me skull drag ya' ass all around this motherfucker!"

"You drag me? Imagine that bullshit! What you need to do is man up and stop tripping. He had some money to spend, so he was good to go. I already told you my car need a new water pump and front brakes, so that's that. The club pay was slow the last couple of days, so yeah— *bam;* somebody had to sponsor paying the mechanic. And I know it couldn't be your sorry X-Box-playing ass." Prying his hands from her throat, Jessica, hard core, didn't skip a beat. "Besides, you smoking the weed his money bought and drinking an extra beer he had in the backseat of his truck where we banged at, so ummm . . . Yeah, get over it; kick rocks!"

"What! So it's like that?" Mike Mike glanced over on the floor where the empty bottle was laying. Feeling like he'd slow swallowed the devil's homemade brew, he wanted to throw up. He wanted to murder both Buzzy and her.

"It's just like that. You heard me. What's done is done. Shit, I was tired of banging that greasy mechanic for fixing my ride, and he was tired of not getting cash," Jessica nonchalantly popped off about bartering with her cat. Unfazed by the impromptu lightweight beating, she finally snatched away, casually strolling toward the bathroom. "Now, like I said, get the fuck over it, clean that bullshit up, and go grab my damn bag!"

"Your fucking bag?"

"Yeah, fool, my fucking bag. The game don't stop around here for me."

"The game?"

"Yes, Mike Mike, *the game!* Money talks and real bullshit walks!"

"J, you's real shady with your shit. Ratchet as fuck. You gave Buzzy the pussy; *my* pussy! I mean, you acting like this a joke or something."

"What's a joke," Jessica paused with more attitude than when he'd just had his hands around her throat, "is you talking about having a roof over my head, eating, drinking, buying what I need when I need it. You talking about that? Naw, you couldn't be. See, I'm gonna have all that and more one day, so that can't even be what you mean!"

"Yeah, what the fuck if I am?" Mike Mike was more in his feelings now than when J-Rite didn't come home for two days saying she unexpectedly went on a trip with some of her girls. "And do Derek know about the messed-up shit you did with his brother?"

Jessica smirked at the question before she replied. "I mean Derek was most definitely down at the club last night for a little while with Buzzy, so probably. But if you asking was he actually in the truck watching us get down or giving blow-by-blow commentary on every gulp, twist, and turn, naw, he wasn't."

Mike Mike felt like he'd been sucker punched in the stomach. "I swear I can't believe you ain't got no type of filter. You crazy like that damn sick-in-the head mother of yours was and Hutch! Not giving a fuck must run deep in all y'alls bloodline!"

"Come on now and miss me with all that shit about my family, dead or not. Play your position, Mike Mike, before you don't have no position to play. I mean, you wanna eat steak tomorrow, don't you? And smoke free weed, that good Kush?"

"Say what?"

"Yeah, nigga; well, I don't see your ass running back out to get another job since Burger King. I mean, shit, McDonald's hires every day too. Collect some empty bottles or some scrap metal or something . . . damn." After a few seconds of dead silence, Jessica laughed taunting "her man" even more as she combed through her weave with her fingers. "Yup, that's what the hell I thought, fool; crickets around this motherfucker! You ain't trying to do shit but what you doing—living off of me. When I did all those parties a few months ago, back to back, you used to come have my back and make sure niggas didn't get too wild with it. But now, you just like forget me, so I'm like forget you too."

"So okay, that's it, huh? You gonna go to work like you ain't just tell me that dumb bullshit about my best friend's brother; me and him practically grew up together." Lighting a Newport to calm his nerves, Mike Mike was still infuriated. *This stankin' bitch! This dirty ho!* He paced the floor in denial. He couldn't believe what he'd just found out. His woman and Derek's brother had smashed—committing the ultimate hood betrayal.

Jessica had just about enough as she was willing to take from a person who added nothing to her life and brought nothing to the table. As far as she was concerned, if he didn't want her being out in them streets and doing what she did, he'd step off wit' that judgmental crap. "All right, Mike Mike, well, let's just say I kept it in the family and kept that shit moving. I'm doing me all the way."

"Bitch." His one-word reply could be heard clear down at the other end of the block.

Standing in front of the mirror, she applied makeup on her slightly red face. Jessica couldn't help but laugh once more before she set the record straight. "Look, crazy, I don't know what in the hell you want me to say. You ain't just meet me, playboy. I dance, and I sells this kitty cat. That's who I am and what I do. Now, what part of that don't you understand?"

CHAPTER TWO

It was nearing one in the morning. Mike Mike had been sitting on the couch in close to the exact same position for hours. Not having turned back on his X-Box or the music, he sat stunned. Still in a state of shock over what his girl and best friend's brother had done, the high he'd been on before Jessica came home dropping the bombshell confession had long since worn off. Left in a completely sober mind-set, Mike Mike was lost in his thoughts about the woman he'd loved since she'd moved on the block. Not to mention the betrayal by Buzzy, whose brother Derek and he had been through hell and back. Feeling as if he could actually hear his own heart breaking into a million pieces, part of him wanted to die. Out of desperation wanting to at least hear her voice, he reached for his cell placing a call to Jessica. After allowing it to ring three times, he quickly hung up before the voice mail clicked on. Trying to call a few more times, Mike Mike did the same thing; ended the call prior to hearing the long drawn-out greeting. It wasn't that he didn't want to leave a message for the female that had caused him to cry, because he did. It was the sad fact, as Jessica had so cruelly pointed out, that he had a government phone; a government phone that was extremely low on minutes. Having exhausted the majority of the 250 allotted minutes trying to call his girl the evening before, Mike Mike was being cautious as well as smart. From past experiences, he'd learned what kind of diarrhea of the mouth he'd have to endure from Jessica if she happened to call late at night after her shift and not be able to get in touch with him. In her eyes, it was one thing if she didn't pick up when he called her. Yet, let the shoe be on the other foot, it would be utter hell for Mike Mike to pay.

Finally getting himself somewhat emotionally together, he stood to his feet. Taking stock of the way the interior of the house looked thanks to his tirade, he decided to keep himself busy. Flipping the coffee table right side up, the shattered-soul youth fought not to shed any further tears. Having gotten a few plastic grocery bags from underneath the kitchen sink, he collected trash, empty bottles, and other items off the living-room floor. Moving in silence, Mike Mike thought of different ways to seek revenge, especially on his girl. Nonetheless, they all ended up with him being without the one thing he desired the most: Jessica.

As he cleaned praying for his beloved to call him, the unthinkable occurred. It was a knock at the door. Snatching his cell phone off the dining-room table, Mike Mike saw it was now close to two o'clock. Shaking his head in disbelief, he knew it couldn't be who he thought it was. Since Jessica had been dancing, Derek had been falling through late night to play the game, smoke weed, and talk shit. However, Mike Mike knew good and well his best friend did not have the nerve to show up at his front door—not tonight—not after knowing his brother had been banging his woman the night before. He felt his blood boiling, staring at the locked door. He was outraged. How could he not feel that way? Out of all the different women in the city he could have picked to get some ass from, Buzzy had picked Jessica, and Derek knew about it. Whether his woman was a willing participant or not, the unforgivable deed was still unscrupulous in Mike Mike's book. To say that Derek's older brother crossed the line would be an understatement.

Now it was time for Mike Mike to let his true feelings be known. He was devastated and ready to be heard. Taking the janky .38 revolver out from underneath the cushion of the love seat, hurt soul, he vindictively headed toward the door. Each step he took was packed with a heavy foot of resentment. Easing over to the window, the beige-colored blinds were moved slightly over to the side to get a better view. It was him. *This fake-ass backstabber got the nerve to really show the hell up like he ain't cross me.* Not hard to spot, he saw the tail end of Derek's car parked in the driveway.

With haste, Mike Mike swung the front door of the small wooden frame bungalow wide open. The pungent smell of the disinfectant products he'd been cleaning with rushed out the door into the night air. With both feet planted firmly in the threshold of the dwelling, Jessica's man disappointedly leered at his ex-best friend. Shaking as he spoke, his words were deliberate and full of malice.

"Are you serious, dude, or what? I mean, what the fuck you doing over here at my crib? I can't believe your rotten-snake ass!"

Derek was high as two kites. He'd been on a drinking and smoking binge all evening; however, he easily recognized the heat in his homeboy's tone. Being born and raised in the hood, it wasn't hard to miss the ghetto fever Mike Mike was throwing in his direction. After taking in account his friend's verbal shade, Derek looked downward. Squinting his weed-weary eyes, he momentarily froze. Not sure of what he was seeing, the inebriated visitor rubbed his bloodshot pupils to ensure he was not dreaming.

"Yo, Mike Mike, my nigga. What's the deal with you? Are you high? Are you gone off some of them pills we had the other day? I mean, you bugging. Why you got that thang out?"

Taking a few steps backward, Mike Mike lived in the celebration of revenge. The element of surprise was definitely on his side. With his chest stuck out, he vindictively raised his right arm. Unlike Derek, he was far from being under the influence of any substance, liquid, pill, or otherwise. What Mike Mike was feeling was raw, uncut, unfiltered human emotion; none other than betrayal in its worst form. He'd been violated, so man code universal wide dictated he returned the disrespectful favor. With deliberate aim, Mike Mike pointed the hairline trigger firearm directly at Derek's face.

Instantly, Derek's confused expression switched to terror as he tried to prevent the surprise confrontation from escalating any further. "Yo, Mike Mike, for real, though . . . Why you pointing that thang at me? What's the deal? What, you and Jessica got into it again? What's the deal?"

"Don't say her fucking name, my nigga; don't. I'm dead ass right now." Deep off into his feelings, Mike Mike set Derek on fire with his eyes, meaning exactly what he'd just demanded.

"Huh?" Derek flinched up, still trying to slow his friend down from pulling the trigger.

"Yeah, come on, dawg, don't come around here playing the role. This ain't what you want right about now. I swear it ain't."

"Mike Mike—"

"You think I'm bullshitting or something? You already know what it is. You know what time it is. That was some real slimeball bullshit you cosigned on."

"Mike Mike, hold up, boy," he pleaded, wanting mercy.

"Naw, slick, I swear on my dead peoples, I thought we was better than that! We been through hell and back since day one, and you gonna go out like that? Damn, dude, you got me all the way twisted; then coming around here knocking on the door like we still a hundred with it!"

It rapidly became apparent there was no calming the escalating situation down. Realizing it was a mere seconds away from things popping all the way off, instinctively, Derek lifted his forearm in some magical attempt to shield the impromptu bullet play attack from occurring. He knew he had to think fast if he didn't want to feel the burn of a bullet and risk prematurely meeting his Maker. With huge beads of perspiration dropping from his brow, Derek knew he had to make his move before Mike Mike got even more amped up and went for his own. Working with limited space on the porch and few options, the time was now.

Getting out of Dodge, Derek shook off his fear as he dove head-first clean over to the other side of the porch. Roughly scraping the side of his face against the weather-beaten concrete windowsill, he sought refuge behind an old lawn chair, praying Mike Mike wouldn't let loose. As blood started to leak down from his injured cheek, he once again tried to get some understanding. "Dude, what in the fuck is wrong with you? You straight bugging pointing that shit at me! You know that throwback joint ain't right. Damn, fam, chill!"

Furious, Mike Mike stepped all the way out of the doorway and onto the porch. Gun still drawn, he was in street-soldier stance ready to do battle. "Naw, Derek, I ain't bugging; not at all. And it ain't no more of that fam bullshit jumping off; at least, not from me. That's dead!"

Derek knew he was on the verge of getting his ass handed to him; that much was obvious. With his best friend holding a gun and nowhere to go, his heart raced and his lips turned dry. Of course, he'd blown any amount of high he'd had still circulating throughout his system since originally knocking on Mike Mike and Jessica's door. Rambling, Derek nervously continued trying to talk his way out of whatever was troubling Mike Mike. Unfortunately, it didn't seem to be working in his favor. His longtime road dawg was livid. In reality, Derek knew that Buzzy had given Jessica some dick the night before, but he honestly believed her actually dry snitching them out to his manz was out of the question. As he perched defensively behind the chair, he couldn't fathom his boy's wifey would be so ballsy, reckless, and out cold to do that dumb shit. The odds of that seemed zero to none, so he was lost where this sudden rage from Mike Mike was coming from.

"Dawg, what is you doing? What is you saying? I'm outta the game with what's the deal with you and all this!"

"Shut the fuck up, Derek. That con game you be running out here on these hoes ain't about to work on me. I ain't one of your little bitches or Jessica's good dick-sucking ass!"

"Whoa, guy! Slow your damn roll. What the fuck is you talking about? What you trying to say?" he continued, attempting to put a cap on the growing resentment Mike Mike was displaying toward him.

More than agitated with the innocent act his boy was putting on, he walked closer to Derek, gun still aimed. "Look, dude, stop trying to play me for some lame. The way I see it, you got a few of these slugs coming, if not all these bad boys. Nigga, I owe you that much, don't you think?" Bombarding his once best friend with questions, Mike Mike revealed what he knew to be true before waiting for a response. "Come on now, guy. Stop playing dumb. How was that pussy? Was it good? Did she suck your brother's dick or what? You can tell me! Did he bust in my woman's mouth? Did she slow swallow his damn nut? Huh? Did she? I mean, I know how Jessica gets down, so I can already imagine she blessed his sneaky ass real proper!"

At that precise moment in time there was no denying the truth. There were no further confusing thoughts about what was going down on that porch in the wee hours of the morning. Derek now knew, fact for certain, Mike Mike had discovered Buzzy had sex with old girl. He didn't know how he knew, but with a janky trigger pistol waving in his face, playing Twenty Questions was not at the top of his list; living to see daylight, however, was. *Damn, this crazy fool knows my brother hit Jessica's hot ass off last night. How in the entire fuck did he find that shit out? I know she ain't said nothing. Fuck, damn, shit! Maybe somebody saw us. But who in the hell? Damn! Fuck, this nigga all up in his feelings and shit. Waving that damn gun around like he done lost it.*

Derek's mind was racing a mile a minute. Peeking out from behind the lawn chair, he saw his homeboy's face. It had murder plastered all across it. At this point, there was no way Derek felt he could explain what'd taken place. What could he say other than the fact that his brother knocked Jessica off because she always looked like she had some good pussy. Or they was drinking and Buzzy said he felt like getting his dick sucked. Maybe he could confess the truth to his best friend that they'd stopped by the strip club Jessica danced at and she cut off into Buzzy first. That she negotiated a price lower than he was willing to pay because she was just as hungry to taste his nut as he was willing to let loose in her mouth.

Whatever he did or said from this point on, Derek knew his life was on the line. Not in denial, he knew how much his best friend loved Jessica. Despite her tramplike ways and sexual treachery antics, Mike Mike felt she was some sort of low-income princess that could do no wrong. He had to make this good. "Okay, nigga. I ain't gonna lie. Me and her was smoking some weed; some of that Kush from around the way. Her and my brother was both buzzed and some dumb shit jumped off. I know it was messed up. The minute they left—"

"And *what,* motherfucker?" Mike Mike sinisterly leered wanting to fire a few rounds off into his boy's head now more than ever. "What you about to tell me about my damn girl? I'm begging you, please tell me!"

Before Derek could get a chance to respond and plead his case, he got an abrupt reprieve. Like a gift bestowed from God, an old-school Malibu with rims roared down the dark block. Distracted by the thunderous sound of rap music blasting from the speakers, Mike Mike briefly looked away from his otherwise intended target. Seizing the moment, Derek leaped over the rusty railing. No sooner than both feet touched the pavement he took off. Darting down the driveway toward the backyard, Derek prayed Mike Mike wouldn't shoot. Making it safely behind a dilapidated garage, he exhaled. He was pissed off that he was suffering the backlash of his brother, not even him getting some pussy from Jessica. As he tried to figure a way to get his car out of the driveway without Mike Mike making good on his promise to shoot him, Derek knew this night was going to have life-lasting consequences.

CHAPTER THREE

"No doubt, you been doing your thing tonight, J-Rite. The crowd is loving your little ass. In between me and you, we making all the money in this motherfucker. Of course, them bitches was hating hard every time you went back in VIP, but what else is new?"

"Right, girl, who you telling? If these local birds spent as much time hustling these dudes, they could get they own revenue count up. They need to stay outta me and your business, and, of course, Raven's, when she here. One day, they gonna learn we three here to make money not fucking friends," she loudly announced in the semiempty dressing room, hoping a dancer would be brazen enough to try her. "Either hoes step they game up or step off. I'ma stunt any way it go. I got bills to pay and tricks to lay."

Out of all the dancers, waitresses, and other staff working at Bare Faxx, Wild Child and her old school-mate Raven were J-Rite's only friends in the club. When it came down to it, she could halfway count on both of them if some shit popped off. Like hood birds of a feather, the money hungry three started at the less-than-upscale strip club a few months back. Renegades from a rival spot that'd mysteriously burned to the ground, they were despised. Each of the club's regular dancers would be heated when the "greedy do anything for an extra dollar" trio would invade their territory. A thousand times worse than other females gracing the stage, J-Rite and

Wild Child had no limits to what they'd say or do in the chase to get that extra bump. Countless times, the housemother stepped to them both about numerous complaints from colleagues. J-Rite could care less. The more illicit she behaved, the more money cash on the floor. If the others couldn't afford to pay their tip out fee after swinging from a pole all night, that was their problem, definitely not hers. Labeled "easily fuckable" by the customers as well as their coworkers, she was amused. Raven had small children at home to tend to most nights so she could not be at the club 24/7 like Wild Child and J-Rite. However, if there was money rumored to be in the house or some scheme to come up on the floor, she was ready to leave her seeds with their grandmother and be a part of the movement.

"Let's bring to center stage that little bit of hell for your ass. That caramel-colored candy that dissolves in your mouth. That H-I-J for your asses—J-Rite live and in 3D living color," DJ What Up Doe hyped the crowd up more than usual.

Not new to the art of seduction, J-Rite was good at what she did. Not just good; some would say an expert at times. And that made others often mad. True to the streets, she understood a long time back no one could get something for nothing. And you always get what you pay for. While it was not just customary but mandatory to tip the disc jockey, she went beyond the call of duty. J-Rite wasn't a dummy by far. Fully aware of the vast amount of shade being thrown at all times in her direction, it made her go harder. If girls could spread rumors and lies about her throughout the duration of her shift, their missions would be dead-on. One, maybe two, customers a night might believe the hype and choose to spend their money on the next female. Ensuring she had the best music on her playlist, and he'd go all out coaxing the cash to stay flowing, J-Rite not only paid the DJ up front, she'd double his tip—sometimes tripled it.

As the first bars of her two-song set began to play, J-Rite made her way through the multitudes of hands trying to get free feels. Dressed in a metallic gold baby tee barely covering half her tits, she adjusted the matching G-string. She could feel the admiration from the men fill the air. The women, however, dancers and just bitches there to hang out alike, were visibly annoyed.

After using her personal rag dampened with alcohol to wipe down the brass pole, she was ready. Armed with her best moves, J-Rite's hips gyrated in a slow, circular motion. Swinging around the pole, she opened her legs wide, allowing potential pervert row gawkers to get a full look at what she was working with. Seeing various denominations of currency being thrown into the air and up onto the stage only motivated her grind even more. With Wild Child standing guard to ensure no random thirsty dancers or bum-ass busters had any wise ideas about swooping up some cash on the sly, J-Rite made her way to the top of the pole. Wrapping her strong inner thighs and lower legs tightly in place, her fingers unlocked from their grip. As she allowed her upper torso to drop backward, the rowdy crowd erupted. Embracing the flashing lights and cheers, the fun-size beauty cupped her bare breasts. Seductively licking her cherry-glossed lips, she then opened her arms so everyone could see her perfect body in all its glory.

Caught up in all the excitement that came along with her sultry performance, Jessica failed to see a set of eyes focused on more than her seminude body. After the second song came to an end, the over-the-top adult performer scrambled around the floor gathering up her tips and the top to her costume. Exiting the stage, J-Rite was immediately met with an onset of admirers wanting special attention and exclusive private dances. Focused on her money, she quickly looked over each person head to toe determining who she thought had the potential to spend the most loot. To J-Rite, cash was king; always was, always would be.

Taking the first winner of the one-song set by the wrist, she started to lead him toward the rear of the strip club where the VIP room was located. Not more than four maybe five yards away, she was stopped dead in her tracks by a guy she was more than familiar with.

"Hey, baby. Dang, two nights in a row? What do I owe this pleasure to?"

"Yeah, girl, what time you breaking out tonight? You staying 'til this thing shut the doors or what?"

"Why? What's good? What you got going on?" J-Rite fired question after question off at Buzzy as her perverted customer took the opportunity to gawk at the jiggling ass he was seconds away from having perched on his lap.

"I got something I wanna give you. Something that's gonna change your life forever," he announced with a crooked grin on his face.

J-Rite's curiosity was piqued. "Change my life? Nigga, what your ass up in this motherfucker talking about? Is you high?"

"Naw, girl, I'm trying to put you on to some real gangstalike game. Now you down or what?" Buzzy held a glass of top-shelf 1738 in one hand and a small wad of cash in the other. Giving Mike Mike's woman the same look he'd given her last night when she blessed him in the backseat of his truck, Jessica realized he was serious.

Leaving from the back door of the club, she had a smile plastered on her face. Oversized dance bag in tow, J-Rite's shift was over. Blessed with having what most would consider a good night, the show didn't stop for Mike Mike's girl. It was a little past 3:00 a.m., and while her dude was at home, probably high, half drunk, and playing video games and still licking his wounds from the blow to his manhood he took earlier, she had her one ready to go. Having no problem with putting in overtime, she was on the chase. Lured with the promise of what she thought was going to be a few more dollars on top of her normal "pay to play" charge outside of Bare Faxx, Jessica's eyes eagerly searched the parking lot. She'd allowed Wild Child to take her vehicle so she hoped this hustle worked out in her favor. Relived, she saw Buzzy flash the high beam headlights from his truck.

The reckless-behavior dancer handed the only security guard that would even speak to her a hot twenty as his tip and took a deep breath. Somewhat tipsy, J-Rite rolled her black bag behind her right side while running her fingers through her hair. Reaching the triple-black SUV, she seductively leaned in the window so Buzzy could get an eyeful of what he was minutes away from paying good money for yet another night.

"Hey, baby, I see you waited for me."

"Yeah, for sure," he replied, turning his radio all the way down so she could hear. "I told you I would. I told you I was gonna change your life tonight, so climb in and let's roll out."

"Yeah, well, we both know what a dude say in the club and out is two different things, especially when the cold night air hits his ass and sobers him up." The sassy tone she was giving Buzzy made him know he'd made the correct choice for what he had in store.

"It ain't no thang, J-Rite. I'm here. I got you. Now, you ain't on no damn curfew with youngblood, is you?"

Jessica laughed, placing her bag in the rear seat where she'd fucked him the night before, then got in the front. "Come on now, Buzzy, it's been a long day. Now stop playing with a tired bitch like me and change my damn life, nigga. I'm waiting!"

Under the assumption they were headed to some hotel on the other side of town to get it all the way in, Jessica leaned back in the plush leather passenger seat getting comfortable. Deciding to not participate much in the small-talk conversation Buzzy was attempting to have with her, she felt her eyelids getting heavy. Fighting sleep was more than a notion as she briefly drifted off.

Finally arriving at what she thought was going to be the room, the eager-to-fuck-to-get-paid J-Rite was thrown off, awakening to the notoriously known East Side street, Bewick. Not wanting to ask questions or appear too nosy, she let Buzzy take the lead, no questions asked. Knowing Derek's older brother was about that life, the also street-raised female got out of the truck at the same time as Buzzy did. A true West Sider to heart, J-Rite wasn't all the way familiar with this part of town. However, she knew any areas located within the city limits of Detroit were not safe to be in, let alone a sitting duck in an expensive SUV. So staying put was not an option.

As she and Buzzy walked up on the porch of the surprisingly well kept duplex, she immediately took notice of the gun he had down at his side. Not having to knock, the door swung open. On the other side of the black steel gated threshold stood not one, but two stocky-built females also brandishing firearms. Still confused about what was about to take place, the brave stripper never flinched and never muttered a word. If she wasn't down for whatever was going to happen after whatever came next, she was putting on a hellava front. Moments later,

Buzzy made the formal introductions using street names; never government.

"Hey, you two, this is my around-the-way homegirl, J-Rite. I'm thinking about putting her on our team. Letting her get a little bit of the black American Dream we trying to live."

One of the women strong stared Jessica up and down from the top of her head full of weave to the bottom sole of her sneakers. Having no problem whatsoever voicing her opinion, she spoke out. "Well, damn, Buzzy, I ain't trying to be funny or second-guess you, but it don't look like she ready for anything but the stage."

"Yeah, man, it's almost four in the morning, and she got on a damn full face of makeup! Where in the entire hell do they do that at?" The other one laughed, giving her partner in crime some dap.

"I'm with her; this chick ain't ready for shit but to catch a couple of flying dollar tips. I mean, she is fine as a motherfucker, but on our team? Naw, Buzzy."

Up until now, J-Rite had been as quiet as a mouse. Fighting the urge to put both women in their place, she casually looked around the foreign domain in hopes of possibly finding a makeshift weapon to use, if need be. As each handed Buzzy rubber banded rolls of money for him to count, they kept ridiculing Jessica's gangster, failing to see what their boy saw in her they were missing.

I swear on everything I love these big-footed hoes is pushing they luck with me. Fuck, I wish Wild Child or Raven was here. We'd manhandle both these bury bears like it ain't jack shit, just like we do at the club. That's what be wrong with these Detroit females with no home training; they think they untouchable. But all it takes is one ruthless and rotten bitch like me to show them life ain't all sweet! I swear, Buzzy got me fucked up over here on this bullshit. Change my life, my pretty ass! He crazy! Seeing how she was at a total disadvantage far on the other side of town, in some random-ass house, getting the once-over by two dykelike bitches waiting for a reason to pounce, Jessica decided it was best to keep her mouth shut and let that disrespectful scene play itself out.

"I see y'all had a great couple of days around here. Shit's really picking up. We should be where we need to be by week's end," Buzzy bragged with his chest stuck out, having ignored all the unwarranted insults and daggers they were throwing at J-Rite.

The female that opened the front door arrogantly smirked, showing the brown-stained bucked tooth that was gapped in her dental. "Yeah, we doing this thing ourself. We don't need no wannabe dressed-up-in-the-face Barbie doll to get on the team. We got this. So you can just take her prissy ass back to that pole she was probably swinging from."

After enduring more than twenty minutes of being spoken about like she was not present, Jessica could no longer hold her well-known fiery tongue. Not caring about being outnumbered by the less-than-feminine goons, she was done. Her gutsy disposition was bursting to get out, and it did. "You know what? A bitch like me is straight tired of you two nothing-ass rats trying to talk down on my ass. Yeah, I know I'm damn near perfect in all y'all's eyes. Hell, yeah, I'm a pretty motherfucker, but so damn what? That don't mean I can't split both of y'all shit clean down to the white meat!" Jessica had once again transformed into J-Rite and was in full effect. "Since I came through the damn door, y'all acting like I asked to come over to this raggedy-ass piece of shit house! Buzzy brought me over here," she shot him the serious side eye while still staying focused on the two bitter haters.

"Now, I don't know what in the hell y'all got going on over in this place besides the obvious; y'all slanging, but here's a newsflash for all three of y'all. J-Rite don't give a fuck! Matter of fact, Buzzy, can you just take me to the crib or do I need to call my girl to come get me? I can wait somewhere up on the corner! It ain't no thang to me one way or another. I ain't got time for none of this petty circus y'all got stirring!"

Buzzy stuck his arm out to stop his two pit bull workers in Nike tracksuits from attempting to physically attack his guest. "Whoa, whoa, y'all, slow down. This is who I wanted y'all to meet; J-motherfucking-Rite in full live color. Not the quiet, laid-back chick Jessica that walked through the door with me, but *her*. This is her *true* self. I'm telling y'all that she is a good fit for the team. Matter of fact, I got something special in store for her that is gonna change the face of our game in the next few weeks to come. Remember, teamwork makes the dream work!"

The two feisty, big-boned women did as demanded, simmering down, as Buzzy stepped up taking control of the increasingly volatile situation he'd seemingly orchestrated. That was the easy part. However, J-Rite was a horse of a different color. The females had pushed her buttons to get a reaction; so now she was posted up to give them one. Fuck Buzzy all of a sudden wanting to intervene. She was hyped up by that time and was not as willing to just let their verbal tirade go unanswered and make shit all good, because it wasn't. Not in J-Rite's book anyhow. For some strange reason, Buzzy wanted to see the true beast in her emerge; well, so be it. There was no putting the genie back in the bottle. Not this time; not this late night, early morning. Do-or-die J-Rite didn't care if she got the brakes beat off her or took one or two or even three of the slugs fired off from the pistols that were now lying on the dining-room table. Foster home raised, strip club bred, and mad at the world for her only bloodline family Hutch having been murdered by the cops, J-Rite was not the pushover they apparently believed her to be. She'd stood silent because she wanted to, not because she had to.

"Look, Buzzy, I don't know what you was trying to do or prove, but I thought me and you was on some other type of shit tonight. This here is messed up all the way the fuck around!"

Wanting to make things right, he dug his hand in his pocket and pulled out some of the money the mouthy women had just given him. Peeling off a couple of hundred dollars, he asked J-Rite to calm down and just hear him out. Like most females, money talks and bullshit walks. Stuffing the cash in her back pocket, she folded her arms waiting to see what his explanation was going to be. Sending the female who initially opened the door out to his truck, she returned with a bottle of Hennessy so they could all have a drink and get down to business. The floor was his. Buzzy claimed he could, would, and was about to change J-Rite's life—so now he had to show and prove.

CHAPTER FOUR

Having had Buzzy take her to get her car from Wild Child, Jessica was caught in the early-morning musical mix blasting on the radio. The sun was up when she pulled up behind Derek's car parked in her driveway. After what she told her man the night before about she and Buzzy banging, the out-for-self diva was surprised Mike Mike would allow his little brother Derek inside the house, let alone spend the night. She assumed their days of playing video games all night and getting high were over. Yet, here the car was, like it was from time to time . . . up in her driveway. *Dang, my dude soft as hell. It damn showl couldn't be me!*

Shaking her head in disbelief, she stuck her key into the deadbolt lock. Not caring one bit if Mike Mike was still caught in his emotions, she strolled through the front door. Finding him knocked out, stretched across the couch, she could only shrug her shoulders. *I got love for this nigga because he used to have my back when I really needed him to. Now, he just who he is; a true lazy lame waiting for me to .get out in the streets and make money. Well, now, he really gonna get his wish.* Her mind replayed Buzzy's life-changing game plan just laid out for her.

Taking notice of the janky pistol they kept in the house resting on the coffee table, Jessica eased over, snatching

it up. It was best for it to be in her possession, just in
case Mike Mike was still in his feelings and wanted to act
a fool. As she put it in her purse, Mike Mike started to
stir. Within a matter of moments, he was awake and sitting up. Watching him raise his hand up to shield small
rays of the sun fighting to get through the closed blind,
she got ready to hear his mouth. He always liked to call
himself going ham on her when she came home at this
time, but so what was her general attitude. Jessica didn't
much care what Mike Mike said or thought one way or
the other. In her book, the person who made the money
made the rules.

"Hey, you up. Where is Derek at? I see his car out there.
I know that fool ain't in our bedroom!"

"Fuck Derek! Fuck him and his damn brother," he
blurted out as he stretched his arms upward.

"So where is he and why—"

"Look, don't ask me nothing about that backstabbing
idiot. Just know it's fuck him; bottom line!"

Jessica was confused as to why a person's vehicle
would be parked in her driveway when there was apparently nothing but fever coming from Mike Mike for the
owner, but whatever. "Look, we can deal with all that
fuck your best friend and Buzzy shit later. I'm on something else now. And, yo, I see you done cleaned up that
mess you made last night, and that's good. But we need
to kick it because I got an opportunity on the floor, and
I'm seriously thinking about it."

"An opportunity?" he quizzed wanting to check her
about what time she'd just come home, but opted not to.
*I know with her it's gonna be some shit a nigga don't
wanna deal with. She keeps my damn head pounding!*

Jessica reached in her back pocket giving Mike Mike
one of the hundred-dollar bills Buzzy had blessed her

with. Tossing him the car keys, she had him go get them some breakfast. Jessica wanted her man to have a full stomach when she broke the news of what she ultimately had in store.

CHAPTER FIVE

"Fuck that, I don't do that credit shit. Beside, I see your ass on the block all the time spending them nickels and dimes with my competition. Now you wanna come over here on that broke tip? Hell, naw, I ain't with that shit," J-Rite angrily barked at the female begging her for free dope. *Fiends always want something for nothing,* she thought, walking over to her home away from home and sat down on the steps. The building was an old mansion that the new landlords turned into efficiency apartments. Thanks to Buzzy and his plans to change her life forever, she'd given up the pole and relocated. Mike Mike wasn't at all keen on what she was doing, not to mention the driving force behind it, but he had no choice. He knew since they were younger Jessica had told him he had to lead, follow, or get the fuck out of the way. Opting for the easiest of the three, he helped his childhood sweetheart pack her bags, even dropping her off in Grand Rapids himself at the address Buzzy had provided. Now it was six weeks later, and she was making her mark getting money in the infamous city located two hours away from Detroit.

J-Rite pulled a White Owl out of her pocket and started rolling her last bag of weed. *Damn, I left my lighter in the house.* Just then, an older addict slow strolled out of the front door of the building. With a pep in his step and a wanna-get-lifted gleam in his eyes, he had broken the number one rule of the game a few years back: don't get

high on your own supply. He was an ex-drug-dealer-trag-
ically-turned-junkie. Sean stood six feet tall, with a wiry
build and a caramel-brown complexion. He had a shaved
face and wore his head bald. With seasoned wrinkles in
his face that read *the streets got the best of me,* you could
still easily tell he used to have the hoes going crazy in his
heyday. He was one of the few customers that Jessica
dealt with she actually liked. Maybe it was because he
was never trying to get over on her. She figured it was
because he'd been in the game himself, so he knew how
stressful things were for her and fought the addiction de-
mons not to be all extra in her sight. "Hey, guy, gimme a
light," she nonchalantly glanced over her shoulder.

He dug deep in his pants pocket handing her a green
lighter with the top torn off. "Here you go, little bit.
Knock yourself out."

After flicking the borrowed flame maker once, then
twice, she got some fire. "Damn, nigga. I almost burnt my
face off; turn this thang down." J-Rite knew it was point-
less to say anything; even though she turned it down to
blaze, he was going to turn it back up. Sean looked at her,
grabbed his lighter, and like most crackheads, walked
off like he didn't have a care in the world. J-Rite took a
puff on the blunt. *I gotta get my shit together and make
some more money. I can't stay up here forever.* She figured that if she hustled small she would stay out of the
way and not be noticed by the police. But as time slowly
dragged by, she missed her old life more and more. Part
of her wanted to ask Mike Mike to come and hang out
with her but knew that wouldn't be in her best interest
or his. She knew it was best just to keep sending him a
few dollars from time to time and let his pill-popping
depressed ass be. Jessica knew if she showed him any bit
of affection, he'd be back tripping. Whenever she would
go by a strip club, it was as if the pole was calling out to

her, but since she was slinging for Buzzy full-time, she'd traded in her moneymaking thong-filled "ho bag" for his "dope bag."

As J-Rite sat on the stairs thinking about what was going on back in Detroit, a midnight-black Durango sitting on 24-inch rims, tinted windows, and music playing loudly swerved up in front of the building. Slamming down on the brakes repeatedly, whoever the driver was attempted to show off, making the SUV rock from side to side.

"Fuck is this," J-Rite hissed while putting her right hand in her hoodie pocket and grabbing ahold of her .380. She knew most of the tenants in the building were her customers. And she knew all their vehicles; at least the ones who were fortunate enough to still own one and had not smoked it away. Bracing up, she readied herself to let loose with her peacemaker, if need be. Up until this point, she had been lucky enough to not go toe to toe with anyone else in the area also slanging, but she had a strange feeling all day long her luck was about to run out. Listening to story after story about this drug dealer and the next, she figured this brazen showboating idiot had to be the latest neighborhood dope man she kept hearing about. At the same time, the music slightly lowered, the driver's window rolled down.

"What up doe, pretty girl?" the driver jubilantly yelled out like they were old friends from around the way.

"Turn that shit all the way down! Fuck wrong with you? Have you lost your damn mind or what?" J-Rite recognized the obnoxious female, taking her hand off her gun. Relieved she didn't have to use the illegal firearm to send anyone to heaven or hell, she walked down the stairs. The closer she got toward the female Buzzy had working the door back at the trap house he'd taken her to, her stomach started to turn. Even though she'd made peace with her and her girl that fateful night, J-Rite still hated the fact he'd send her ratchet pussy-lurking ass up to check on her or collect money when he couldn't.

Asia turned the Durango off and hopped out. She was tan skinned and seemed to be a good eight inches or so taller than Jessica. At least 230 pounds, she definitely outweighed the once-petite stripper. Nevertheless, J-Rite was ready to do the same as she had back in Detroit when dealing with Asia: straight hold her own.

"Damn, pretty girl, ease up. I was just having a little fun; mixing a little business and pleasure. You feel me?"

"Yeah, okay, whatever. Well, when you cop this? Last time you came up here you was pushing a Caddy," J-Rite remarked before taking a half-smoked blunt out of her pocket. She handed it to Asia to show her there were no hard feelings for her checking her behavior, but she refused.

"I'm good on all that. A bitch caught a case, and I gotta drop once a damn week now. And, yeah, I got this last week for my birthday. I needed a come up. A little some-thing something to keep them simple-minded hoes dropping them panties."

"Well, I don't know about all that, but I ain't gonna front; this bitch right! You hooked it up; rims, sounds, the whole nine." The last time they were together they had some words for each other about the ticket being correct, and Buzzy swore she'd never have to deal with her again; yet, here she was. *I wonder what the fuck she doing up here? I hope she ain't come up here on that bullshit,* J-Rite thought to herself watching Asia like a hawk. "So what made you come up this way? It ain't time for me to make no move on that tip," J-Rite finally asked curiously knowing she hadn't gotten the heads-up di-rectly from Buzzy about this, that, or the third.

"Well, J-Rite, to be honest with you, I ain't up here about Buzzy's business. Well, not really. I don't know if you heard or not, but the feds knocked him a few days back, so we done," she sadly announced, dropping her head.

"What! Are you fucking serious? The feds! Hell, naw! You lying!" J-Rite's eyes bucked, and her throat got dry. As her heart raced she immediately became paranoid. Her head twisted from side to side looking around as if the cops were in the bushes waiting to jump out and yell *surprise*, gun and handcuffs in hand.

"Girl, I'm serious as two or three fucking heart attacks. Shit's all bold back home. The streets is going crazy, scrambling around, praying they don't get hit next. Detroit hot as fuck!"

"Damn, Asia! I was damn near ready to re-up in a few days. Shit, this is all the way messed up! Damn!"

Asia's first mind-set was to run game and tell J-Rite that Buzzy had sent her for whatever cash she had to aid in his legal fees. But after picking up for him a few times in the past, the hustler in her whispered into her ear, *Naw, Asia, fuck that short bread. You and this li'l pretty bitch can link up and get some major paper. Fuck the middle man!*

"Damn. So, I mean, why you up here? You just wanted to deliver the bad news in person?" She arrogantly looked her up and down the same way she'd done her the night Buzzy had taken her to the trap house.

"Naw, girl, I got a few other irons in the fire I wanted to kick it with you about. You know . . . a way we can both eat."

Both eat? Bitch, please, I'm already eating! Suspicious over Asia's true intentions, Jessica was interrupted by her cell ringing. *Saved by the fucking bell!* Glancing down at the screen, her mood changed. It was her sister-in-law

Leesa. Immediately, a smile graced her face. Anytime she'd hear from the female that her deceased brother Hutch considered his better half, she was ecstatic.

"What up, girl?" she gleefully asked putting the phone up to her ear.

"Shit, my baby. I've been trying to make a few things happen that would be good for both of us. I bumped into your boy Mike Mike the other day at the weed spot. He told me you had temporarily moved up to Grand Rapids."

"Yeah, you know I'm up the way here in Gun Ru, doing what I do. Detroit was getting kinda dry for me, and you know his crazy ass is lazy as fuck. So I'm done dancing for now."

"Oh yeah?"

"Yeah, fam, I'm making my ends another way."

"Right, right," Leesa signified her li'l homie's statement. "Mike Mike told me something like that. Well, we need to meet up like ASAP. I gotta holla at you."

"Okay, sis; so when you wanna hook up?" J-Rite turned her body slightly around trying to get some privacy from Asia who was blatantly ear hustling.

"Can you meet me in Kalamazoo, at the bus station in about two hours? I got some shit in the oven up there. If not then, let me know when a good time is for you."

"Naw, I'm on point. I can meet you there; no problem. And, yeah, sis, can you grab me some weed too before you come my way?"

"I got you, girl. And thanks for coming to meet up with me."

"Anything; anytime for you." J-Rite hung up the phone, then refocused her attention back to her surprise visitor. "Look, Asia, I gotta shoot this move real quick. But you already know my number, so hit me up later if you still in the city. I know whatever it is will keep."

Not even bothering to wait for Asia to say whether she'd call later, Jessica left the blue jeans sagging, high top sneaker-wearing female standing at the curb. Lost in thought, the suddenly popular-in-demand small-framed boss wondered about what Leesa wanted to talk about. Not totally in the dark, she knew more than likely it was about getting money, because that's what Leesa was all about; that cheese. She was never legally married to J-Rite's brother Hutch, but she and Leesa had still become close every chance J-Rite ran away from one of the many foster homes she was forced to live in. It was hurting J-Rite to know that Leesa had lost the love of her life. She and Hutch had met back when they were in the ninth-grade. The two fell head over heels in love and started living together right out of high school. Leesa had schooled J-Rite about boys and everything else she didn't know or needed to know. Out of all the females she'd encountered over the years, Jessica never had a bond with anyone like the one she had with Leesa. Wild Child and Raven were indeed her road dawgs when it came down to the streets back home, but Leesa was family—streets or not.

Looking forward to seeing a familiar face from Detroit, Jessica headed into her building to at least change her shirt, wash her face, and brush her teeth. She wasn't out in the streets looking unkempt, but she just wanted to freshen up. Only a few feet from the glass door entryway J-Rite heard a voice from behind call out to her. *I know this thirsty dyke ain't still on the curb calling my damn name when I told her I was busy.* Hoping it wasn't Asia being all extra, she turned to see it was another one of her regular customers and drug runners. "Oh, hey. What's up, Rhonda? What's good with you? You trying to get on or what?"

Rhonda, in her late forties, was a hard-core smoker and a certified hustler. If no one else in the neighborhood was going to get high, you could best believe she was. She was down for whatever; whenever; especially if it meant a blast. "Yeah, J, I need a fifty right quick for somebody."

After J-Rite hurriedly served Rhonda, she rushed up to her apartment to get herself together and call for a cab. While waiting, her mind drifted to a terrible dark place, receiving the awful news her brother was dead. Unfortunately, she remembered the tragedy like it was just yesterday.

It was her fourteenth birthday. Jessica was planted on the couch watching a rerun of *Saved by the Bell,* waiting for Hutch to come back from his boy's crib. She'd run away from yet another foster home and at this point, didn't care if she ever went back to the horrid conditions she was forced to live under. All she knew was that by the time this episode was over, her big brother would more than likely be coming through the front door of the house he shared with Leesa bearing gifts. She asked for a few new outfits, a pair of small square diamond stud earrings, and, of course, the new Jordans. She'd suffered and done without so long, even if he returned with just a balloon in hand she'd be thankful. Sure, she'd be disappointed, but thankful just the same that he cared. Their life had not been charmed by far. However, at least they had each other's back as much as possible, even though Jessica was under the state of Michigan's jurisdiction. The impressionable teen didn't particularly like the fact that her only blood was out in the streets, taking penitentiary chances with his freedom, but Hutch was never one to sit by and just let life pass him by. He knew if he, Leesa, and his little sister were going to have any chance at living a decent life, it was up to him. Hutch did whatever he had to do whenever he had to do it; the risk of consequences be damned.

After Jessica's television show went off, another one of her favorites came on. Then that went off as well. Checking the time of her flip phone, she noticed that it was getting late and still no Hutch showing up and showing off. Selfishly as most were at that age, the orphaned teen prayed he was just held up at the mall ensuring she had everything she desired for her special day. She'd never once had exactly what she wanted on her birthday, so she was excited believing this was that day. Camped out on the couch, Jessica soon fell asleep, dreaming about what life could've been if she and her brother were blessed with a mother that was not crazy and had cared enough about them to want to live and make things right.

Seconds turned into minutes and minutes quickly became hours. Startled by the sound of the front door being slammed shut, Jessica leaped to her feet. Wiping a small bit of sleep from the inner corner of each eye, she focused in on Leesa, realizing her usual high-spirited facial expression was not there; instead, it was replaced with one of horror. Jessica knew something was wrong. After watching Leesa fall to her knees and start to wail, she got in panic mode herself. Originally, the day-to-day hustle life naïve Jessica thought Hutch was in jail; possibly had got knocked with a gun and some enormous amount of drugs. Tragically, that was not the case.

After a few minutes of trying to get Leesa to calm down and stop hyperventilating, Jessica was hit with the news. Her big brother, her constant protector, was dead and not coming back. He'd got killed; shot down like a stray dog in the street. Just as hysterical as Leesa was, Jessica had become. She was in denial. She didn't believe it. She couldn't believe it. She started calling Hutch's phone and received his voice mail. Despite pleas from her sister-in-law to stay put and deal with the awful reality of the truth, Jessica bolted outside onto the porch. In tears, the distraught sister rushed to the location her sibling was supposedly at. Face-to-face with yellow crime-scene tape and countless news cameras and residents mulling about, the normally strong willed and strong-minded Jessica broke all the way down. Throwing up all her stomach's contents onto the curb, her life would never be the same. Hutch was gone and never coming back.

The word on the streets was, of course, much different than what law officials claimed. Hood rumor was Hutch was on his way to link up with his peoples when old boy said he needed to holler at him on the 911 urgent tip. Being a stand-up dude everyone could count on if need be, Hutch put his own business on hold. A female visiting inside the house revealed when Hutch arrived, his man acted as if something was off. Something didn't seem right. She confessed to Leesa she, like Hutch, felt the strange tension as well. Their host started acting funny to them both. She told Leesa the guy just broke out in tears repeating that he was sorry. Hutch didn't bother to ask ole boy what he was talking about and just left, she exposed. When he jumped in the car, the police surrounded it. "Girl, he tried to get out and surrender or run; but the police opened fire, murdering him like he wasn't shit to them." She shook her head in utter disgust.

Through multiple cross investigations in the police department as well as the streets, it came out that a couple of dirty on-the-take officers on a task force cut a deal setting Hutch up. Leesa was devastated. She couldn't understand how and why they'd do something so heinous. Livid, she attempted to sue, but the police had planted a gun on Hutch, claiming he tried to open fire so they returned fire in self-defense. Leesa knew her man and knew that was a blatant lie. Hutch never took his gun to meet his connect. He didn't need to, for they were too close for that. The dry-snitching rat who set Hutch up got six months for his cooperation. Ironically, they found him dead in the shower.

Rattled out of her dreadful daydream, J-Rite heard a car horn was honking like there was no tomorrow. Looking out the window, she saw it was her cab. Snatching up her money and gun, she was ready. *Better to be caught with this motherfucker than without it.* She placed it in the small of her back. J-Rite then hopped in the cab and was at the bus station ten minutes later purchasing a ticket.

CHAPTER SIX

J-Rite was awakened by the bus driver shaking her left shoulder. She got off the bus and called Leesa to let her know her whereabouts. "Aye, girl, I just got here. We just pulled into this bad boy. Where you at?"

"Give me about thirty minutes or so and I'll be there. I got caught up in something that need my attention ASAP."

"All right, big sis, no problem. I'm good. Just hit me up when you get here to the station. I'm gonna grab something to eat." Taking a quick inventory of where she was at, she saw a McDonald's and headed toward it. Not being able to get the fact that her connect and friend Buzzy was locked up facing God knows what consequences, she ate her meal thinking of her future. *I know I can get rich up here in this motherfucker. This place a damn gold mine just like Grand Rapid is. If I hustle hard for six months maybe I can get my money all the way up and get out of the game. Maybe I can go back home to Detroit and see if Mike Mike done changed.* Her thoughts momentarily drifted back to her old life. *I know I did him dirty just busting up like I did; but me and him been on two different levels for the last few years.*

After she ate her food she walked back to the bus station and waited. Finally her cell rang. "Yeah, what's up?" J-Rite said, answering her phone.

"Hey, sis, where are you at?" Leesa asked.

"I'm inside the station."

"Well, I'm outside; c'mon, let's ride."

J-Rite walked outside and saw Leesa standing next to a nice sports car sitting on chrome rims. "Damn, girl, I like this." She admired the vehicle while walking over, hugging Leesa.

"Thanks, sis. You know how I do." She winked her eye as they got into the car. After tossing an ounce of weed on Jessica's lap, she informed her they had to make a stop. "We gotta stop and get some blunts. We can go to the store right up the street." They pulled up in the parking lot of the liquor store and parked. "You want something outta here, Jessica?" Leesa asked as they entered the store.

"Yeah, a juice. I'll grab it," she replied, walking to the cooler. J-Rite grabbed her juice and walked to the counter where Leesa was standing.

"Well, damn! How are you doing today, Ms. Lady?" a male's voice from behind J-Rite asked, standing a little too close for comfort.

"Who in the hell is you talking to?" Wanting to stay aware of her surroundings and who had invaded her inner space, with an attitude, she turned to see who it was. Face-to-face with the man, she noticed he was nothing short of gorgeous. She was hoping he was talking to her.

"Stop playing; you know I'm talking to you, with your pretty self. How you doing?"

"I'm fine, and how about you?" J-Rite smiled while trying to look cute still holding her juice.

"I know you fine. That's why I'm trying to see what's good with you." The fact that his pickup line was so cornball made the usually hard-core-disposition J-Rite blush and giggle. "A guy been wanting to holla since you walked in."

"Oh, so you were stalking me? Is that what you do?" she teased with an even bigger smile on her face.

"Of course," he said flashing his dental as well. "I'm Dino, and I'm a stalker of a beautiful woman named . . ." He waited for her to hopefully reveal her name.

"Well, I'm J-Rite."

"Well, can I call you sometime, J-Rite?" he said, staring directly into her eyes.

"Yeah, I guess you can." Dino had hazel-brown eyes. Six feet tall, with a medium build, honey-brown skin, and 360 waves, J-Rite wasted no time telling him her number to lock in his phone after Leesa had paid for their items and they were headed out the door. "Well, Dino, hit me up whenever; I'm around."

"He was a cutie, girl." Leesa said when J-Rite joined her in the car.

"Yeah, he really was. Now, okay, girl, where we headed? Clue me in."

"Well, I want to show you this house I'm thinking about getting. You know me. It's some low-key type of shit, you feel me? Besides, with you not too far away, I think we can lock things down around here. There's money in these streets up here. And real talk, I got a major plug outta this world. We gonna get it in!"

"Dang, Leesa, that would be really freaking boss status shit. I was thinking the exact same thing. You know I'm with you no matter what." *Besides, I need money in a major way, especially since Buzzy is ass fried.* J-Rite thought about the reality that she was almost out of product as she broke down a blunt, then started rolling up some weed. "I'm down for whatever when it comes to getting that money," she proclaimed while lighting the blunt.

"I know; since Hutch been gone, things done changed for you, J-Rite. But trust me, you my girl for real, for real. Matter of fact, forget that; we're family."

"Yeah, we all we got, Leesa. My big brother ain't here, but we always gonna be good."

After Leesa started laying out her plan for them in the weeks to come it became apparent J-Rite was about to be moving in a different crowd and on a much different level in the game than she was in with Buzzy.

"So, okay, sis, you got anybody you wanna bring in with us? Because we gonna be moving a lot of work; I mean a lot! And we need all hands on deck that can be trusted. None of these lames from up here, though."

J-Rite thought for a minute about who she knew wanted to hustle and make money and who wanted to just get paid and showboat. *I could bring in Asia, but that ain't a good idea. She's cut from a different cloth, so she gon' be on that stunna shit and probably make us hot.* After doing another brief rundown off people she could trust, her mind kept going back to the obvious two: Raven and Wild Child. J-Rite knew that Wild Child slanging dope was out of the question. She was true to the game of stripping and selling pussy and nothing more. That left only one choice. "Yeah, I got somebody. It's my homegirl Raven. Remember her?"

"Oh yeah. How's she doing? I ain't seen her in a minute."

"She doing straight. She still be dancing up at the club from time to time, but you know them three kids of hers be slowing down her grind. But trust and believe, if the money's right, that bitch will put in work. Plus, she one of the few people beside you I really truly trust."

As the pair of them drove through the inner city and into the suburbs, Leesa finally crossed over into what seemed like the difference between heaven and hell. "Look around, sis. This is the hood I'm talking about getting the house in."

"Wow, I ain't gonna front. This looks low key for real. Some old cornball movie type shit."

"I told you. And it's a lot of money out here. The people I've been serving all got good-ass jobs. So none of that 'I got a DVD player you can hold until I get paid' bullshit! Straight-up cash and carry."

As J-Rite sat back and peered out the window, she couldn't believe that the people that lived in these houses and drove these nice cars were drug users. This is the life she always wanted: big house, nice car, a family, and less drama to deal with. Yet, here, her dream was tainted. She faced the harsh fact that no matter where you live in the world, drugs, crime, and corrupt behavior would follow.

"This is the house right here," Leesa blurted, bringing J-Rite out of her thoughts. It was a two-story brick house with a yard full of green grass, a white picket fence, a two-car garage, and a long driveway. "So, sis, what you think of the house so far? Nice, right?"

"Yeah, girl. I like it. It's nice."

"Well, I'll know if I'm going to get it in a few weeks. I like it a lot. The real estate agent said I'll probably get it, so we'll see. All I need to do is get with this plug and put the deal he offered all the way into motion."

"Yeah, that sounds like a plan to me." With Buzzy out of the picture as a supplier, Leesa was right on time with her offer. He'd brought her up to Grand Rapids to change her life and inadvertently, he had. *Good luck with jail, boy! See ya and I wouldn't wanna be ya!* J-Rite grinned, thinking about all the money she was promised to be raking in.

CHAPTER SEVEN

Riding around getting high, the two soon-to-be ballers set to take over a new territory pulled into a crowded parking lot.

"So you wanna hit this club with me or what? We might as well celebrate now. Because after we get started, ain't no slowing down."

"Yeah, we can roll. I'm game." J-Rite finished off her tail.

"Now you know they ain't gon' let you in with your gun."

"How you know I got my gun on me?"

Leesa gave her a strange look and laughed. "*Really, girl? You forgot I just ain't meet your wild ass! You my little sister; I ain't yours!*"

"Damn, this place is packed." J-Rite was buzzed looking around at the three-ring circus that was taking place out in public. There were people in the parking lot popping bottles, blowing weed, shooting dice, and just having a good time. *Look at this nigga getting his dick sucked on the side of his car. He must be getting money to get it like this 'cause he ugly as hell.*

They pulled up in valet and got out. After paying the cover charge and getting searched, the duo entered. The interior of the club looked like an old warehouse. It had a huge waterfall in the middle of the floor, with an oversized oval-shaped bar to the side. People were dancing and having what appeared to be the time of their lives as music blasted through the speakers. The elbow-to-elbow crowd was packed like sardines. With drinks accidentally spilling on several women and the pungent stench of a few musty men, the two of them had just about enough of being average.

"Hey, girl, let's go find the VIP section. I can't live like this!" Leesa fanned her face with her hand trying to get some air.

"I think it's upstairs." J-Rite pointed to the carpeted staircase that was roped off from the rest of the club.

When they got upstairs, there was a bouncer looking like a gorilla standing guard in front of a rope. Posted and ready to attack, he looked as if he devoured steroids for every meal. "Yeah, that's a flat fifty for both y'all, and that's because I think your girl cute," he said with a deep, sultry tone while smoking J-Rite over head to toe.

The booth they sat in was close to the corner. A girl in a black skirt, white shirt, and black heels walked up to the table pretending she was happy to be doing her job. "Hello, I'm your waitress for the evening. Can I help you ladies?"

"Yeah, can I get a double shot of Cuervo and a Corona with lemon?" Leesa asked matter-of-factly.

"And how about you, miss?"

"I'll have a double shot of Rémy and a MGD, that's all," J-Rite yelled over the loud-playing music.

The waitress disappeared into the semidarkness getting their drinks. After a few minutes, she returned delivering their drinks and checking to make sure all was well. Moments later, the visibly irritated waitress walked back up to the table, tray in hand. "Here y'all go. Enjoy." She forced a smile setting a bottle and two glasses down.

"Hey, hold up! What's the deal? We ain't order this," Leesa stopped her before she could walk away.

"I know you didn't order it. It's with compliments from the owner of the club, Tyrus," she announced, nodding her head back in the direction of a table near the rear.

"Look at you. I see you still got it, girl," J-Rite said, smiling as she poured the champagne for them.

"Shut up, girl! The last thing I need is for some nothing-ass nigga to bother me trying to be a big shot. I'm good on all that."

A mere few seconds after Leesa said that they were rudely interrupted by a visitor to their table. "Hey, how you ladies doing this evening? Y'all good?"

"We're both doing fine," Leesa said speaking for her and J-Rite.

"Well, I hope y'all enjoying the champagne. It's the best we have in the house," he boasted, flashing a slight smile so that his gold diamond-encrusted tooth could be seen.

Leesa was all up in her feelings and wanted to let the seemingly generous wannabe mack playa know exactly where she stood. "Yeah, about that . . ."

J-Rite sat back already knowing Leesa was about to set Tyrus, or whatever his name was, straight. *This nigga used to having hoes fall all over his ass. My girl 'bout to get him all the way together.*

"You didn't have to do that; you know, send no bottle over. We good. We can buy our own drinks, you feel me?" Leesa said with a mug on her face. She didn't believe in letting a man take care of her if it wasn't Hutch. She was the strong, independent type who didn't want, expect, or take any handouts or free shit. Leesa knew sometimes free shit ends up being the most expensive thing you can ever have.

"No no no. It's nothing. I like doing things for beautiful women like you two. Maybe we can go to the room later and y'all can do something for me. What y'all think?" he said, still smiling, letting the knot in his pocket be seen.

"Nigga, you got us fucked up! Fuck you think this is!" Leesa shouted as she threw her drink in his face. "I don't know what kind of bitches y'all got up in this motherfucker, but me and my little sister ain't none of them! We ain't home grown from this part of town or city. Bitch, we from the D, and that disrespect shit don't fly with us. Your money and bottom-shelf bottles ain't nothing to us. We move in circles with real bosses—*not* chumps!"

One of his bouncers saw as well as heard what was going on and rushed over to the table. "Is everything good, man?" he asked, ready to earn his paycheck or possibly get killed.

"And if it wasn't, nigga, you wasn't gon' do shit but get your feelings hurt too!" J-Rite said, grabbing a beer bottle ready to go to work.

"Yeah, man, shit is good; it's all good," Tyrus said to his boy, wiping his face, then licking his fingers. He was a thinker before a reactor; that's what made him who he was. He was definitely going to make these two fresh-mouthed females pay for embarrassing him; just not now. "They don't know any better. They not from around here. They from Detroit . . . so they say." He walked off smiling, plotting, and scheming on payback for their asses.

"All right, let's go, J-Rite, before I have to kill that fake idiot and his boy." Leesa fought to be heard over the music while getting her purse and heading toward the steps. They made their way to the front door when J-Rite noticed two women in leather outfits watching them all the way to the parking lot.

"Hey, Leesa, look at them hoes over there. You think they up to something? I mean, they staring at us all extra and whatnot."

Leesa looked in the direction of the women. "I don't know what they want, but fuck 'em; let's go. Let's ride."

"That country-reject nigga blew my fucking buzz anyhow!" J-Rite said, leaning back in the passenger seat.

"Niggaz always on some bullshit. That's what I loved so much about Hutch. He was real," Leesa said, pulling out of the parking lot and into the street.

"Yeah, I miss that boy too."

J-Rite looked in the side mirror and saw two motorcycles coming up behind them at a fast pace. The bikes rode past for a distance. She thought they were going to keep going, but the bikes suddenly slowed down, then stopped altogether. Instantly knowing something was about to jump off, she grabbed her gun from under the seat. Leesa, taking her gun from its stash spot, got ready too.

"Hey, that's them thirst buckets from back at the club!" J-Rite shouted.

The bikes tried to block the car, but Leesa maneuvered the vehicle and swerved around them and kept going.

"Okay, sis, dig this. We can't outrun these chicks so we gon' have to handle our business! So get ready. I'm about to stop." Leesa pulled up in a parking lot and slammed down on the brakes, bringing the car to a screeching halt.

The bikes roared up aggressively, stopping in front of them. J-Rite was hyped up; definitely ready to go to battle. With a vengeance, she jumped out of the car pointing her gun directly at one of their out-of-the-blue pursuers' heads. "What the fuck y'all want with us? Why y'all following us? Huh? What's the deal, bitch?"

"Look, ladies, we don't want no trouble, but we got a job to do," she responded, not fearful of the pistol being aimed in her direction.

"And what the fuck type of job is that?" Leesa barked, also heated.

"Hey, our boss Tyrus wants to talk to both of y'all. He said for us to bring y'all back to the club. That's it!"

"Bring us back for what?" J-Rite hissed, gun in hand.

"Look, bitch, I don't freaking know. We just follow orders. We don't ask questions. He asks; we deliver!"

"Well, bitch," she returned the insult and fever thrown her way, "that's an order you won't be able to comply with. So fuck y'all and y'all boss! We about to be out."

J-Rite and Leesa started easing their way back to the car. One of the women posted on J-Rite's side tried to reach for something. It was useless. Leesa fired off one round, striking the female in her kneecap. As the girl fell to the ground, Leesa let off one more, ripping a gaping hole in her victim's shoulder.

"Hey, you! Don't fucking move!" J-Rite shouted to the other one who was now in tears. She walked over to the lady. "Me and my sister make our own moves; call our own shots. You can go pick yo' friend up off the ground and go tell that nigga Tyrus if he wanna war with us, bring his A-game, because we Detroit bitches, and we don't break!" Raising her gun, J-Rite put several holes in each of the motorcycles, rendering them undrivable.

About forty-five minutes later, Leesa pulled up at J-Rite's building. "Look, we gonna link back up in the morning and start to get things popping in a major way. So, if you can, get in touch with Raven and whoever else you think we can trust; we'll be good. You see, after to-night, these lames out this way be straight jealous to see females doing they own thang. So we gotta be ready!"

J-Rite let Leesa know she was thankful for the chance and wouldn't let her down.

CHAPTER EIGHT

J-Rite woke up thinking about the awful news Asia had delivered about Buzzy, and the blessing Leesa had dropped at her feet. She only had a small amount of product left, and, of course, the ticket money that was now all hers to keep. Since she was sitting on so much free money, so to speak, she decided to pass on her good fortune. It was incredibly windy and J-Rite feared a tornado warning was about to be announced. Not wanting to run the risk of getting caught in a brewing storm, instead of going to the corner store to send Mike Mike's good-begging depressed ass a few dollars, she used the Western Union app on her cell. After receiving the confirmation information online, she texted it to him. As she expected, Mike Mike started calling, trying to beg her to come back to Detroit, but as usual, Jessica pushed *Ignore*. She wanted to help him because they struggled together when times were hard; nothing more, nothing less. She always thought he was going to be the love of her life, but after being away from him for some months, she realized she didn't even know what love was.

Next, she called Raven, hoping to get her hustle hard ducks in order.

"What up doe, Ms. J-Rite? Ms. Moneymaker!"

"Shut up, girl, what's up your way?"

"Same old shit. I'm struggling taking care of these damn kids and my grandmother."

"Okay, then, fam. How are the kids and Granny?"

"They all good. The kids bad as hell, and you know Granny; still straight bugging on how I live my damn life. But enough about me. I heard you're still up the way, shooting the Rapids."

"Yeah, Raven, that's why I called you. I got some real hellava shit cooking up this way. I mean, some *major* paper on the floor." J-Rite was beyond geeked as she spoke. "It's the kinda lick we always used to talk about back in the dressing room when shit was slow."

Raven could just about feel her friend's excitement through the phone. "Damn, girl, are you serious? It's a hit like that?"

"Yeah, we just gotta put in a li'l bit of work. I need your help. In a few weeks, I need you to come up here for a while. You think Granny will watch the kids?"

"Shidddd, with money on the table, her old crazy ass ain't got no choice!"

They each laughed about Raven's determination to hustle or die and caught up on the other hood gossip that J-Rite had missed out on while being in Grand Rapids. Raven even had some firsthand 411 on Buzzy getting busted since the feds had apprehended him down at the club smack-dab in the middle of getting a lap dance from their homegirl, Wild Child. After finally ending their conversation, J-Rite smiled to herself thinking about her immediate future. *Hell, fuck, yeah! Shit 'bout to change around here. Shit really, really about to change.*

By midafternoon, the storm had blown over. Ready to get in the streets and grind out the rest of the, as well as the last, package she'd be getting from Buzzy, J-Rite grabbed her cell and stuck her gun down in the small of her back as she got ready to cook up. Since the building where she lived at was big and the people were always in and out, the conniving drug diva figured that she could cover her tracks, and the police would never be the wiser. She, like most people who were breaking the law, felt they had the game and how to win it all figured out. J-Rite, having been a product of the hood since birth, was no different. She'd learned how to cook dope from Hutch when just a preteen. Having skipped school one day, she crept over to Hutch and Leesa's early, thinking the house would be empty. When the truant youth walked into the two-story dwelling, Hutch was preoccupied in the kitchen. He heard the door close and came to see who it was with gun in hand. J-Rite was, of course, startled at first.

"Dang, boy! Why you got that mask on your face like some bank robber or something? You think you a doctor?" she smartly quizzed Hutch while walking toward the kitchen. When she entered, she saw Leesa standing and a whole bunch of dope on the table.

"Hey, li'l bit, you don't need to be in here," Hutch advised, walking up behind his sister, pulling at her shoulder.

"Wait, hold up, Hutch. Show me how to cook dope too."

At first, the older, overly protective sibling was reluctant, but he knew she was going to find a way to learn one way or another, so he decided to show her. And like they say . . . the rest was history.

After J-Rite was finished cooking, she broke the drugs down into nickel rocks. Packaging them in small baggies, she then put her "work" in her bootleg Gucci book bag. With a few on her person, she was ready for the evening customers. As if on cue, when she got outside, Rhonda and Sean were sitting on the porch drinking a bottle of cheap wine.

"What's up, y'all?"

"Shit, baby, just chilling. You want some of this?" Rhonda asked, holding out the bottle as if J-Rite would ever take shit to the head behind either one of them.

"Naw, girl, I'm good. But look, I got a hookup for y'all."

"Oh yeah? What is it?" Sean inquired, not willing to do anything for a hit like Rhonda.

"For every fifty y'all bring me, I'll give y'all a free one. Plus, a free bump now to get y'all out of the gate."

"Yeah, I like that shit!" Rhonda replied, knowing she was bold.

A few days had passed before J-Rite was completely sold out. Rhonda had earned her just due spreading the word how good J-Rite's sack was. The Detroit-born and -raised hustler's clientele had picked up extremely fast. Counting her funds, she then decided it was time to buy a car and stay out of the cabs where she could get got at any time. With cash in hand, she found a lot that had a no-questions-asked policy. If you had the money, you'd be good to go; in and out.

CHAPTER NINE

J-Rite pulled up to the bus station. Elated, she saw Raven standing with her hands on her hips next to two black-and-yellow trimmed suitcases. Five foot seven, caramel skinned with perky breasts and an apple-shaped butt, Raven was dressed like she had left straight from the strip club the night before and jumped right on the Greyhound. Unfortunately, no matter how hard her granny had tried, Raven suffered from absolutely no home training.

"What's up doe, Jennifer?" J-Rite joked, using her girl's government name.

"What up, Jessica?" Raven returned the favor as they both laughed and hugged.

"How are those babies doing? Granny ain't bugging?"

"They good, with their bad asses. And yeah, she was trying to go on me, but I went harder. I mean, shidddd, here I am; up here hanging with your crazy ass about to get paid outta of minds."

"Hell, yeah, I heard that!" J-Rite knew Raven wasn't gonna let her down.

"So you like living up here or what, 'cause a bitch like me thinking about relocating some damn place with a better school system and less crime? Hell, I'm the only hustler and criminal my bay-bays need to be seeing act a fool."

"Yeah, it's tight, but I can't front. I miss home, and, of course, the club," J-Rite confessed, helping put the suitcases in the trunk.

"Fuck the D and that brass pole! You ain't missing nothing but a bunch of bullshit! So tell me, what's up with this money? I'm ready to get it pumping!"

"Me, you, and Leesa are gonna hook up in a few."

"Cool, I ain't seen her in like forever. How she doing?"

"She's all right. Let me call her now and see what's good."

After talking to Leesa, they headed to the local steak house where they agreed to meet and discuss business.

"What up, girl?" Leesa greeted Raven while hugging her.

"How you been, Leesa?"

"I've been good. How the kids doing?"

"They are all right. They're getting big. They at home with my granny."

Each female ordered what seemed like everything on the menu. Finishing their meal, they had a few drinks, then got down to the business at hand.

"Well, look, I got the work in the car, so we can be out whenever y'all ready."

Standing in the parking lot, the trio made a pact to not stop slinging until they each had enough cash to live comfortably for the next few years. Leesa then looked around to see if there were any prying eyes. Cautiously, she opened her trunk, removing a medium-size brown paper bag.

"Hey, real talk. Y'all let me know how this shit is. Oh yeah, I was so busy yapping about this work, I almost forgot to tell you. I got the house, J-Rite. The movers over there now putting all the stuff in. So I'm gonna get at y'all later."

Parting ways, the girls stopped at the store to grab some blunts and a bottle of dark liquor.

"You already know I got that Detroit fire for us to blaze," Raven bragged as they were headed to J-Rite's place.

"That ain't shit, girl! I got that Kush on deck."

"That's what's up, J-Rite; either/or. As long as I get high tonight that's all that matters!"

Putting her groceries in the car, Leesa was lost in thought about how long it was going to take to get her money right. When she closed her trunk she took notice of a guy walking her way. On guard immediately, she wished she had her gun on her hip.

"Excuse me, miss, but I think you forgot your bag."

Leesa looked the guy top to bottom sizing him up. *Damn, he sexy.* He was six foot four, dark skinned, with grey eyes, a low fade, and a goatee. But his beauty still didn't stop her from being standoffish. "Naw, that ain't my bag. I mean, that's not my bag." He smiled, still holding the bag in his hands. "What's so funny?"

"I mean, hey, I'm not a college professor. You don't have to speak proper English to me."

"Is that right?" she gave him the serious side eye.

"Yeah, I think you're gorgeous no matter how you talk."

Leesa held her laugh in. She didn't want the tall, dark, handsome stranger to know she found him and his compliments flattering. "Well, thank you, but like I said off rip, that's not my bag; nice try, though," she giggled, walking to the door of her car.

"Oh, this ain't your pair of stockings or pack of razors?"

That was her bag. She must have forgotten, so now she had to eat crow. "Oh dang. My bad. I'm sorry, can I have my bag?"

"How about this . . . You can just give me your phone number. That way, we can call it even."

It had been years since Leesa lost Hutch. Sadly, she was still holding on to the memories; yet, she knew she needed to move on. Hutch would want her to be happy; however, today would not be that day. "Sorry, I can't. I'm married," she proclaimed, holding up her hand to show a ring Hutch had given her one Valentine's Day.

"Oh, I apologize. Please forgive me," he said, holding out her bag so she could easily take it.

Leesa took the bag and got in the car. She didn't want to start dating again. Even though it had been years since the love of her life was killed, her emotions were still running high. Besides, if she did start dating, would she be betraying Hutch? Would J-Rite be mad at her and think she was unloyal to her big brother? As thoughts raced through her mind, Leesa figured that the best thing for her to do was to stay single and chase that money. *Maybe when the time is right, me and J-Rite can talk, and I can see what she thinks.* When Leesa pulled up to the house, the mover's trucks were gone. She walked in her new house and exhaled. *Now I just gotta maintain by any means necessary.*

J-Rite and Raven were both buzzed, but not enough to slip on taking care of business. Spreading everything they needed to hook up on the table, they were interrupted by the sound of J-Rite's cell ringing. Rolling her eyes after seeing it was Asia, J-Rite answered, knowing she was about to hear more of the same: Asia practically begging to be down. Hearing out the worrisome womanizer Asia, J-Rite hung up with a headache. "Yo, Raven, peep this shit out. That was the trick Asia that used to run with Buzzy. She wanna hook up and get money with us. She keep calling me about it almost every other day, like a stalker."

"Well, what you gon' do?" Raven asked while puffing on a blunt, then passing it to J-Rite.

"Hutch used to always tell me that money and bullshit don't mix. And I know damn well Asia on some bullshit!

She be on some flashy shit I ain't with. She gonna bring a lot of attention I don't want or need, making us all hot," J-Rite said, blowing out weed smoke.

"Well, you know what you gotta do then."

"Yeah, I'm gonna tell her I'm good for right now, and if she can't deal with that, fuck her! She ain't gonna fuck up my money. I might hit her back when we finish doing what we do and give her the bad news."

They went over to the kitchen and started handling their business. J-Rite was glad that she didn't have to show Raven how to cook dope. All her babies' daddies were drug dealers, so that trait was passed down.

"You know, girl, I think I'ma get a house up here for me, the kids, and Granny. Detroit getting more ruthless and rotten as the days go by."

"Yeah, that's what's up. I mean, I ain't gonna lie, I miss the city and can't wait to get back home."

"Yeah, and to Mike Mike?" Raven quizzed, giving her girl the side eye.

J-Rite knew Raven was trying to peep her out and laughed. "Naw, fool, not him. I mean, I ain't mad at his dumb ass no more for having no real hustle in him; some niggas is straight lame like that, and he one of 'em. Besides, Mike Mike ain't trying to step up and be no real man I need him to be. He just wanna play that damn game, smoke weed, and pop them pills he takes for depression. I'm tight on all that."

"Oh yeah," Raven sarcastically replied with a smirk.

"Yeah, girl, I need a real damn man; not a boy."

Raven slowly shook the Pyrex and grinned. "Oh, you mean like ole boy Dino you said you met the other day?"

J-Rite didn't verbally respond. She just played off the question and kept it moving.

After what seemed like forever, they were done cooking. J-Rite called Leesa to tell her what they'd hooked up while Raven, who had the munchies, made a run, pulling up in the parking lot of KFC located only a few blocks away from J-Rite's apartment. "Damn, this bitch packed in the inside," she mumbled getting out of the car. Waiting what seemed like an eternity, it was finally her turn. Raven stepped to the counter and placed her order. Heading out the door, a short stocky guy held the door open.

"Hey, you," the man spoke in a flirtatious manner.

"Oh, hey," Raven responded.

"My name is Benji, and yours?"

"I'm Raven, nice to meet you." She licked her lips while holding her bag of chicken in one hand and her soda in the other.

Raven thought Benji was really something to look at. He was light skinned with green eyes, had long hair, and a baby face. He looked no older than twenty-one.

"How old are you?" she blatantly asked, blushing.

"I'm twenty-two. Why? I'm too old for you?"

"Yeah, right. Why don't you give me your number, and I'll call you."

"Oh, we gonna play that game?"

"Play what game? I'm gonna call you; seriously," Raven exclaimed.

Not trying to act brand new, Raven knew exactly what Benji was talking about. Women would get a guy's number, and then would never call them. It wasn't only a thing that a woman did to men. Men also did it from time to time. As Benji stood looking at Raven, he was hoping that she wasn't going to play him like that, because he really wanted to get at her. Not just because of her looks and body, but he felt a certain way as he stood there with her. He couldn't quite put his finger on it, but there was something about her that made him want to get to know her better.

"Look, if you give me yo' number I will call you. I'm too grown to play games, so let me get that number so I can go handle my business," she said, leaning on one leg.

"All right, ma, I hear you. Let me see yo' phone." She handed him the phone, and he put his number in it, then handed it back. "The ball is in your court." He walked inside the restaurant, leaving her to enjoy her meal and the rest of her night.

CHAPTER TEN

J-Rite was serving a few customers when her cell rang. Glancing down at the caller ID, it read *Private*. She was going to ignore it, but her curiosity got the best of her, and she answered it. Hearing the voice on the other end made her glad she did.

"Oh, dang, hey, Dino. How you doing?"

"I'm doing okay. I just had you on my mind, that's all."

Hearing this made J-Rite smile. "Seriously?"

"Look, I'm sorry I ain't called you, but I've been having bad luck like a motherfucker."

"Oh yeah? What kind of bad luck?"

"I lost my job, and some punk stole my car. Look, I would love to fuck with you, but right now, my paper ain't right." Dino was running game on her like he was known around Grand Rapids and Kalamazoo to do to females. "But when my paper is back tight, I'm coming for you."

"Where you at? I wanna see you so we can kick it face-to-face." J-Rite was playing into his deceptive hands and didn't even know it.

Grabbing a blunt, two twenty-dollar bags of weed, and placing the items into her purse, J-Rite was out the door. Stopping at the gas station for a juice, she was on her way. A few minutes later, she was parked in front of the address Dino had given her. When she got on the porch the door opened, and she was at a loss for words. Dino was standing with his shirt off. His chest was chiseled, and he had a perfect stomach. *Damn, this nigga fine; he got it going on.*

"What up doe?"

"Hey, Dino, what's up?"

"I just finished cutting grass, so a nigga might smell a bit."

J-Rite didn't care if he smelled like a sewer; she just wanted to reach out and touch his handsome ass. However, she tried to focus. She needed to keep her head in the game and stay getting money on the regular.

"Let's go to my car and talk. So you wanna smoke this blunt with me?" she asked, rolling up after they each got comfortable.

"Naw, I'm good, ma. I don't smoke."

Now, that's what the hell I'm talking about; a nigga that don't lay around smoking blunts all day like Mike Mike. "Wow, that's what's up. Well, do you mind if I smoke?"

"Naw, go ahead."

After hitting the blunt twice, she blew the smoke out the window and coughed until her eyes watered. "Look, I know you had my number and was sitting on it, trying to leave a sista hanging, but—"

"Naw, ma, it wasn't like that. My situation is just on hold right now. But when I get right, we gonna hang out and do that shit all the way."

"Real talk, Dino, you never know when shit might change for you! You can never tell where a blessing might come from." J-Rite handed him some money and an eight ball of dope.

"What's this for? I'm confused," he puzzled, holding the cash and drugs in his hand.

J-Rite sat back in the driver's seat feeling like she was a true female boss. She was trying her best to impress Dino, even if she had to pay the price to pull it off.

"Yo, I ain't gonna front; I never met a chick like you before."

"Is that a good thing or bad thing?" she asked, hoping it was the better of the two.

"It's a damn good thing, but damn. So, can I take it you out here in these streets?" Dino insinuated, already knowing the answer.

"Why you ask me that?"

"Well, most girls don't give niggas dope and cheese just because."

"Naw, guy. I got this from a friend that owed me some money. So since he blessed me, I thought I would bless you."

Needless to say, he knew better. He didn't believe her. He'd already done his homework on her pedigree. "Yo, I can't take this from you."

"Yeah, you can; just consider it a favor 'til I need a favor," she winked, blazing up once more.

"That's good looking; you know you a real one. Most people have ulterior motives. But I feel that you genuine with this."

"It's just that I've been through so much shit my damn self, so I know what it feels like when the world is on your shoulders." She tried her best to make her speech seem genuine, but the truth of the matter was, she was trying to run game on him while he was busy doing the same to her.

Abruptly, Dino leaned over, kissing her. This caught J-Rite off guard. She hadn't been with a guy in so long she thought she was going to go crazy. The softness of his lips, the warmness of his tongue, the way he smelled made her want to get banged on the spot. After they stopped kissing, they just sat and didn't speak. They both wondered what the other schemer was thinking.

"Hey, what you doing tonight?" she finally broke the ice.

"Nothing too much, why?"

"You wanna go out? My girl just got in town, and I want you to meet her and my sister."

"Yeah, that's cool. What time you talking?"

"I don't know for sure but probably around eleven. I'll text and let you know."

"All right, do that then."

They kissed one more time. Then he got out of the car.

As J-Rite drove off, she watched him in her rearview mirror hoping that this feeling she was having was real. She then dialed Leesa to tell her to add one more person to their VIP list.

Raven and J-Rite had hit the mall earlier to ensure they were going to stunt later at the club. Texting Dino to let him know they were on their way, the two friends walked out of the building looking like models. When J-Rite pulled up to Dino's house she was nervous, hoping he cleaned up well. Thank God he wasn't with that thug bullshit. In all his glory, he walked out wearing a black suit, gold-striped tie, and Kenneth Cole loafers. When Dino walked up to the car she got out and hugged him.

"Damn, you look good!" He rubbed his hands together looking her up and down.

"You ain't looking too bad yourself. Oh, hey, I want you to meet my girl."

Raven got out of the car as well. "Hi, I'm Raven." *He is fine!* Raven thought as she headed to the backseat so he could ride shotgun with J-Rite.

Arriving at the club, J-Rite called Leesa to let her know that they were there. She found a parking spot, and the three of them started walking to the entrance.

"I thought y'all might have a problem finding me so I came to the door."

"How you doing? I'm Dino," he smoothly stated, walking up to Leesa.

"I know who you are. I was with J-Rite when y'all met, remember?"

"Oh yeah, that's right. I guess I was way too busy focused on J-Rite, to notice anyone else. My bad, but anyway, nice to see you again."

Hearing this, J-Rite smiled.

"Our table's over here." Leesa walked off assuming they would follow. When they got to the table there were three bottles of champagne already chilling on ice.

"Dino, you want me to pour you a drink?" J-Rite was ready to get the party started, snapping her fingers to the beat of the music.

"Yeah, but not too much. I don't really drink. My mom was a drug addict and a drunk, so I try to stay away from it. You feel me?"

J-Rite and Dino decided to skip the champagne and head straight to the dance floor. When they returned to the table, sweaty and parched, Leesa and Raven were talking about the guys in the club that were trying to holla at every female with a big butt or chest. Just as Leesa was getting ready to open another bottle, Asia walked up, interrupting their good time.

Damn, I forgot to call her begging-to-be-down-ass back, J-Rite thought, sensing some shit was about to be jumping off. "Oh, hey, now. What up, Asia?"

Asia rolled her eyes and smacked her lips. "You tell me because that's what I'm trying to find out. So what up?" she barked with attitude.

J-Rite was hoping that Asia wasn't about to make a scene, but Asia had other plans as she looked around the table. She knew everybody but Dino and Leesa. "No wonder you ain't called me back. You too busy trying to fuck with this funny-style duck and hang with these hoes!"

Raven never really cared too much for Asia when she'd come in the strip club with Buzzy. She only tolerated her because she was making it rain from time to time, trying to stunt. But now, not only were they outside of the club, they were in an entirely different city. "Who you calling a ho, fat, pussy-slobbering-tongue bitch?" Raven yelled, getting up, ready to do battle.

"Hey, look, honey, you better watch your mouth. The only reason I ain't up right now kicking off into your burly ass is because you my li'l sister's peeps. So don't press your luck."

J-Rite jumped up. "Chill, y'all, I got this. Asia, you need to watch your damn mouth! You always extra, and that's what the problem is. That's why I ain't fucking with you like that. You wanna be on that stunna shit, and I don't."

Damn, so she is out here in the streets heavy. I knew she was the chick from Detroit they keep talking about is on the come up. Dino leaned back in his chair with his arms folded. He wasn't in the habit of hitting women, but if he had to sock this Asia carpet muncher in the mouth to get her off his soon-to-be girl, then so be it. Asia would be nursing a bloody grill.

"Oh, it's like that, J-Rite? Buzzy locked up, and you like fuck me!"

"Yeah, you be on some other shit, so it is fuck you!"

"Fine, don't rock with me. But remember, I was the one that was bringing you that work every week, so watch how you move, pretty girl," Asia dry threatened as she stormed off all up in her feelings.

"Sorry you had to see that." J-Rite turned her attention to Dino who had remained silent taking the whole altercation in.

"Naw, bae, you ain't gotta apologize. You handled your business. But why don't we just break out before she come back and y'all get to thumping. She seems mighty heated still."

"Fuck that bird; she don't want it." Leesa stuck out her chest talking shit, and Raven followed her lead. "But Dino is right. Niggas all looking at us like we some animals on display. Let's just call it a night. I'ma have Leesa drop me off. I'll see you later at the crib, I guess," Raven giggled, winking at her.

As they were walking to the door, J-Rite noticed two guys looking at her. She walked closer to get a better look. To her surprise, it was her friends from back home, Tone and Mario. Both were caught up in the foster care system as she was so they bonded together. They were her surrogate brothers when Hutch had not been around. They always went hard for her, and she would return the favor if need be. They'd lost touch over the past few years, so seeing them was nothing more than a blessing.

"What up, Jessica?" Tone excitedly shouted, swooping her up in his strong arms as Dino looked on, not saying a word.

"Hey, Tone! What y'all doing up here?" her smile was as wide as it could get as she was hugging him.

"We heard there's money up here, so you already know," Mario, the younger brother, nodded his head while rubbing his chin, checking both Raven and Leesa out.

J-Rite wrote her number down, telling them that she had some work on the floor and to get in touch with her ASAP. "Call me, y'all, so we can get it all the way popping."

Leaving the club, they saw Asia near the entrance trying to push up on some female. Wanting to avoid any more confrontation, Dino ushered all the women out the door, urging them to just let the petty bullshit go. After making sure Leesa and Raven drove safely off, he and J-Rite got in her car and headed to get a room just as they'd discussed on the dance floor when a slow song was playing. Asia may have messed up the evening with her over-the-top antics, but the rest of the night belonged to them.

CHAPTER ELEVEN

"I like the way these look; they so cute," Leesa mumbled to herself referring to the strapless heels she was trying on. No matter how she was feeling, shoe shopping always put her mind at ease.

"They look really good on you," a male's voice suddenly chimed in.

Here we go with this shit! She turned around, surprised at who it was. *What the hell he doing in a lady's shoe store? He was probably shopping for his girlfriend.*

"Hey, Miss Lady. How you doing?" the guy from the grocery store who was holding her bag hostage inquired.

"I'm fine, and you?" Leesa replied, not caring to speak, just being polite.

"I never properly introduced myself. I'm Q."

"Q? What's that, a nickname? You kinda old for a nickname, don't you think?"

"Well, my first name is really weird, so I go by my first initial."

Damn, he got a gorgeous smile. Leave it alone, girl. Does it really matter what his name is? It ain't like I'ma go out with him.

"Do you wanna know what it is?"

"What? What is it?" Leesa frowned.

"My name? Oh, you lost focus . . . probably fantasizing about me, huh?"

Damn, it's like he reading my mind. "Now, why in the entire hell would I be fantasizing about your corny ass?

And, no, I don't wanna know your name! Plus, I told you I'm married once before; now stop bothering me."

He was surprised. His ego was bruised. He began to walk off feeling defeated. "You don't have to worry. I'll leave you the fuck alone. No disrespect intended. Have a blessed day."

Leesa felt horrible about the way she carried on. She didn't mean to act like she did. *He really wasn't bothering me. Why do I feel so bad about it?* She grabbed her things and walked toward the counter where he was in line paying for some shoes. *I wonder who he's buying shoes for.* She got a look at the shoes. They were stiletto heels. *I know he ain't buying them for his mom. The nigga in here trying to talk to me, and he got a woman. Just like a nigga. I'm really 'bout to give him a piece of my mind soon as we leave this store. Here I am feeling bad, and this nigga out here trying to get his mack on. He done tried the wrong bitch!* Leesa hated to be taken for a fool. Her pride and attitude were two things that made her make most of her decisions—good or bad.

Q paid for the shoes, then walked out of the store. Leesa didn't know exactly what she was going to say, but he wasn't going to like it. She knew that for sure.

Why does it even matter if he tried to talk to me and he has a woman? It ain't like I gave him my number, but he did try to play me. An older woman in front of Leesa purchased her items and also left. Leesa was next. She paid for her things, then started walking around the mall in hopes of finding Q. Finally she spotted him and headed in his direction. He saw her coming his way and gave her the coldest look any man has ever given her. That expression made Leesa momentarily second-guess her next move. *Why the fuck is he looking at me like that?* Leesa noticed a very pretty lady walking toward him. The lady's presence made his hard look turn into a smile. *Oh, this must be his woman.* The lady walked up to Q, and they started talking.

"Hey, Q. So how in the hell you gonna try to talk to me and you have a woman? That's the problem with niggas now. They think they can do whatever the fuck they want!"

"What are you talking about?" the lady interjected with a frown.

"I'm talking about how your man was just all in my face trying to kick it when you wasn't around."

Q shook his head in disgust. *If I knew she was this crazy, I would have never tried to talk to her ass. But she does look good mad. It's always the fine ones; that's a damn shame.* "Okay, lady, are you done?" Q finally had enough of her behavior.

Am I done? This nigga got a lot of fucking nerve! And she ain't said shit. She must know he ain't shit. "Yeah, Negro, I'm done," Leesa fired back while starting to walk off.

"Naw, don't go now. I want you to meet my sister. This is . . . Well, sorry, crazy lady; I never got your name."

"Your *sister?*"

"Yeah, now if you don't mind, we have things to do." Q shook his head as he and his sister walked away leaving Leesa standing there to act a fool by herself.

And she felt like a complete idiot. *What the hell's wrong with me? I'm acting real fucking stupid. That shit doesn't make sense. This ain't even my character.* Back in her car, as she drove, she was having a hard time getting Q off her mind. *I wonder if I'll ever see him again. I know he think I'm crazy as hell.*

Pulling up in her driveway she noticed a box sitting on her porch. Upon opening it, Leesa discovered several dead roses. *Who the fuck sent this shit?* After checking for a card and finding none, the hood diva went in the house, gun in hand. Checking every room, thankfully, she found nothing. *I'm starting to slip. I gotta watch my ass. I know it ain't the nigga from the club. He couldn't have found out where I stay, so who the fuck could it be? And if it is him, then, he gonna have a real problem on his hands.*

When J-Rite walked in the apartment Raven was stretched out on the couch. Hearing the door shut, she leaped to her feet. "Okay, tramp, I want to know *everything,* and don't leave shit out!"

"Girl, yo' ass is crazy," J-Rite giggled like a small girl about to share a secret. "All I can say is, I don't have any complaints."

"Well, damn, the nigga must've torn that ass up, 'cause you walking funny as hell."

J-Rite went in the bathroom. Taking a hot shower she felt refreshed. No sooner than she stepped a foot out, her phone started to ring. Wrapping a towel around her wet body, she prayed it was Dino. Looking at the caller ID it read *Private.*

"Yeah, who is this?"

"How are you doing, Jessica Sanders?" a male's voice spoke, but she didn't recognize who it was.

"Who the hell is this?"

"You know who this is, you little bitch."

"Look, I ain't got no time for games!" J-Rite hung up, not in the mood for no dumb shit.

The phone rang once more.

"Yeah, nigga?" she shouted, answering the phone.

"Just keep being tough. We'll see if you and your sister Leesa like begging for y'all life. Thought y'all were gonna get down on my girls and it was gonna be nothing behind it. Naw, I don't roll like that! Get ready for a real playa to step up to the plate!"

"Bitch, I'm from the D, so fuck you, pussy nigga! Eat a dick." J-Rite knew from that point on, they were going to have to handle Tyrus much sooner than later.

"What the fuck was that all about?" Raven burst into the bathroom having overheard her homegirl yelling.

"Hold tight. I'ma tell you in one minute. Let me just call Leesa and see if she good her way," J-Rite answered. "Hey, sis. I just got a call from that old fag Tyrus."

"About what?" she suspiciously barked. "Wait a minute, how the fuck he get your number in the first place?"

"I don't know, but he knows my freaking government name; yours too."

"You know what? We need to take care of this nigga. We need to put together a team before shit really gets outta order."

"I got the perfect goons for the job. Leave it to me. I'ma 'bout to hit 'em up."

Raven had stood mute long enough waiting to hear what the deal was. "All right, damn, you gonna tell me what the fuck is going on or what?" Raven sat listening. When J-Rite was finished, she then asked questions. "Well, what Leesa talking about? Y'all got a plan or what?"

"First, she gonna try to find out all about this lame. We know his first name and the club he owns, but that's it. We need to know where he lay his damn head at!"

"Fo'sho! Well, we gonna have to take care of this! You know how I feel about playing games with beef." Raven didn't believe in sitting around and letting things happen. She lost her parents like that. Her father had gotten into it with a guy and took the situation too lightly. It ended up costing him and his wife both their lives. Raven made sure that when she had a problem she would handle it quickly.

J-Rite looked at her ringing cell phone. Although the call wasn't *Private*, she didn't recognize the number. "This better not be that fuck boy again."

"Yeah, who this?"

"This Mario. What up, girl?"

"Yo, I was just about to call y'all. Come through. Let me give you the address."

"Who that?" Raven wondered as she went to look out the front window.

"That was Mario and Tone. They on they way over, and we can handle this Tyrus situation quick. Like you say, a nigga ain't got time to be beefing when you trying to get that money."

J-Rite was happy to have everything going how she wanted it. She felt that the problem with Tyrus was a minor setback. *This nigga couldn't leave well enough alone. Now, it's a whole bunch of bullshit about to start. But we gonna end it real quick.*

Twenty minutes later, Tone and Mario were at J-Rite's place. Tone was the older and calmer one. He was twenty-seven, six foot two, and 220 pounds. He wore his head bald. He was brown skinned with a nice personality. He had dark eyes and wore a goatee. His brother Mario towered over him. He was twenty-five, six foot four, 250 pounds, and wore his hair in a bald fade. He had the same eyes as his brother. They were the wrong guys to be beefing with. They could be the best or worst thing that ever happened to you.

"Yeah, like we said last night, we heard there's money up here, J-Rite," Mario stated before taking a sip of the Hennessy she'd poured. "And these pussies be acting like straight-up hoes up here. They act scared to give us a damn connect!"

"Acting? These busters ain't acting; they is who they is! So y'all wanna fuck with us and get this money or what?" J-Rite planted her hands on her hips while holding court.

"It's just you and her?" Tone smiled looking at Raven.

"Naw, my brother's wife Leesa's rolling with us. She's the one that's got the plug. I used to be copping from that nigga Buzzy before he got knocked."

"Yeah, we know. That ho-ass motherfucker got the whole East Side of Detroit hotter than the middle of July. That's why we up here about to rape these streets!" Mario spoke up. "So, when we gonna start getting this bread? We ready to start slanging."

"Just gimme a few days, y'all, then we on." J-Rite looked at Raven. Strangely, she decided not to say anything about Tyrus and his threats yet.

After the two brothers left, Raven sat down to talk to her friend. "Why you ain't tell them about that creep?"

"I want to see what Leesa finds out first; ain't no need to say shit just yet."

When J-Rite and Raven pulled up to the apartment building, police were scattered everywhere.

J-Rite and Raven went to collect some of the monies owed to the team. After picking up nearly three grand, they went to the mall to shop and grab something to eat. Getting back to the neighborhood they could easily see there was sheer pandemonium taking place.

"Hey, Raven, go find somewhere to park and post up. I'll find out what the fuck's going on!" J-Rite said in a panicked tone as she jumped out of the car. She wasn't worried about the police bothering her because as far as she knew, she wasn't hot; just another face in the crowd.

Rhonda and Sean saw her coming and ran up, revealing that the building had been shot up.

"Rhonda, what the fuck happened?"

"We don't know!" Sean cut in, looking back over his shoulder.

"Damn, well, did anybody get hurt?"

"Naw, girl. Not that we know of, but who you think did this?"

"Shit, who you asking? I don't know." J-Rite knew who was responsible, or who, at least, she thought was; she just wasn't telling Rhonda and Sean. *This shit done got out of hand. I can't be trying to make money here. Ain't no telling when this nigga gonna strike.* J-Rite called Raven and found out she was parked a few blocks over. Bending a few corners she saw the car. "Yo, girl, this nigga gotta die! We can't keep letting this nigga get the upper hand on us like this! At first, I thought he was on some playing shit, but now things done got real. We gotta find out some shit on this nigga." J-Rite was heated as she ran down what she knew had to pop off.

Raven's phone rang before she could respond to J-Rite's declaration of Tyrus's demise. It was her daughter. "Hold on, J, let me take this real quick. Hey, baby! Is everything all right?"

"Yeah, Momma, everything's good. I just called to say I love you. When you coming home?"

"I'll be home soon. How is everybody?"

"We're all doing well. Granny misses you too. She said we getting to be too much for her."

"Well, look, baby, Momma gotta go to work. I'll call you later. I love you, okay?"

"I love you too, bye."

"Damn, J, I wanna bring my family out here, but I can't bring them out here like this. No need to put them in harm's way, so we gotta get this shit over with."

J-Rite was caught in her feelings, knowing Raven was right. "Don't worry. That asshole about to fall! Now, let me call Rhonda to see if shit done died down around there and call Leesa."

After J-Rite made sure Leesa was good, she and Raven headed back to the building. J-Rite knew with the shooting, the police were going to be watching the building more carefully. She knew that if she didn't play it right, she ran the risk of getting busted. At this point in the game, she couldn't afford to take any losses. Not naïve, J-Rite also had to wonder if Tyrus was going to make another move more serious than the last or was he just trying to scare them. Either way, she knew she had to get her money and get it while the getting was good.

After they were done cooking up, J-Rite called Tone and Mario, asking them to come back over.

"It's time we move the speed up a li'l bit on our hustle, you know."

"Yeah, girl, if this idiot gonna try to get us, we need to be ready."

Shortly after, there was a knock on the door. J-Rite and Raven both grabbed their guns.

"Who is it?" J-Rite said in a deep voice.

J-Rite let her Detroit-born goons in.

"What's up, Raven?" Tone said, show stunting through the door. *Damn, she thick as all outside.*

"What up, boy?" she cooed in the sexiest voice she could.

"Hey, y'all, I know I said a few days, but I got a building for y'all. It's right up the street."

"Yo, is anybody posted up there that called they self holding it down?" Mario eagerly asked, cracking his knuckles.

"Naw, it's all y'all's. It's wide open."

Mario looked disappointed, and Tone and J-Rite knew why. Mario had a bad habit. He liked to talk with his guns.

"That's all your ass think about is killing motherfuckers." Tone took his focus off Raven to laugh at his brother.

"Fuck whoever ain't on our team, our family! You know our motto: do unto others what the hell they can't do to you."

J-Rite announced she was leaving the apartment and would be right back. Since she and her team of runners started gaining more clientele, she low-key rented the apartment across the hall. There she stashed all the work. Once inside the apartment, she swooped up the work, placing it in a Footlocker bag. When J-Rite returned, the three of her friends were all shooting dice.

"Yo, sis, I'm breaking these niggas!" Raven bragged, holding a pile of money with a blunt hanging out of her mouth.

"Man, fuck this shit! I'm done." Mario stood up from the crouched position.

"Yeah, me too," Tone cosigned, looking at Raven like he never seen a female beat a guy at anything, let alone shooting dice.

J-Rite handed Tone the bag. She then explained to them the potentially deadly situation with Tyrus and told him she'd get with them later about the ticket.

"So what you want to do about this old-style nigga?" Tone asked with his chest stuck out. No sooner than he said it, he felt stupid for asking. He already knew what needed to be done.

"That was a dumb question." Mario showed the handle of his gun.

"Well, as soon as Leesa give me the call, y'all can handle all y'all business."

"Okay, that's a bet. Y'all watch all y'all's ass; we out!" Mario headed toward the door.

"We will," J-Rite said.

"Oh yeah, Raven, let me know when you gonna let me get my money back from your cheating ass." Tone held the dice, shaking them in his hand.

"Yeah, whatever you say, nigga!" Raven grinned from ear to ear.

CHAPTER TWELVE

Asia sat at the bar thinking about how J-Rite was making her miss the opportunity of getting paid. She didn't try to look at it from J-Rite's perspective that she was a tad bit over the top. She felt that J-Rite crossed her. Asia was infuriated that the streets were talking. It was noise that things were going well for J-Rite and her team. Asia resented the fact that J-Rite didn't want her on her team, especially after she was bringing her Buzzy's package weekly before he got knocked. In Asia's mind, now J-Rite was trying to be better than everybody else, especially her.

"How are you doing? Can I buy you a drink?"

Asia turned to see who it was that was interrupting her pity party. *Oh, damn, she hot.* "Yeah, you can; and then I can return the favor."

The woman took a seat next to Asia, making sure she brushed her dainty hand across her newfound friend's leg. "Yeah, I'd like that."

"So what's yo' name?"

"It's Hazel, and yours?"

"It's Asia."

The bartender came over, and they ordered their drinks.

"So are you waiting on somebody, Asia?"

"Naw, I just stopped by to get me a drink. What about you? Are you waiting on somebody?"

"Yeah, I'm waiting on my girlfriend."

Asia's attitude changed a bit. She had been hit on by
plenty of women since coming out, but these Grand
Rapids women just didn't give a damn. They were brazen, disrespectful, and off the chain in general. "Damn,
shawty, you cocky like that?"

"I mean, damn, even though I got a girl, can I still call
you?" Hazel asked before taking a sip of her drink that
had just been placed on a napkin.

*If she don't care that she got a girl, then I damn sure
don't care either.* "Yeah, you can still call. It ain't no
thang to me, but I ain't gonna have to beat your girl ass
and risk catching a case, am I?"

Oh, I like her she straight aggressive. "Naw, you ain't
gonna have to do that. I'm good with mines. So just write
it down on this napkin." Hazel opened her purse showing
Asia her gun. Like most women in Michigan, she carried
a pistol.

Leesa knew with Tyrus having Kalamazoo and Grand
Rapids under his grasp he had eyes and ears everywhere.
She and her team didn't want any trouble. They were cool
with him doing his thing as long as he left them alone.
They thought for sure that he would have made another
move against them. But to their surprise, he didn't. His
seemingly lack of caring that they were taking a huge
chunk of revenue from drug sales was suspicious if nothing else. His silence didn't make them feel more relaxed.
The Detroit immigrant team made sure that if Tyrus or
his cohorts did attack, the playing field would be even.

Over the past month or so, business had picked up
and J-Rite and Dino's relationship had most definitely
done the same. The two were always together doing this
or that. She'd dropped more than a few thousand dollars
on hotel rooms so they could get some much-desired

privacy. Thank God the beef had died down and Raven had just copped a small three-bedroom bungalow on land contract. She was waiting for her three children and Granny to relocate to where she was doing her dirt at. It was never a good idea to shit where you sleep at, but obviously, Raven hadn't received that memo. Now, J-Rite was happy to say she was laying down roots to Dino's hometown as well.

J-Rite pulled up to Dino's house. As she got out heading toward the porch, she noticed her man was standing with three guys. "Hey, baby!"

"Hey, boo-boo!" one of the random guys blurted out to J-Rite.

"Shut the fuck up, fool! She was talking to me." Dino elbowed him in the lower side.

The supposedly loving couple hugged and kissed. Then Dino introduced her.

"This is my girl, J-Rite. J-Rite, this fat nigga right here name Marlon, this Rell, and the nigga with the weak jokes is Dre."

"What's up doe? Y'all good?"

"What's up?" they said in unison.

"Dino, I need to talk to you if you got a second or two." They walked off the porch and to her car. "Look, Dino, my biggest fear is not having shit and being alone like I was in all those foster homes I told you about. And like how I felt when my brother got killed. I'm about to make major moves in these streets, and I want you with me."

"So, you're admitting in the game now, huh?"

J-Rite had kept denying that she was selling drugs. She told him that Leesa had gotten a lawsuit and gave her the money she was always stuntin' with. Even though she was all in for Dino, she didn't know how he was going to react to the fact that his girlfriend was a confirmed drug dealer. So once more, like she'd done so many times throughout their brief relationship, she denied. "Nah, bae. Stop pressing me about that. I already told you the deal. I'm just thinking about opening a small boutique or something like that. I just want us to get a place together and chill."

She's trying to play me sideways. I know she in the game. Why doesn't she just tell me? She acts like she can't trust me. "Look, do you trust me, or do you think I'm some goof-off lame like that ho-ass nigga Mike Mike you told me you used to fuck with back in Detroit?" He was going hard about her lying to him while he was doing the exact same thing as she—even worse.

This caught her off guard. "Yeah, I trust you. Why would you ask that? And why you bring up his name?"

"Why you keep lying to me? I know where the money coming from. You out in the streets slanging. You didn't think that I would find out? All Grand Rapids singing your name out they mouths! So real talk, what else you lying to me about? Maybe all that bread you keep sending his crazy ass? Yeah, bitch, I saw some of them damn Western Union and Money Gram receipts with his name on them."

Not only was he yelling, questioning her like he was the police. He'd called her out of her name. This was a first. J-Rite felt hurt and angry at the same time. *If I wanted him to know, I would have told him. Why he keep pressing me about this shit? It ain't cool to do that!*

"Dino, why you keep asking me that? What's that all about?" she fumed, irritated, as her voice rose to the same disturbing level as his. J-Rite felt like Dino couldn't take a hint. She hadn't told him before now for a reason, so he should have left it alone. "If I am out here in the streets, why you so upset about it? You should be happy your girl getting money. And Mike Mike is in the past. I'm just looking out on the strength."

"It's not that I'm not happy. It's just that I don't want you to get in nothing. The streets ain't safe; especially for no female," Dino backed up, not wanting to seem like he was in his feelings.

"Chill. I don't want you to worry, baby. I'll be all right. So we gon' move together?"

"Girl, I ain't got money like that hanging around."

"I'll take care of everything. Just say yes, Dino."

A nigga is feeling her, and it would be a good look for what I got going on. "Yeah, okay. But we gonna talk one day about who you really are and what you doing out here day to day," Dino proclaimed before she drove off, leaving him to return to his friends.

CHAPTER THIRTEEN

Raven was bored. She didn't think Benji would remember her. Yet, to her surprise, he did when she called. In their thirty-minute conversation, she found out that Benji had no kids. Sure, he said he liked kids, but had none. He was twenty-two, but had been on his own since he was eleven. He was street smart and book smart. While most guys Raven knew had dropped out of school, Benji graduated and was taking night classes at a college. Raven found those qualities in him attractive. She knew that no one ever graduated from the streets. The single mother of three had seen too many big hustlers fall because of their greed and ego; two of her baby daddies being included. As the two of them finally met up, they continued to feel each other out.

"When we kicked it on the phone, you seemed like somebody I wanted to get to know. So here the hell we are."

"Oh yeah, and why is that?" Raven quizzed.

"You just didn't seem like one of the many airheads that I've been bumping into lately. They all been outta their damn minds," Benji announced, shaking his head.

"Naw, not me, I'm good. But I thought guys liked airheads as long as they have that body; you know, a big ass and all of that."

"Not me. I want a woman with some damn brains."

She was surprised to hear that. With Benji being so young, she figured he only wanted some arm candy dangling. Truth be told, even though she could hold her own, it never occurred to Raven that she would catch his attention like she did.

"So what's it you looking for?" he asked her.

"I don't really know. I'm ready to settle down, but I need a real man to do that. I don't need a guy to take care of my kids. They get everything from me. I need a man to make me happy, mentally and physically. You feel me?"

"That's the type of relationship I wanna be in, but at the same time, I can't be feeling like I'm giving a one-hundred percent and getting nothing in return but a female who is trying to run game. Plus the sex has to be on point!"

"And . . . ummm, are you saying that like you referring that to me?"

"Yeah, I might be. You open for the challenge or what?"

"You're talking about the sex or the relationship?"

"Maybe I'm talking about both."

"Well, real talk, Benji, we gon' have to see about the relationship part because I don't just bring my kids around anybody."

"Well, that's good to know, because I don't want to get attached too quickly."

Raven gave him a strange look. "What you mean?"

"When I say attached, I mean to the kids. I used to date a girl that had a daughter. I loved her like she was my own. When we broke up, it hit me hard, because I couldn't see the baby anymore. I like kids, and I wanna have some one day. I know that might seem odd, because most niggas don't really want any. But I'm a different type of man and, hopefully, you'll get to see."

Damn, a guy that loves kids. That's something you don't see often. I might have met a nigga that's a keeper. I'ma find out. "You're talking a good game. We gonna see if you can back it up. I just wanna know one thing."

"What's that?"

"If you such the perfect nigga, why you ain't got a woman? Now, *that's* the million-dollar question." Raven had never met a man that had all the qualities she wanted, so naturally, Benji had her curiosity piqued.

"Truth be told, a lot of women my age don't want to be tied down."

"Yeah, I understand." Raven knew that with Benji being only twenty-two he more than likely dated chicks his age or younger. When she was his age, she didn't want to be tied down either.

"One female broke up with me before the summer. She claimed it was because she didn't wanna feel guilty if she fucked somebody else. I guess in reality she knew she was going to be out cheating. I mean, I respect her for telling me 'cause that's a bullet I dodged."

"So she wanted to be summer ho, huh? That's crazy." Raven didn't really feel like that. She just wanted to see what Benji was going to say.

"I don't really look at it like that. It's funny you say that. If a nigga fucks a bunch of rats, he's a playa. But if a woman fucks a bunch of guys, she's a ho. Now, how the fuck is that fair?"

Damn, he on point, I was hoping he looked at it like that. "All bullshit aside, I was hoping that you said that. You seem too real, Benji, like you jumped outta a damn fairy tale."

After they finished their meal and a few drinks, they knew it was getting late. Paying the bill, Benji walked Raven to the parking lot. Having driven separate vehicles, it was time to say their good-byes. Stopping in front of a black Yukon, Raven lightly grabbed his arm.

"This it right here. Thanks." She hit the alarm.

Her truck's hard as hell. I wonder where she works at. I ain't gonna ask; it ain't my business. "I like yo' truck. I wanted one like this when they first came out."

"Thanks, I got it for the kids."

"So you gonna let a nigga get a hug or something?" He smiled, showing his perfect teeth.

Raven was attracted to Benji strongly. She figured because of his looks a lot of guys hated him. And she knew he probably had women falling at his feet. But he was the total opposite; humble.

"That's what you want—a hug or something?"

"Yeah, can a nigga get some type of affection?"

She opened her door and set her purse down on the driver's seat.

"So you want a hug?"

"Don't say it like I'm forcing you."

As much as he wanted to hug her, she wanted to be hugged by him. He held her in his arms. She put her nose into his neck and could smell his Sean John cologne. Raven felt as if time had stood still. She didn't care if he let her go. She could have stayed like this forever. Benji seemed to be too good to be true. Only time would tell.

CHAPTER FOURTEEN

Leesa sat at the table eating her food. Glancing around the restaurant she caught a glimpse of Q. He was standing behind the counter. He looked over in her direction, and their eyes locked. *What the fuck is he doing back there?* He gave her a half smile, and she flashed a forced one back. Oh God! *He might have done something to my fucking food!* She dropped the fork onto her plate, then reached for a napkin. *Now he's coming over here. What the fuck he wants?*

"How you doing today?" he stood by the table's side.

"Fine, and you?" Leesa didn't want to speak, but felt she had no choice.

"Look, I'm sorry. We got off on the wrong foot. My name's Quintay."

"Damn! Where you get that name from?" Leesa couldn't help but ask as she fought not to laugh in his face.

"I told you it was weird the day I met you. That's why everybody calls me Q."

"Well, I kinda like your name, Quintay! It makes me smile when I say it!"

"Oh, okay, I see you got jokes. But since you like my name, do you think it's all right if I sit down?"

"Yeah, go ahead." Leesa felt a little silly about the way she acted before at the mall and thinking he may have poisoned her food.

"Are you enjoying your meal?"

"Yeah, I guess. So what were you doing behind the counter?"

"I was making sure that everything was going as it should be."

"Oh, so you're the manager?"

"Naw, I'm the owner. You like my li'l place?" he asked, being modest.

Leesa looked around the interior, then looked back at him. "Yeah, I like it. It's a nice place. I'm impressed. What other secrets you keeping? You have a girl or wife or just your sister from the mall?"

"Nope." Q busted out laughing, immediately getting her reference.

"Okay, smart guy, any kids?" When she asked that, Q stared off into space and his mood changed.

"Hey, you're all right? Did I say something out of order?"

"Naw, not at all. It's just I had a son, but he got hit by a car. He was running after a ball."

"Oh my God, I'm so sorry to hear that! I never had any kids, but I know how it feels to lose someone close to you." Leesa didn't know this man from a can of paint, but for some reason, she felt like she could keep it real with him as he'd done with her. "Well, I'm a widow . . . well, kinda. My fiancé was killed some years back. I'm still dealing with it. I guess that's why sometimes I still say I'm married and keep my engagement ring on my finger."

"Damn, I'm sorry to hear about your loss as well. You wanna talk about it?"

He wants to talk about my feelings! "I've never met a man that wanted to talk about another man. You must be some kind of special."

"Well, when I'm interested in a woman, I wanna know all about her. Most guys don't understand that in a relationship you have to be equal and give it your all."

Leesa hadn't met many guys that thought like that. In fact, the only guy that she met that did think like that was Hutch, who was everything she wanted in a man. *Q is a lot different from what I thought he would be; he seems like he's more grounded.*

Before the two became more engulfed in their conversation and confession session, a waiter came over to the table interrupting. "Excuse me, Q, we got a problem."

He pulled out a business card and handed it to her. "Look, I better go take care of this; meal's on the house. Call me, ummm . . ." At that moment he realized after all that exposing of deep inner feelings, he still had yet to know her name.

"Leesa," she blushed, reaching out to take the card before he hurried away to fix whatever was wrong.

Rell, Dre, and Marlon were standing in front of the building that they had just opened up to hustle out of. They'd grown sick and tired of all the Detroit castaways migrating to their city and raping all the homegrown revenue from the drug trade.

"Yo, Marlon, who that?" Rell said, pointing to the silver Benz truck that was parking in front of the building.

"Fuck if I know. I'm standing here with you."

Suddenly, Dino jumped out of the car, throwing his hands in the air. "What up, niggas?"

"Damnnnnnn . . . When you get that?" Marlon ran up to the passenger side admiring the molded trim along the bottom.

"My girl copped it for me as a birthday gift. It's hard as hell, ain't it?"

"Yeah, it is."

"So how big is it, bitch?" Dre stared at Dino laughing his ass off.

"How big is what, nigga?"

"That dick J-Rite's fucking you with, faggot!"

"Fuck you, nigga!" Dino said, walking over to him like he was gonna swing.

"Fuck yourself, the pussy better."

"Whatever, nigga, but what's up with this money?" Dino got serious, ready to get down to business.

"Everything looking good. We can re-up in a few days."

"That's what's up. Yo, get yo' ass behind the wheel. I need to shoot this move real quick," Dino publicized, tossing him the keys. "Y'all watch the spot and don't fuck shit up!"

"All right, lame, where we going?"

"I gotta meet J-Rite at a house we thinking about getting. And that means I need more cash on hand, if need be," He punched the directions into the GPS system and leaned back in the passenger seat. "Dawg, you think we should open some more spots or what?"

"Yeah, my nigga; you know, mo' chedda, mo' betta."

"Yeah, you right. We give Rell crazy ass that building and get Marlon another one. I'm trying to rape these streets like my girl slick ass and the rest of these cats up here."

"Damn, this crib sweet." Dre was impressed as they pulled up to the address.

"Yeah, I picked this motherfucker out." J-Rite was sitting in her car talking on the phone when they walked up on her. "Hey, baby, sorry I took so long. I had to pick up Dre."

"What's up, Dre?"

"Shit, ma, I like this crib."

"I know, right? It's boss status. Ya' boy picked it out." She gave credit to her man.

As they walked in the house, J-Rite felt like she was living in a fairy tale. *I got my castle and my king. I got everything I want.* "Baby, I just wanted to give you your set of keys to the house and the burglar alarm code. That was Leesa on the phone. She needs to talk to me about something real quick, so I gotta bounce. I'll see you tonight at the club. Happy Birthday again, sweetie."

"Thanks for everything, bae. You know I love you," Dino blessed her with a long embrace and a deep kiss.

After J-Rite pulled off, Dino walked back in the house.

"Yeah, man, you got it made. Your girl and you on point. Y'all straight living the white man's dream!"

"Whatever, fool, let's go. I gotta shoot this other move real quick. I just had to swing by here first and grab them keys to my new castle."

This time, Dino drove his new truck, allowing Dre to ride shotgun. Twenty minutes later, they pulled up to a small house and parked.

"Who stay here?" Dre wondered, looking around.

"My li'l friend, that's all," Dino bragged, getting out of the truck.

"Your li'l friend? Fuck you talking 'bout?" Dre scratched his head as they stepped onto the porch.

Dino pulled out a key unlocking the door. Like he belonged there. He stepped inside. "Hey, baby?"

"Hey, bae," the seductively dressed woman got up, kissing Dino on the lips. Then she turned toward Dre and spoke. "Hey, how you doing? I'm Monique, and you must be Dre. It's so nice to meet you. My honey told me so much about you."

Well, he ain't told me shit about you, Dre thought to himself. "It's nice to meet you too."

"So you want a beer?" Dino asked his homeboy, walking toward the kitchen.

"Yeah, man, that's good lookin'. Can I sit down?" Dre turned, asking Monique.

"Yeah, of course. Make yourself at home."

Dre sat down on the couch. Confused, he attempted to take everything in. He couldn't understand what was going through Dino's mind. *J-Rite is bad as hell, and she got money. So why the fuck would he cheat on her with this bird? This nigga done lost his damn mind!* Dre wished he had a girl like J-Rite. He wanted to settle down but couldn't find the right girl.

Dino returned from the kitchen handing him a beer.

"So what we gonna do tonight, baby?" Monique gleefully chimed in, caressing Dino's chest while shamelessly licking his earlobe.

"It don't matter. It's whatever." He felt his manhood stiffen.

"Yeah, it do, Dino, considering it's your birthday."

"Yo, I ain't trying to be rude and shit, but remember, Dino, we got that thang to go to tonight."

"What thang?"

"That thang, *remember?*" Dre insisted, hoping that he would remember J-Rite was giving him a party.

Done playing dumb, Dino snapped back to his senses. "Oh yeah, *that* thang. Sorry, baby." He slapped Monique across the ass. "But I'ma take a rain check."

After they finished their beers they left.

"Man, you done lost yo' mind or what?"

"Come on, man, what the fuck you talking 'bout?" Dino started the engine, then peeled out into traffic.

"Dude, why you cheating on J-Rite good-caking ass?"

"Nigga, you sound like a broad all up in my business."

"Naw, Dino, I'm just being real. You ain't got no reason to cheat."

"Man, I don't give a fuck what your good-hating ass talking about. Monique's bad as hell. Don't act like you ain't see all that ass she working with! And besides, Monique know 'bout J-Rite."

"So *that* should tell you she ain't shit."

"Dre, pump your brakes. You reading too much into it. It's just sex. That ho got that porn-star pussy going on!"

"You ain't fucking her raw, is you?"

Dino didn't answer.

"Man, you dumb as hell. You better start strapping up because if J-Rite find out, she gonna kill your dumb ass!"

CHAPTER FIFTEEN

The club was packed. J-Rite was sitting at the bar with Leesa and Raven having drinks.

"So what's up with Tyrus?"

"I heard nothing from him." Leesa shrugged her shoulders.

"Tone and Mario said they been trying to find out some more shit on the nigga. He must be hiding out because he knows we own the game," Raven interjected.

"Where are those niggas at anyway?" Leesa questioned.

"Yeah, I'm trying to break them niggaz!" Raven mocked referring to dice.

"I know, right? Well, they said they were coming," J-Rite said.

"What's up, y'all?" Tone said as they walked up to the bar. "Hey, J-Rite, I need to talk to you ASAP."

"Okay, fam, we can go out to the car so we can have some privacy and hear over all this music."

When they got out to the car, Tone gave her a large envelope. J-Rite opened it. It was some photos of Tyrus standing on the porch at a house.

"Where's this at?" she puzzled but still happy to have the information.

"It's here in the outskirts of Grand Rapids. I found out he got a few spots here and some businesses popping off here. So when you ready to take care of him—It's on!"

"Look at what they got for us." J-Rite handed Leesa the photos going back inside their favorite place to hang out at.

"Yeah, this is what we been waiting for."

"I told him I'll let him know when we're ready to handle it."

"Well, I think we should wait until we have some more problems out of the nigga before we get his ass," Leesa said.

"Naw, fuck that! We should handle that nigga now," Tone jumped, in ready for war.

"Yeah, you probably right; fuck letting him get the drop on us," Leesa changed her mind agreeing. "Now we need to get our game plan airtight. But right now, let's gets some drinks and get our buzz on."

"Damn, who's on their way over here, baby?" Dino asked as J-Rite was hanging up her phone.

"Mario and Raven. They need to holla at me about something real quick."

"Good, now you can hook my nigga Dre up with Raven."

"Naw, that ain't even 'bout to happen. That's my girl, and that's your boy. If it don't work out, they gonna have bad blood in the air. And ain't nobody trying to hear that!"

"Damn, that's fucked up," Dre laughed, knowing she was probably right.

"Nigga, don't even worry 'bout it. Just holla at that bitch with all them baby daddies when she get here," Dino taunted before taking a sip of his drink.

"You better watch your mouth. And when did you start drinking anyway?"

"I have to drink because I smoke. It keeps me on my toes. Plus, why drink and don't smoke?"

"So you smoke now too?"

"Yeah, a nigga blow Kush. It ain't like I'm strung out like you, so chill."

J-Rite hadn't noticed Dino smoking or drinking before. She'd been too busy trying to keep her money right. She did notice, however, they seemed not as close as they used to be. She knew that in order to keep a happy home she had to make sure Dino was a hundred percent happy. If things between them were going bad, it would affect how she acted in the streets. And now wasn't the time for her to be off of her square. Truth be told, that was one of, if not the main reason, she and Mike Mike never worked out. J-Rite was brought out of her thoughts by the door-bell ringing. She walked to the door.

"Hey, now," J-Rite let her friends in.

"What up doe, y'all?" Dino said, trying to sound like he was from Detroit as they walked inside.

"Dre, this Mario and Raven." J-Rite made the intro-ductions. She could see Dre's eyes ready to pop out of his head when he saw Raven.

"How you doing, Raven?" Dre was trying to get his mack on.

"So what's?" J-Rite asked, sitting down next to Dino, tired of keeping him in the dark about her business.

"Is it cool to talk in here?" Mario suspiciously asked, looking over at Dre and Dino.

"Yeah, nigga! What the fuck! I'm her man, so it's always gonna be whatever," Dino barked in a hostile tone.

"Slow down, slick, I was talking to her," Mario said with murder in his eyes.

Nigga, you ain't no killa. You talk that rah-rah shit! Dino thought to himself, sensing things were on the verge of getting heated.

Dre sat back and watched to see how things were going to unfold, praying his boy would just fall back. He was hoping that he would be able to get a shot at Raven.

I can't let this shit go down. They 'bout to kill each other. "Dino, be quiet, baby."

"Be quiet? What the fuck! I'm a grown-fucking man. I got some shit to handle anyway. I'm out. Let's roll, nigga."

"Okay, well, damn, it was nice to meet you, Raven."

"Yeah, yeah," she said, uninterested, waving her hand at him, glad Mario ain't have to clown on J-Rite's man.

"Look, word on the street Tyrus got a few niggaz from outta town, and he plans on taking shit all back over again. He got a nephew up here too. So maybe we should pay him a visit. You know, send his ass a message that we ain't fucking around with his old ass."

J-Rite thought about what Mario had just said. She liked everything except involving the nephew. She didn't want to get innocent people caught up in the mix just because. "I wanna get him. I don't have beef with the nephew, so leave him out of it."

"All right, we leave him out of it . . . for now," Mario conceded.

"Okay, cool. Get at us later, J, we out." Raven nodded as they left about, to make some more crucial moves.

J-Rite took that opportunity to call Dino and make sure he was good; that they were good. "What's wrong with you? You know I got business to handle, and that comes first." She'd finally confessed to Dino that she was indeed in the streets. She felt he was mature enough to handle it, even though he had been acting like a straight pussy lately.

"I'm tired of this shit."

"And what shit is that?"

"Do you know what it's like to date a girl who a big hustler? Nobody respect me because they think you take care of me."

"Okay, so what? Big deal. I do take care of you. Fuck them anyway! They wish they had it that good. Them the same niggaz I feed on these streets. So let them know that." She was hoping that made Dino feel better.

After she told him that she did take care of him, he stopped listening. *Bitch think she better than me. I don't need her. Me and my boys about to come all the way up and send all them Detroit niggas packing.* "Look, I'm not jealous. It's just that I worry about something happening to you." He decided to just play the game and continuing getting what he could until he was ready to make his power move.

"Ain't nothing gonna happen, bae. I gotta get this money."

"But we got enough money."

"I never got enough money. It ain't enough money in the world."

"That's greed talking—one person can't never get all the money." *What she mean she ain't got enough money? It's like she ain't even including me in the shit. I guess she all for self.* Dino's ego started getting the best of him. In his book, it was now secretly game on: her versus him.

Leesa had been thinking a lot about Q lately. They had talked on the phone a few times. Every time he called, she got excited. She wanted them to go out but felt she wasn't ready. Leesa still hadn't told J-Rite about him to get her opinion, knowing full well what it would be considering the fact she still was loyal to the memory of Hutch just as she was. Every time Q would ask her on a date, Leesa would make an excuse, although she really had growing feelings for him. In her mind, he had the potential makings to be the next guy she was supposed to be with in life. She knew nobody would ever replace Hutch, but he would want her to be happy.

I'm going to open my heart. I just hope that I don't get hurt. She picked up the phone and dialed Q. He answered on the third ring. She got nervous and hung up. The phone rang and startled her. She looked at the caller ID. It had Q's number on it. *How stupid am I?* "Hello."

"Hey, how you doing?" he asked in that sexy voice she lusted to hear.

"I'm okay, and you?"

"I'm fine, and you a li'l too old to be playing on the phone, ain't you?"

"Oh yeah, about that . . . I wasn't playing on the phone. I dialed the wrong number."

"Yeah, all right, I'll let you go then," he said, calling her bluff. He didn't wait to hear her say "don't." He just hung up.

No, the hell he didn't just hang up on me! Before Leesa could call him back, her phone rang. "You done lost your damn mind! Who the hell you think you is, hanging up on me like that?" She heard him laughing on the other end. "What the hell so funny?"

"I know you ain't heated. It's just that you sound so damn good when you mad. I really like you, but you giving me the runaround, and I don't deserve it. I know you still hurt about . . ." Q paused before he spoke. He didn't know if he should say the name. *I don't want her to bug out, but I gotta get through to her.* "Look, boo, I know you still in love with Hutch, and I can respect that, but you have to understand that I have strong feelings for you as well."

Leesa was at a loss for words. Of course she knew he liked her, but didn't know how much until now. "I really like you too, so where do we go from here?"

"Well, how 'bout dinner Saturday night for starters?"

"All right, where are we going?"

"It's a surprise. You just gon' have to wait and see. Trust me, I got you."

CHAPTER SIXTEEN

Tone went to the door of the apartment he and his brother had been hustling out of. "Yeah, who is it?"

"It's Meka."

He unlocked the door and opened it while clutching his .45. "What up, Meka?"

"What up, Tone?" Meka was a customer that J-Rite had introduced them to. Since J-Rite no longer had a spot, Meka would cop from them on the regular. "I need a fifty, and here go that ten dollars I owe you."

"Good looking. I thought you forgot about that."

"Naw, baby, y'all show me so much love and respect even though I smoke. Y'all don't treat me like a fiend."

"We only as big as you make us, girl," Tone served her.

"Oh yeah, I almost forgot to tell you it's this nigga name Tiny running around robbing customers."

"What the fuck? Good looking on that intel," Tone replied with that look his brother was familiar with as he let her out. "But don't even worry 'bout it. You're always safe when you come to our spot."

"No problem, bro. I'll take care of it, but right now, I gotta go hook up with Raven at the mall," Mario said, rolling up a blunt.

"What's up with y'all?"

"Come on now, you know me. I'm really feeling baby girl."

"Yeah, all right, good luck with that. But remember, we got real shit to do."

After his brother left Tone sat on the couch and rolled a blunt as well. He had to make sure that his plan was thought out before he made his move. He didn't know that his brother had caught strong feelings for Raven and much like J-Rite felt, he didn't think it was a good idea for them to be mixing business and pleasure. *Fuck! I gotta get this asshole that's robbing niggas. He might try to hit my customers or my spot. Then it's really gonna be a problem in the streets of Gun Ru.*

Mario walked in the mall and saw Raven sitting down where she'd said they'd meet. His heart started beating fast. She made him nervous for some strange reason. "Hey, girl, I should have brought you flowers."

This caught her off guard. He'd never acted like this before. She gave him a strange look. *Fuck wrong with him?* "Nigga, are you crazy?"

"Naw; why you say that?"

"Why are you talking 'bout flowers?"

"What, you don't like flowers?"

"I mean, yeah, but it sounds funny coming from you."

"I mean, you putting it out there, and I want you to know I'm noticing it."

"Is it something you wanna tell me?"

"I mean . . . yeah. A nigga like me really feeling you."

Raven was flattered. "I think it's cool you feel like that, but I don't feel the same way. I like you like a brother. You don't hate me now, do you?"

"Hell, naw! I still got mad love for you. I just thought it was something it wasn't. So let's just go to the movie and chill." He was hurt but didn't want her to know. The last thing the hard-core hood warrior wanted was pity.

As they were walking, a female holding a cup bumped into Raven and spilled pop on her. "Damn, bitch! You made me spill my pop!" the female lashed out ready to buck.

Before she could say anything else, Raven attacked. Enraged, she punched her in the face, knocking her to the floor. She then stomped the helpless girl everywhere her foot would land.

A seemingly random guy saw what was going on. Rushing over, he roughly shoved Raven away, who fell back and tried to catch her balance and get right back into the brutal mix. Before the guy knew what was coming next, Mario was all over him. Attempting to be some sort of Captain Save a Ho, it had backfired. The stranger too fell to the floor and started getting kicked in the face until he, like the female, became unconscious.

"I'm 'bout to kill this bitch!" Raven yelled as she continued her tirade.

As Mario watched Raven in action this made him like her more.

J-Rite woke up in an empty bed. She rolled a blunt and started smoking. *I wonder where the hell Dino at?* She looked at her phone to see if she had any missed calls, but there were none. *We gotta work this out. I don't wanna lose a good nigga over some bullshit.* She dialed his phone, and the call went to voice mail. She dialed Leesa's number; it went to voice mail as well. Before she got out of bed, her phone rang. It was Leesa sounding cheerful.

"Hey, girl, what's up? I just called you!"

"Nothing. Just enjoying life. It feels good to be alive," she cheerfully responded.

What the fuck wrong with her? "So, sis, you wanna hook up for lunch?" J-Rite was hoping that she did.

Thankfully, she said yes. *I wonder what the hell is going on with Leesa. Maybe she just in a good mood. That's the way I'm supposed to be. How are Dino and I falling apart? This just doesn't make sense.*

J-Rite got dressed and headed to meet Leesa. On the way, she called Dino but still got no answer. She was thinking about going to do a drive-by to see if he was at his family's house but didn't want to seem like she didn't trust him or she was a stalker.

"What's up, big sis?" Jessica sat down at the table with Leesa.

"I'm good, what's up with you?"

"Girl, Dino and I are having problems—a lot of problems. The bad thing is, I don't know why."

"Well, did you talk to him about what's going on?"

"Naw, sis, one of us is always on the move."

"Okay, Jessica, first thing first; put your big-girl panties on and sit down like adults. But have you ever thought it might just be time to let Dino go? I mean, look at it like this . . . You love him and would do anything for him. But he's been treating you like shit on a stick. That ain't right."

"So you saying end it right now?"

"I ain't saying that, but you have to know where he stands. Does he want you or not? If not, then for real, for real, move on; fuck playing games!"

"Yeah, you right. As soon as we bump heads, we gonna talk. I got too much shit going on to be chasing his ass, or any nigga, for that matter. Either he with me or fucking against me!"

CHAPTER SEVENTEEN

"Mario, that gots to be Tiny." Raven blew out weed smoke, watching their intended victim like a hawk.

He'd told Raven what Meka claimed. Once she found out, Raven insisted he take her with him. At first, Mario told her that she couldn't go. But she told him that since he was copping from them, it was like the guy was stealing from her also. She had a valid point, so he brought her along.

"Yeah, it's him. It's gotta be. It's damn near 90 degrees out here, and this fool rocking a hoodie."

"So, how we gonna handle it?" Raven asked, really for whatever.

"I'm gonna walk up to the house and tell him to get in the damn van."

"That ain't gon' work."

"Yeah, it will. I'ma put that Glock in his spine. He ain't gon' have a choice."

"Yeah, whatever you need to do, let's make it happen."

Mario got out of the van, casually walking over to the house. "My man, can I get a light from you?"

"Yeah, here you go." The guy naïvely fumbled in his pocket.

While he was getting his lighter out, Mario stuck the gun in his face. "Put your fucking hands to your side, and you betta not move!"

"Yo, dude, just don't shoot me, please." His face showed panic.

"Shut the fuck up!"

"I'm sorry, please just don't shoot me! Please, I have a family."

"Get the fuck over here and shut the fuck up! I swear to God I ain't gonna tell you no more!" Mario vowed, snatching him up by the collar.

"Look, please, you got the wrong person," he begged and pleaded with tears forming in his eyes.

Mario slapped the guy on the side of the head with the gun. Blood started gushing out of his head. He started yelling for mercy once more. "Shut the fuck up!" Mario fumed, shoving the barrel of the gun in the man's open mouth. "You weren't begging when yo' ass was running round robbing motherfuckers! Now get the fuck in the van!"

"I'm not getting—" he tried to speak one final time.

Before he could finish his statement Mario knocked him out cold with a blow to the jaw. He easily yanked the smaller guy up off the ground, tossing him in the van. "Tie him up," Mario ordered Raven as he was pulling off from the curb. "I know the perfect spot to take this nigga. We won't have shit to worry about." Mario was getting a lot of enjoyment out of this. It had been awhile since he'd done this type of thing. The Detroit-raised lunatic liked getting money, but he felt that just sitting around was making him soft and lazy. Minutes later, they pulled up in front of a run-down apartment building. "We can leave his ass in here."

Raven seemed like a natural at this. She didn't have a love for it like Mario, but from her father's untimely death, she knew that sometimes things had to be handled. They got out, and Mario carried the guy in the building over his shoulder.

"Come on. Let's take him to the apartment right here," Mario nodded, referring to the first apartment on the left. Once inside, he threw the man on his stomach.

"I'll finish this nigga off," Raven bravely said, placing her gun to the rear of the guy's head.

"Naw, shorty, any nigga can kill a buster like that, but a real one looks them in the eyes." Mario turned the guy over, smacking him in the face until he woke up. Regaining consciousness, the guy was startled. As blood dripped down his face, he thought it was a bad dream . . . until he saw Mario and Raven towering over him. "Now put the gun to his head and handle your business." Mario instantly picked up on her hesitation. "Look, baby, if you want me to, I'll do it. I don't want you to do shit you ain't comfortable with."

The man they were about to kill was praying that with Raven not being able to do it, they would let him live. Mario had no such thing on his mind.

"Look, all you gotta do is think about something or someone that made you mad, then handle your business."

Who can I think about? Raven started to cry. Pointing the gun at the man's face, she pulled the trigger.

"Damn, baby, three slugs? That was cold-blooded! Let's get the fuck outta here. I'ma torch the van," Mario schemed as they walked out of the building.

Raven didn't know how she was supposed to feel. Caught up in having mixed emotions, the ex-stripper-turned-drug-dealer-now-murderer didn't know if she should've cared or not about the deadly deed she'd just committed. *I gotta call my kids and see if they all right. I hope they better than me right about now.*

"Damn, Rell, you look fucked up!" Dino said to his friend as he sat in a chair next to his hospital bed.

"Fuck you, nigga!"

"Naw, my man, I'm just messing with you. Me and Dre gon' find out what the hell happened."

"Fuck you mean what happened? Don't you mean who did this shit to me and my girl?"

"Yeah, man we got this. So tell me again, what jumped off?" Dino knew there was more to the story than Rell was saying.

"I told you some bitch started hating on my girl for no reason. They started fighting, going at it. Tiffany was winning when a few lames jumped in. It was like four of them. Them bitch niggas just got the best of us. Man, they got Tiffany real good. I mean, dawg, I'm salty. They ain't even have to do her like that! She in surgery now."

Rell was always in some beef. One time he didn't like some guys that stayed around the corner from him, so he claimed one of them robbed him. When Dino and the rest of his homeboys went around there letting them thangs go, they found out the guy that got shot had nothing to do with anything. Rell lied, saying he said the guy kinda looked like the guy that robbed him. Come to find out, he never really got robbed.

"All right, nigga, call me and let me know what's good. Keep me posted." Dino got up and walked out the door. *Damn, I hope baby girl be all right. I gotta find out who did this shit. Let me call Dre and see what's popping.* Dino dialed up Dre as he was getting in the car. *Where the fuck this nigga at?* Dino thought after Dre didn't answer his phone. *I wonder what the deal is with his weird-acting ass. He been bugging lately . . . like he avoiding me or some shit.*

CHAPTER EIGHTEEN

"So now I gotta keep you," Q joked with Leesa as they were leaving his grandmother's house.

"Why you say that?" she blushed.

"Besides the fact that I like you, my family loves you. My mother and grandma told me that if we don't stay together, they gonna boot me out of the klan! And they never liked any of my ex's."

"So, you take all your girls home, huh?"

"Hell, naw! Just two; my first date and my son's mother."

At first, Leesa was flattered to hear that, but then she became suspicious. "Why just two? What you hiding?"

"What? I ain't hiding shit! It's just I haven't found any other woman that I've dated worth taking home. And why you always do that?"

"Do what?" Leesa played the role knowing exactly what Q meant.

"You know what I'm talking about."

"If I knew, then would I be asking?"

"You always looking for the worst. If you don't want to fuck with me let me know!" Q meant it looking directly into her in the eyes. The same eyes that he hoped would be the first he saw when he woke up and the last he saw when he went to sleep.

"Hey, Q, I swear it's not like that. I just always hope for the best but expect the worst."

"Well, that's something we gonna have to change."

"It's something that I wanna change, but it's just so hard. I've been like that my entire life; skeptical."

"Well, I want to be with you for the rest of my life, so I'm going to do whatever I have to just to see you happy."

Leesa started feeling a funny feeling in her stomach. *This nigga must really like me. We been kicking it for a li'l bit, and he ain't said nothing 'bout the pussy. Any other nigga would have asked for some.* "I want you to know that after Hutch got killed, I thought I'd never be with anybody else. But then you came along and changed that. I'm glad to know that you have the same feelings for me that I have for you. I've been unhappy for so long that I didn't think I would ever find someone to be with me. I guess today is that day."

J-Rite and Dino still hadn't sat down to talk. It seemed that lately they were seeing less and less of each other. *I don't know what the hell I'ma do about this nigga, but I'm getting tired of this shit!* She went and took a shower. After she got out she was hoping he would be at the house, but she had no such luck. Deciding to lie down for a while, she climbed in the bed not even bothering to put on any clothes. As she was sleeping J-Rite started sweating. Tossing and turning, memories of Mike Mike haunted her. She'd cut him off completely with no verbal or text contact and no more money wired to him. The guilt must have subconsciously kicked in, tormenting her sleep. Feeling someone's touch, J-Rite opened her eyes seeing the top of Dino's nuzzled head between her legs. Instantly she cupped the back of his head and started humping his face while gyrating her hips in a small circular motion.

"You love me?" he asked, briefly looking up.

"Yes, very much, bae. Now put that dick in my mouth."

Dino flashed a big smile, sat up, and took all his clothes off.

She loved the size of his goodness. Just looking at it made her wet. She took ahold of it softly and put it in her mouth. She sucked and slurped like it was the best tasting chocolate Popsicle in the world.

"Damn, J-Rite, baby, this shit on point!" Sounds of his moans filled the air.

"It tastes so good. Let's 69," she suggested. Just as she sat on his face her phone began ringing. J-Rite could tell from the personalized ring tone that it was Tone. She stopped sucking on Dino's dick, reaching for her cell.

"Yo, is you crazy, woman? Don't answer it," Dino demanded as he was just getting off into nibbling on her clit.

"Hold up. I gotta. It might be important."

"What about me? Ain't I important? Every time I look up, you on the phone or in them streets on some money prowl. I bet it's Tone. Am I right or what? Matter of fact, you know what, J-Rite? I think you fucking that nigga!"

"You crazy! Is you high or something? I ain't fucking him."

"Well, you fucking somebody. And if you ain't, you might as well start because you won't be fucking me any more if you answer that damn phone."

J-Rite wasn't going to answer it, but since he tried to put his foot down, she decided to answer it. *Who this nigga think he is? Nigga, you ain't calling shots. You got me twisted.* "Boy, bye. You off the chain!"

"Yeah, what the fuck ever." Dino stormed in the bathroom, then downstairs to the basement.

Defiantly, she pushed *Talk,* listening to what Tone had to say, then hung up with an attitude with her so-called man. Hutch always taught J-Rite to never let anybody run over her, especially a dude. She knew that she was hurting Dino by being headstrong, but also knew that he was trying to hurt her as well. He wanted her to stop hustling just to soothe his bruised ego, when low key, she'd heard him and his boys were trying to make moves in the street as well. *How can he love me if he doesn't support me? He didn't have a problem with me getting money when I was spending it on him. Maybe I'm wrong; maybe he's right. Hell, can I live? I wish I could just go back to the way things were before I started getting money. It was a lot easier when I was dancing. Maybe I can go back to Detroit and fix things between me and Mike Mike. Fuck, naw! Dino the one on the bullshit. I made that nigga who he is; now he gon' come fronting on me.* J-Rite was having a personality split with Jessica. She didn't know what to do.

I gotta get outta this house, I can't think in here. She took a quick shower, then left.

Dino was pissed at the world for the disrespectful way he felt his woman was treating him. His pity party and sulking in the basement was interrupted by an incoming call. *This betta not be this bitch begging me to come back to bed.* "Yeah, what you want?"

"She gone, man," Rell mumbled in a solemn tone voice.

"Huh? What the fuck is you talking 'bout?" Dino asked, shocked to hear his boy on the other end instead of a remorseful J-Rite.

"My girl, nigga, she's dead! She's gone."

"Say what? Hell, naw! How, man? Damn!"

"Fuck you mean? The doctor said severe head trauma and internal bleeding they couldn't stop. I'm fucked up, my dude." Rell started sobbing like a small child.

"Yo, where are you at?"

"I'm at the hospital."

"All right, nigga, I'm on my way." *Damn, my peoples need me right now. Shit, I don't know what the fuck I'd do if I lost J-Rite.* Even though Dino was still cheating with Monique, he loved J-Rite with all his heart. Old girl just gave him the attention that he craved and wasn't getting from home. Heading up the basement stairs, he called his girl's name to tell her he was about to break out, but got no answer. *This bitch done fucked around and left!* As much as he loved J-Rite, she made it difficult at times. He believed in his heart that she was messing around on him with Tone. He had even gotten into arguments with Monique about it. Being a bitter jump off, she insisted she was growing weary of discussing the problems that he and the next female were having. Initially, she didn't mind, but then it seemed that it never stopped.

As Dino drove, he thought about his next move. Pulling up to the hospital he saw Rell standing in the rain looking like death had stolen his spirit. Dino got a lump in his throat. Unlocking the doors, he let Rell in.

"I'm killing the niggas that did this; them and they entire damn family," Rell angrily vowed, slamming his closed fist inside his palm.

Dino knew that a distraught Rell meant every word. He also knew it was his job to ride with homeboy until the wheels fell off. "I'm right here with you, nigga. I don't give a fuck who it is! I swear to you on my life, when we find out who did it, they gon' pay." Riding in silence, they swerved up to the spot. "Yo, where the fuck Dre at?" he yelled out to Marlon.

"I can't tell you. I ain't seen or heard from the nigga."

"Well, hold it down. Me and Rell 'bout to shoot over to the nigga crib real quick." Dino had been having a funny feeling about Dre lately. When he did come around or pop up, he acted real strange. *I hope this nigga ain't out here on some bullshit!*

When they pulled up to Dre's house, he was sitting on the porch. The rain had stopped so he was out enjoying the partial sun. "What's up, niggas?" Dre said when they stepped on the porch.

"Fuck you mean what's up? Where the fuck you been?" Rell shouted, throwing his hands up.

"Aww, man, I been chilling, baby, you know."

"Nigga, is you getting high or something? Why you lookin' like that and whatnot?" Dino interrogated Dre, already knowing the answer.

"Dawg, hold up. I'm a grown-ass man. I do what the fuck I wanna do! If I wanna get down a li'l, that's my business."

"Get down a li'l? Nigga, if you wasn't my boy I'd bury your ass!" Dino stepped in Dre's face ready to knock him out if he kept running his mouth.

"What the fuck wrong with you? Tiffany dead, man, now this shit?" Rell lowered his head trying to regain his composure.

Dre couldn't believe how his life had spiraled out of control. "I'm sorry, y'all. Don't turn on me. I need y'all."

"It's all too much for me right now, but I still got you." Rell gave him some dap.

This was Dino's worst nightmare. He never wanted any of his people to be strung out. He always thought they were better than that. *How the fuck this nigga gon' get hooked on this shit? Don't he know this the same shit making us rich? He out here on this same bullshit that these fiends on. I can't let him get too far out there. I gotta put a stop to this shit and put my foot down!* "Nigga, I'ma tell you what, if you keep fucking wit' that shit, then we done with you!" Dino said, looking at Dre with cold eyes.

How this nigga gonna play me? "You got a lot of damn nerve to try that shit! I been with you since we was li'l niggas. Now you talking 'bout turning yo' back on me! Fuck you, nigga. You lucky I don't take all your shit and smoke it up."

"I know you just talking that shit 'cause you high. So I'ma let it go."

"Naw, it ain't because I'm high. Nigga, you got the perfect life, and you out here fucking it up running with the next bitch!"

"Pump your brakes, nigga. My world don't concern you."

"Then my damn business doesn't concern you."

"Whatever. Rell, you heard what the fuck I said!"

Dino turned and started walking off the porch. Rell got up and followed. Neither one of them looked back. They couldn't deal with Dre right now.

CHAPTER NINETEEN

Raven woke up to loud laughter. She got out of bed and walked in the living room and stared at the sight and smiled. Her kids and Benji were playing. She had been seeing a lot of him lately. Her kids liked him, and he liked them as well. She, like her granny, was hoping that this was the real deal. He was everything Raven ever wanted or desired in a man. Benji was everything her three baby daddies were not.

Benji looked up seeing Raven leaning on the wall. He flashed a smile and blew her a kiss.

"Hey, y'all," she said. Closing her robe good, she leaned over to kiss him.

"Don't, girl! Your morning breath is enough to kill us all," he teased as he sent the kids in the basement to help their granny sort clothes.

"Can I talk to you for a minute, baby?"

"Sure, just let me go use the bathroom, then I'll meet you in the room."

Benji walked to the bathroom barely able to control his thoughts. He started hardening up just thinking about having sex with Raven. He loved having sex with her. It was like something straight out of a dream. Seconds later, she walked in the room with her top off and her nipples erect.

"Did you lock the door?"

She nodded, then turned on the stereo to drown out her noises. Benji made her scream and climax like no other man ever had. "Damn, daddy, I see you ready to play." She licked her lips looking at his hard dick.

"I'm always ready for you."

Raven got in bed and grabbed his manhood. In awe, she gazed at it in her small hands and admired the way it looked. "I love the way you do this pussy. You be beating it up."

"I gotta beat it up. It's too good not to."

As she licked and sucked Benji, he felt like he was about to explode. "Damn, this shit on point! It's hard not to fall in love with you."

"You think we should get married?" Benji brushed the side of her face with his fingertips.

Raven was stunned, shocked—almost speechless. She lifted her head up staring him in the eyes. "Are you serious?"

"Yeah, I'm dead serious. Why? You don't want to marry me?"

She didn't answer right away. It never crossed her mind that he would be ready to get married at his age. "You know marriage is a big step, and I do have three kids."

"Look, you don't have to make up all these excuses why you don't want to marry me. I can take a hint."

"That's never going to happen, I can promise you that. Of course, I'll marry you! And you better not ever think of leaving me!"

"I would never leave you or the kids. I love them like they my own. So you think your homegirls gonna be happy?" Benji had met J-Rite and Leesa briefly and liked them, but he didn't know if they felt the same.

"They ain't never said they didn't like you, and trust me, if they didn't, they would have said something. We good on my end!"

"Yeah, what up doe?" Tone asked when his brother picked up the phone.

"Shit, nigga, just chilling. What's up?"

"Where are you at?"

"Over this broad's house," Mario replied, lying back like a boss getting his dick sucked.

"Damn, nigga, well, turn the news on. Somebody done killed an undercover cop in the hood. They left him stanking in an empty building."

"Yeah, I see it. Dang, that's fucked up." Mario had turned on the television while his female friend continued to handle her slurping business. "Whelp, I'm 'bout to come holler at you real quick, bro. See you in a few."

I wonder what the fuck wrong with this nigga? Tone thought after he hung up with his little brother. He knew something was wrong—it was like he had a sixth sense. He could tell when something was wrong, when his Mario wasn't feeling well, or when he was in trouble. *Let me call J-Rite. Something might be about to pop off.* He then called J-Rite and told her he needed her to come over too. Twenty minutes, later they were all sitting together.

"All right, what's up?" J-Rite was confused as to why she was summoned to rush over, even though she had shit of her own she wanted to kick about.

"Soooo, I killed that cop," Mario confessed matter-of-factly.

"The one on the news this damn morning?" J-Rite shouted, pressing her hand to her chest.

"Yeah, that's the one," he confirmed, dropping his head in shame. "He's a guy that Meka said was robbing niggas' spots. But I guess it turns out it wasn't the right nigga."

"What!" J-Rite couldn't believe what she was hearing.

"So you killed the wrong fucking nigga?" Tone sat back in the oversized chair rubbing his chin.

"Yo, hold up. This is what happened. One of our custos told us about a nigga that was robbing spots. Me and Raven checked it out, and we seen a nigga posted like he was casing the joint."

"Raven too?" J-Rite rolled her eyes to the top of her head.

"Yeah, J, so then we snatched him up and handled our business. We left him at an empty building. Now come to find out, the nigga was an undercover cop. My bad."

"*My bad!* Y'all know how fucking hot this shit is 'bout to get?" Tone leaped to his feet and paced the living-room floor.

"Yeah, but, bro, we ain't think it was no cop. He ain't say shit!"

"Okay, but y'all Bonnie and Clyde asses can't just go around murdering motherfuckers because some dope-fiend said a nigga ain't right. That shit was dumb as fuck." *This is why stupid niggas and money don't mix,* J-Rite thought to herself. She had never been mad at anything her people did before in the name of getting money, but now, she was heated.

"Look, I know you mad, but I was only doing what I thought was best for us."

"Yeah, they should have played the game a li'l bit better, but all we can do now is fix this shit." Tone starting thinking about their next move.

"Yeah, Tone, you right. No need to cry over spoiled milk. So, the only one that knows what happened is the dopefiend. Well, y'all know what's got to be done."

"I'll do it, J-Rite, don't even trip." Tone stepped up.

"Naw, I fucked up; me and Raven. I'll take care of it."

"Naw, y'all, I'ma take care of it. I'ma put in the work." J-Rite had a lump in her throat no sooner than she made the statement.

The brothers gave her an awkward look.

"You?" Tone kinda laughed.

"Yeah, me. Why? You two don't think I know how to handle my business if need be?"

"It's just that we know you a hustler. We never looked at you like a killer."

"I ain't a killer; it's just how you handle thangs. Now, is there anything else all y'all wanna tell me?"

"Yeah, sis, me and Raven got some beef on the floor."

"I be damned. With who? What the fuck else all y'all busy asses been up to?"

"We don't know. Some nothing-ass busters we stumped out at the mall."

"Well, I'll put the word out and see what's up. Speaking of Raven, anybody heard from her today?"

They both looked at Mario.

"Why are all y'all looking at me?"

"'Cause y'all seemingly thicker than thieves." J-Rite joked but was as serious as ten heart attacks.

"Naw, I ain't heard from her."

"Well, like I said. I'll take care of Meka, and you try to lie low. Ain't no telling who these other people is, but I'm on that too. After I stop by my crib, I'ma go ride and press my ear to the streets."

"Yeah, I can do that, and again my bad," Mario repeated as J-Rite left.

Dino walked in the house. J-Rite was still very much pissed off from the disrespectful comment about her and

Tone. As he walked past with tears in his eyes, as much as she wanted, she couldn't stay mad at him.

"Dino, what's wrong, baby? What happened?"

"Dre shooting dope getting high!"

"What? Naw!" She covered her mouth as her jaw dropped.

"Yeah, bae, and Rell and Tiffany got into a fight in the mall awhile back with some niggas. She died from head injuries early this morning. Shit's really fucked up! I'm fucked up!"

"I'm so sorry, baby. Do you know who did it?" she grilled him wiping away his tears. She prayed it wasn't Raven and Mario, but knew it was.

"Naw, not yet. The mall cameras didn't catch it, so who knows? But when we find out, they all gonna die!"

J-Rite held him tight in her arms. *What the fuck am I gon' do now? How can I choose between the man I love and my family?* She felt like the walls were closing in on her. With a pounding headache, she couldn't think of any way to solve the problem. She knew that eventually she would have to pick a side. "Look, Dino. We gotta make it work between us. I love you. I'll be right here for you."

"J, I know you probably have to go out to handle your business or whatever, but can you stay here tonight? A nigga need you!"

How can I tell him no? Dre's like a brother to him, and he's on dope. That same shit that hooked his mom got his boy. "Yeah, baby, I'll stay with you tonight." J-Rite didn't know how Dino would act if he found out that it was her team that ultimately killed his people, but she had a pretty good idea she wouldn't like it.

"Hold me, baby," Dino whined until they both fell asleep.

***

J-Rite was walking back and forth across her kitchen floor. She'd called Leesa and got her voice mail. *This shit done got out of hand. What the fuck am I gon' do now?* Just then, her phone rang. It was Leesa. "What's up, girl? I called you a li'l while ago."

"I was asleep." Leesa glanced over at Q who was just waking up as well.

"Girl, for real, 911. I need you to meet me at Starbucks ASAP!"

"All right, sis, I'm on my way."

J-Rite hung up, then walked around the house hoping that Dino was down in the basement; he wasn't. She called his phone and got no answer. Born in the streets, she could only assume he was with Rell looking for the dudes that he had beef with. She jumped in her car and headed to Starbucks. When she stepped inside, she saw her big sis. It put a smile on her face to know that Leesa could still be counted on when she needed her. "Girl, I don't know what to do! That damn Raven and Mario stumped out Dino's boy Rell and killed his girl."

"Naw, girl!"

"Yes, then on top of that, they are the idiots that killed an undercover cop that's all on the news." She leaned in to make sure no one else was listening.

"What in the entire hell! Those two are reckless as hell! Does Dino know they fucked his people over?"

"Naw, he don't know yet, but I'm scared it's only a matter of time before he finds out."

"Okay, well, who know that they killed the cop?" Leesa was speaking just as low as J-Rite.

"This dopefiend named Meka from around the way. Her dumb ass sent them on the dummy mission."

Leesa gave her a hard cold stare. J-Rite already knew what it meant. "She the one that told them a nigga was kicking in doors and robbing custos, so they call they self getting to got him before they got hit."

"Well, li'l sis, we all in this shit together. Just because they fucked up don't mean we not family anymore."

"You think I should let them know who they stumped out?"

"They don't know yet?"

"Naw, I ain't told them."

"Well, you better go tell them. You know how they are." Leesa was growing weary of all this drug life, falling deeper in love with Q. "They might think it's all fun and games."

"All this bullshit madness they done got into together, and they ain't even fucking!"

"Well, they need to. And seriously, they might all need to bounce back to Detroit and let things die down."

"You right, Leesa, but what if Raven don't want to leave?"

"What you talking 'bout?"

"You know her and that dude Benji getting pretty serious. I think her hot-box butt in love."

"Well, if she don't wanna go, then she gonna have to figure something out."

"Yeah, you right. What do we do about the Dino situation?"

"I don't know. That's kinda hard. What would you do if it was one of us that got killed?"

"It would be hell to pay. It'd be blood spilled all over the streets of Grand Rapids."

"All right then, it's the same way on his end. Let's just see how shit gonna play out. But I guess ending y'all relationship is out of the question, right?"

"Yeah, girl, I think so. I do love him."

"So, y'all have been trying to work shit out?" Leesa questioned.

"Yeah, we have. Crazy as it seems, this shit done brought us closer."

"Well, let's just see what happens. Even if they go back to Detroit, we still got a problem."

"Yeah, you right. I'm 'bout to go let them know what's up. We'll talk later."

On her way over to see Mario she couldn't stop thinking about how she would feel if the shoe was on the other foot. *I hope I'm never in a situation like this again.* J-Rite pulled up to Mario and Tone's house and saw Raven's car parked in the front. "What up, y'all?" she spoke as she was walking in the house.

"You want something to drink, baby girl?" Tone asked her, closing the door behind her.

"Yeah, gimme a Hennessey straight; no ice."

Raven and Mario were preoccupied playing NBA Live.

"I need to holla at y'all," she said nervously. She was trying to think of the best way to tell them. She wondered if they would even care that it was Dino's people. *How this gonna affect our relationship? How can I tell a motherfucker who they can't beef with, like I'm some sort of dictator?*

"Spit it out, girl!" Raven said, blowing out weed smoke through her nose having paused the game.

"Y'all know that guy and female y'all got into it with at the mall?"

"Yeah, what about them?" Mario said, cutting her off. "You know where them lames at? What's the intel?"

"Yeah, I know who they are. And now the girl's dead."

"So fuck that bitch! Where the nigga at? We need to get at him before he get at us," Mario raged with his chest stuck out.

"Negro, they Dino's people. The guy is his boy Rell and his girl Tiffany." She raised her voice, tired of them not taking shit seriously.

Nobody said anything. They all just looked at each other. They knew they were caught up and how serious things had just become. First, the undercover cop; now, this conflict of interest.

"So now what?" Raven placed the controller down on the coffee table.

"I don't know," J-Rite said, shaking her head. "I know he gonna want revenge."

"Yeah, true that! He gonna want blood! Just like if it was us, we would," Tone cracked a halfway smile.

"Leesa and I decided it may be time to really lie low. We thinking it might be time for y'all all to break camp and head back to Detroit. What y'all think? We can set something up there."

"Man, I don't know." Raven shrugged her shoulders undecided, ignoring the fact she was actually the one that'd murdered the undercover in the first place.

"Why? What's wrong?" Mario gave his partner in crime the side eye.

"'Cause me and Benji talking about married, that's why. Besides, I just moved my kids and Granny up here."

"That's what's up? But maybe you can talk him into moving too. Your ass is about to be hotter than July if they find out about the cop . . . and Tiffany."

Raven knew her best friend was on point in what she was saying, but didn't care. She knew Mario couldn't understand, but tried to make shit right. "Look, Mario, you know I love you, and we gonna always be tight, but I'm in love with Benji. Can't you just be happy for me, bighead?"

"A nigga is happy. I just hope that you making the right decision staying up here in the long run, that's all."

"I am. Benji is really good to me, plus he loves my kids like they his."

"Well, I hope so, because when you doing life in prison behind two murders, they gonna need all the love they can get," Mario taunted, storming out the door to soothe his battered ego.

CHAPTER TWENTY

"Is it good to you, baby?" Q asked Leesa as he sat on his knees with his face buried in her love spot.

"Yeah, baby!" she moaned out, grabbing his head, pushing his face deeper so that his tongue would hit the right spot.

Q hadn't had a lot of luck with women, no fault of his own. With him having a nice house, money, and cars, he attracted the wrong type of women. Usually, it was with women that wanted flings, showpieces, money, or just sex. He never wanted that from a woman; he always wanted to settle down. And having that type of want hurt him. He couldn't understand why women didn't want the same. He came from a two-parent family. He'd seen the love his parents shared for each other and wanted the same life for himself. Leesa was the perfect fit for him he thought, outside of the fact she needed to leave the streets alone.

He held her legs up and licked from bottom to top. The more he licked the more she moaned. Hearing her cries of pleasure made him want to do the best job he could. Leesa groped her own perky breasts and started pinching her nipples. Q was bringing her closer and closer to the edge. She hoped this moment lasted a lifetime. He stuck his fingers inside, and she moaned loudly.

"Stand up," she begged in her feelings.

Wasting no time, Q stood up, and she kissed the tip of his dick. She could taste his juice. She started kissing his manhood softly, like she wanted him to beg. Finally she put it in her mouth, inch by inch.

"Oh shit." His body lifted, and he was standing on his toes. He never felt anything so warm and nice in his entire life. He could have died right then and there. When he thought it couldn't get any better, it did. She put all of him in her mouth. He looked at her and smiled. She looked beautiful. He was so hard he thought he was about to break. She sucked like it was nobody's business. He didn't know where she learned how to do this so good, but he wanted to thank the person that taught her.

In total freak mode, Leesa could feel him on the verge of exploding. *I'm working magic on this dick! Whoa, my pussy never been this damn wet!* She took her hands off him and started playing with herself.

Leesa eased his dick all the way out, then put the tip of him back in her mouth. It was apparent by his veins bulging, it was only a matter of time before he let loose.

"Can I have some pussy now?" He was ready to rape her if need be.

"Naw, maybe later, baby, but this all you getting now," she giggled, pulling him down on the couch. Ready to get even freakier, she sat on his lap putting him in her tightest hole. Leesa didn't know what had come over her. She rode him until she was on the verge of screaming. Suddenly, she hopped up—no warning.

"Bae, what's wrong?"

"Nothing, baby." She bent over getting in doggie style. "Now, come over here and finish what you started."

"Dre, you hogging it all up," a neighborhood fiend said to him as they were getting high.

"So what, bitch? This my shit. Now wait 'til I'm done."

"I'm sorry, baby, I just wanted a li'l bit." She tried a softer approach as her stomach grew nauseated.

"All right, damn, girl, come here; gimme your arm."

The fiend eagerly did as she was told.

"Damn, I can't find a vein. I'll put it in your foot like last time if you want."

She quickly took her shoe off. Dre shot the drug directly in between her toes and sat back watching her nod.

"This shit good, baby," she said smiling a toothless smile. "Do you love me, Dre? Do you?"

Dre looked at her and started thinking to himself, *This bitch ain't got no teeth, she ugly, and this bitch smell. This is what the fuck I've become. I used to fuck any bitch I wanted. Now all I can fuck is crackheads. This shit's crazy. I gotta kick this shit and do it fast. I'm going to use the last li'l bit, then I'm done.* Disgusted with himself, he got up and walked over to the window. It was a hot day, and the block was full of people, especially hustlers. He could see all the up-and-coming hood stars, and it reminded him of when he and Dino were teenagers.

"Y'all just wait 'til I get back in the game. I'm going to show y'all how real niggas shine," he mumbled half out of his mind. He pulled a half-smoked Basic out of his pocket, lit it, then took a long puff. *I wonder if Dino and the niggas still got love for me. If not, fuck 'em. I don't need them niggas! Dino getting soft anyway. He should have been got J-Rite's plug like he claimed he was gonna do from jump.*

J-Rite had just gotten out of the shower when she received the call from Rhonda letting her know Meka was on her way to get high. J-Rite was hoping that she could get this over with so she could tie up all the loose ends. She grabbed her gun and jumped in the car. J-Rite was exhausted from all the things she had on her plate. Full of guilt, she had a hard time even lying next to Dino.

She didn't know if he knew or how close it was before he knew. Every minute was making her more and more stressed and paranoid. She was sitting at a red light on Division when a black van pulled up alongside of her. A guy suddenly jumped out. Before J-Rite could do or say anything, he stuck a gun in her face.

"Bitch, get the fuck out! Hurry the fuck up, bitch! Check this motherfucker in!"

J-Rite got out and started walking backward. He shoved her out of the way and hopped inside her vehicle. The van he jumped out of screeched off. Before he could get away, J-Rite whipped out her pistol and shot through the back window twice. The driver lost control and crashed into a telephone pole. Infuriated, she ran up on the van and shot twice more. Hearing police sirens coming her way, J-Rite luckily saw Sean coming around the corner. "Hey, grab this and get rid of it," she demanded, handing the firearm off to him.

The great hustle gods had to be watching over her, because no sooner than Sean ran off, the police pulled up. J-Rite's perfect plan of getting paid in Grand Rapids was starting to unravel. She had butterflies in her stomach. She wanted to throw up.

"Freeze! Put your hands up, lady, and don't fucking move."

"I ain't did shit! They just carjacked me," she insisted with her arms in the air.

A fat white cop ran up on her with malice. "Lay your ass on the ground! Now! Lie down!"

His partner, a young black guy, walked up behind her even more aggressive than his colleague. "I got you covered. Watch this sneaky looking thug!"

I hope Sean got that gun stashed, J-Rite thought as they handcuffed her, throwing her in the rear of their squad car without hearing her side of the incident.

When they got her down to the station, they finger-printed her and put her in a cell. When she walked in, she smelled urine, and that made her dizzy. The lights were dim and the place was filthy. Thankfully, she was the only person in the cell.

This some real bullshit! I gotta get the fuck outta here. J-Rite wasn't so much worried about catching a case, getting into it with anybody, or getting hurt. Her only concern was taking care of Meka before she fucked the entire team over. *I gotta call somebody and get the fuck back on the streets.* She walked over to the pay phone, picked it up, and wiped it off.

"Fuck," J-Rite yelled, slamming the receiver down. She realized that she hadn't memorized anyone's numbers but one person. Picking back up the phone, she dialed a number that she was wishing she didn't have to call. The person on the other end picked up. J-Rite heard the operator ask if they accepted the charges. They quickly accepted. "Thanks, Asia, for accepting the call."

"What the hell are you doing in jail?"

"I got picked up on some bullshit!"

"Are you all right?"

"Yeah, I'm good. I need you to take care of something for me if you still up here in Gun Ru."

"Yeah, what is it? Even though you don't fuck with me like that."

J-Rite didn't have the time or option to cuss Asia out right now. She needed her to do exactly as asked. "Look, I need you to find my sister and tell her where I'm at."

"Yeah, okay," Asia happily agreed, wanting to be able to have a one-on-one face-to-face meeting with Leesa, who she knew had the plug, for months on end. Now was her time. "I got you, J, but you gotta promise to put me on when you touch back down."

It was two in the morning when J-Rite finally got to her cell. There were about twenty other women in the unit. She had talked to Leesa and was told she would have a lawyer first thing in the morning. She started making up her bunk, and the girl that shared the cell with her woke up.

"What up? I'm Shay." She was honey brown, five foot six, and 130 pounds, mostly in her chest.

I gotta watch my back. "What up? I'm J-Rite."

"J-Rite. I heard that name before." Shay said she was waiting on the feds to come pick her up on a case that she caught. They were holding her here until she finished trial. J-Rite didn't tell her too much. She'd watched enough of *48 Hours* to know that sometimes they put undercover cops or informants in the cell to get dirt on you. She knew at this point they didn't really have a case on her so there was no need to help them build one. After she and Shay talked for a while, J-Rite decided to get some sleep the best she could. She knew Dino was probably worried sick about her.

"Jessica Sanders! Sanders!" She was awakened by a deputy calling her name the next morning.

"I'm Sanders."

"You have court," a female deputy said to her as she did her rounds.

After J-Rite washed her face and brushed her teeth, she was taken to a holding cell waiting for court. There were five other girls packed in the small area. After sitting there for an hour, a male stepped to a small window and called her name.

"I'm Sanders," J-Rite spoke up stepping to the window.

"Sanders, I'm your attorney Jason Jefferies. I was hired by Leesa Jones. She's waiting out in the courtroom."

"Look, all that is good, but can you get me a bond?"

"I don't see why not. They don't really have anything on you. From what I can tell, this is a weak case. What's about to happen is we going out in the courtroom and they gon' present what they have, then I'm going to do my part. Then I'll try to get you home. Is there a certain amount of money that you can't afford to pay for bail?"

"No."

"All right, let's go."

J-Rite was anxious. She was led in the courtroom by two deputies. Once inside, she looked around. Everybody was there for support but Dino. The judge let the prosecutor speak, then J-Rite's attorney said what he had to say.

"Attempted murder? There's no proof of that."

"Well, we have a witness willing to testify. The victim is in the hospital."

When J-Rite heard that, she got nervous. Her stomach was doing flips. It had been hurting since she got arrested. After being giving an extremely high bail, she was led out of the courtroom. When she got back to the cell she started throwing up. *What the fuck wrong with me? I gotta get to a doctor when I get outta this stankin' motherfucker!*

"Damn, Monique, this shit got me pissed. How the fuck could a nigga play me like this?" Dino said.

"You want some head, baby? You know that always make you feel better."

That's all this bitch thinks about is sex—nothing more, nothing less. "Naw, I'm good on all that."

Dre had hurt Dino very bad. They had a joint account set up for emergencies. Dre had gone and took the money out to get high. Even though half of the cash did belong to him, it was the point and principal. "Yo, did you call Rell and Marlon like I asked you to or what?"

"Yeah, I did, boy, and you ain't got to keep asking me that. I'm not stupid like that other ho you keep fucking."

"Oh my God! I'm getting tired of your damn mouth!"

"You wasn't getting tired of it when I was swallowing dick, your balls, or you was slow nutting in it. But you know what? I'm starting to think that this relationship done ran its course. Maybe we should just call it quits."

"Is that what you want to do?" Dino asked, hoping deep down inside that she didn't really mean what she was saying.

"Naw, I don't, but you keep taking your problems out on me, and that's foul as hell."

He didn't mean to treat her bad. However, he didn't have time to cater to her all-over-the-place emotions. "Okay, my bad. I'll get off that bullshit, but, baby, can you please call them guys back and tell them I said get their fucking asses over here right now!"

Ironically, the phone rang before Monique picked it up. "Hello," she said answering it.

"Hey, Monique, can I speak to Dino. This is Marlon."

"Yeah, hold on."

"Yeah, what's up? I been calling your punk ass!"

"Nigga, get your face out of the pussy and come through. We got a big problem brewing."

"Where are you at?" Dino asked while putting on his sneakers.

"I'm at the spot."

"Cool, I'm on my way."

When Dino pulled up to the spot, Marlon and Rell were talking to a short, stocky guy standing next to a Silver Tahoe. The guy's back was turned so Dino couldn't see his face. Dino got out and started walking toward them. "What's up, nigga?" Dino said as he and Marlon stood face-to-face.

"Yo, fam, he repping the new owner of the building."

When Marlon said that, the guy turned around. "What up? I'm Benji," he made it known with a hardened look. "And I'ma cut to the chase. It's my understanding that y'all running a nice li'l operation. The deal y'all had with the previous owners, we can have the same thing."

Dino wanted to tell him to go fuck himself! There was something about Benji he just didn't like. But he knew that if he did that, it would put him in a bad place. He didn't need more headaches or beef right now. "Can we get a few days to, you know, think it over?" he asked, upset for having to even consider the deal.

"Yeah. Here's my number. You got three days tops," he announced, handing him a business card.

As Benji got in his truck and pulled off, Dino watched him, heated.

"What you think, Dino?" Rell asked as Marlon continued to stand silent and await his response.

"I don't know what's up with that nigga. We need to do our homework on him!"

"Speaking of doing homework, we need to get them motherfuckers from the mall." Rell was pumped up to kill, and rightly so.

"Yeah, nigga, I'm working on that. I'm real close to finding out who they is. Just hold on. We gonna get revenge in due time, trust!"

CHAPTER TWENTY-ONE

"So how did it go?" Tyrus asked his nephew, awaiting an update.

"These niggas be hoes. They ain't gonna be a problem, I gave them three days to get at me."

"Okay, youngblood. You know I always tell you never underestimate anybody, and respect every man for who they are."

"Yeah, I know, but these niggas nowadays be straight-up hoes. I don't see how come the whole world ain't like us . . . our crew, our family."

"Sometimes I wonder about you, boy."

This made his nephew give him an awkward look. "You ain't got to worry 'bout me. Benji gonna be all right."

Tyrus shook his head in disappointment. "Didn't I tell you that a grown man doesn't go by a nickname, and why you still dressing like some punk? Have some respect for yo'self! You represent me when you out in the streets."

Tyrus had been taking care of Benji since he was little. His mom felt that being with Tyrus would make him tough. Benji's mom knew what kind of life he lived and was hoping that Benji would learn how to use the streets to his advantage. Tyrus taught him, and he learned fast. The older man's protégé was both street smart and book smart. Yet, Tyrus would get upset when Benji didn't do things exactly his way. He hated how Benji thought he had life figured out. Sometimes he felt that the boy was too smart for his own good.

"Unk, why do we always gotta go through this? I'm who I am. You gotta live with that. You made me this way." He leaned back in his chair on the two rear legs.

"Yeah, yeah, that shit sound good. Just take care of my business. And, oh yeah, how you and your lady friend doing that keeps you away from the club family?"

This put a smile on Benji's face. He loved to talk about Raven. "We good, Unk. I'm 'bout to go over there now."

"You know before you and her get real serious I need to meet her."

"Yeah, I know, Unk. I'm gonna bring her over for dinner." Benji was lying. He had no intentions of bringing her to dinner. He didn't want his uncle to meet her. Period. Well, at least until they were married. It wasn't that he was ashamed of her. It was just he didn't want his uncle to say something about her having three kids by three different men.

"Okay, then, but now, I need you to take care of something else for me, Nephew."

"Anything for you, Unk."

Tyrus opened his desk, pulled out a big yellow envelope, and handed it to Benji.

"What's these pictures of? A building you buying?"

"Naw, I need it burned down."

"Burned down? We into arson now?" Benji grinned, trying to make a joke.

Tyrus gave him a look that meant this was no joking matter. "Look, boy, take care of it, and it better be done right."

As Benji flipped through the photos, he wondered why it had to be done. "Why you want me to burn this down? It looks okay," he said foolishly.

"Since when do I have to explain myself? Or ask you something twice?"

"You don't, Unk. I was just wondering, that's all."

"Well, don't! Just do as you're fucking told!"

"Yeah, all right. When?"

"I want it done this fucking week!"

As Benji drove to Raven's house he couldn't under-stand what was going on with his uncle. They had always been so close. Now, it seemed that they were bumping heads a lot. *Unk been on some bullshit lately. I don't know if the nigga going crazy or what. I wonder why he keep tripping on everything I do. Maybe my old girl knows. Let me give her a call.* Benji snatched his cell up off the passenger seat and dialed his mother's number. It took four rings before she answered.

"Hello, Boncellia," he said, calling by her first name. This was something he had been doing since he was lit-tle. She had him do it. When she had Benji, she was very young and didn't want to be a mother, so she always acted like he was her little brother.

"Hey, baby, how things going?"

"Fine. I need to know if Unk sick."

"Huh? Why you ask that?"

"'Cause he's been acting funny."

"Naw, he ain't sick; well, not that I know of."

"All right, cool. I gotta go." He cut the conversation short.

Benji pulled into Raven's driveway, parked, and got out. *I hope J-Rite get outta the shit she in.* He didn't really know what was going on. He just knew that Raven told him her girl was locked up. Although he and Raven were together, they never discussed their individual street business. When he walked in the house, Raven's grandmother was sitting on the couch. "Hey, Granny," he spoke as he leaned over kissing her on the cheek.

"Hey, baby."

"Where is everybody? I didn't see Raven's truck."

"Jennifer is at court seeing about Jessica, and the kids are in the backyard playing."

"Hey, baby!" Raven greeted him walking in the house.

"What up?" He winked in return.

"How's Jessica doing?" Her granny anxiously asked.

"She's all right; she'll be home soon." Her grandmother got up and left the room. "So how the meeting with your uncle go? You good?"

"It was straight."

Raven and Benji had spent a great deal of time together; they both could tell when the other had something on their mind.

"What's wrong, baby?"

"I don't know. It just seems like me and Unk run together 'bout to come to an end. He trip on all the shit I do."

"Well, bae, have you tried to talk to him?"

"Kinda, but he stuck in his ways. You know how people are."

"Yeah, I feel you on that. Oh dang, I forgot Granny's prescription. Come run with me to CVS right quick. I just gotta use the bathroom first."

Benji was preoccupied with the business he had to take care of for his uncle, so he wasn't doing too much talking before they left. After Raven walked to the truck he looked in the envelope once more. He couldn't see the building too good because the pictures were taken at night, but he had the address. *I've seen this place before. Well, I'll take care of it tonight. This nigga gon' give me damn instructions on how to burn down a fucking building. We gonna have to talk real soon or part ways.* He set the envelope down on the couch and walked out of the room, then he went and joined Raven in her SUV and discovered she wanted him to drive, but as he was pulling off, she told him to stop. She had forgotten her phone. When she got in the den, she picked up her cell off the couch. "What's this?" she said, picking up the envelope that was lying next to it. Going through it, she came to the photos and a piece of paper. After reading it, she got upset. She had to sit down. She was stunned. *I can't believe this shit! This nigga was playing me the whole time.*

Benji walked in the room to see what was taking her so long. He saw the love of his life with the envelope in her hand and tears in her eyes. "What you doing with that? And what's wrong?"

"I'm telling you the truth! Why the fuck would I lie? I'm a grown man. I ain't gotta lie about shit!" Benji yelled at Raven sitting in the passenger seat of her truck. He had explained everything he knew about what he was supposed to do to the building, which wasn't much.

"So you didn't know that we was beefing with your uncle?"

"Look, girl, I don't play these types of games." Benji loved Raven very much and was willing to do whatever it took to keep her. "Just tell me what I have to do to make you believe me, and I'll do it."

Raven didn't know what to do or say. She loved Benji with all her heart, but he was on the side of the enemy. *Now I know how J-Rite must feel . . . the man she loves or the only family she got? What do I tell him? I do believe him, but how can I make this shit work? My peeps ain't gonna trust me if I keep him, but I can't just break up with him. I found my soul mate. What do I do?* "I could talk to your uncle and see if we could solve this problem . . . That might work."

Benji knew what type of man his uncle was; he wanted to destroy the girls. He'd heard talk but never any names. "Naw, bae, it ain't gonna work. The beef too damn serious in his stubborn eyes. We gonna have to try something different."

"I don't know how we gonna fix this, but we will. But in the meantime, I need to holla at my girls and let them know what's up."

"Raven, baby, I don't think that's such a good idea. They might wanna get in they feelings and make shit really pop off." Benji knew that Raven was about her business when it came to drama, and more than likely, so was her team.

"You gotta trust me. I'm gonna handle my part. Can you stall your uncle or what?"

"Yeah, I'll think of something. Don't worry." Benji meant what he was saying. He wanted peace between him and his girl and both their teams.

After he got out of her truck, Raven went in the house to sit down and think. She never got a chance to go to CVS as planned.

"Are you okay?" J-Rite was awakened by a voice and someone shaking her. She opened her eyes. It was a nurse with a jailhouse ID pinned to her white uniform.

"What happened? Where am I?" her eyes scanned the room from the stretcher.

"You were found passed out cold in your cell."

"What!"

"Yes, Sanders. Now I've got good news and bad news. The reason you passed out is because you're pregnant. Now brace yourself for the bad news. You apparently have gonorrhea."

Gonorrhea! Gonorrhea! Gonorrhea! When the nurse said that, J-Rite just kept hearing it over and over again in her head. *How in the fuck did I get this shit? Dino been fucking around on me.* She'd been fucking, dancing, and tricking for years and had never once been burnt; now this.

"Sanders, are you okay?"

J-Rite wanted to cry, but she knew she needed to stay strong. "I'm just kinda fucked up about it."

"Yeah, well, it's not the end of the world. You can still have a healthy baby. Plus it could be worse. You could have AIDS. You might want to contact any sexual partners you've been with."

At those words, J-Rite went off. "I don't have sex partners! I have one man. We been together for a while." Usually hard, she covered her face and sobbed.

The nurse had seen this before. One person in the relationship steps out, and it hurts both parties. She didn't know what to say to J-Rite. "Well, look, I'm going to give you some meds. And when you get released, don't go kill your boyfriend and end up back behind bars. He ain't worth it."

When J-Rite got back to her cell, she walked over to her bunk and sat down to think. Before she could get good and comfortable she was called for a visit. When she got in the visiting room, her eyes lit up. It was Dino. She was having mixed feelings. She was happy he was there but also mad for what he had done to her. *What the fuck wrong with him? He got the nerve to look pissed. If anybody should be heated, it's my ass!* she thought, looking at his facial expression, but she was still worried because she had never seen this look before and hoped he hadn't discovered her secret about the mall.

"What's up, J-Rite?"

"Hey, I'm waiting for Leesa to get me out. I ain't see you in court."

"Yeah, well . . ." He was dry.

"Well, I gotta surprise for you. And I got something to cuss you the fuck out about." She decided that even though he hurt her, she was going to try to make it work for the baby's sake.

"Look, it's over, J-Rite. A nigga straight done with your fake ass!"

"What! Why? What you say?" Her voiced got louder forcing a guard to tell her to keep it down or he'd terminate the visit.

"I told you I'm tired of this shit!"

"Get off that bullshit! There's more to it than that, and we both know it. So tell the truth. Be a man for once in your weak-ass life," she cut in, going for the jugular.

"Bitch, I know you had Rell's girl laid out!" He verified he knew her secret pertaining to her friend's dirty deed.

"Bitch! I got yo' bitch! I didn't have shit did to her. They didn't even know them was your peeps. Plus, dawg, you gave me a damn disease, nigga!"

That took him by surprise. He just gave her a look and didn't say a word as he gathered his thoughts. "Naw, shorty, you must've got that from Tone."

"Oh yeah, ho-ass nigga? I'm pregnant, Dino, so now what?"

Dino was caught off guard by her last statement. *She 'bout to have my baby? Naw, it ain't mine. She fucking Tone.* Even though he had no concrete proof, he made himself believe it. "Naw, J, it ain't mine. It's probably Tone who gave you that shit and that baby. So go be with him and leave me the hell alone!"

J-Rite was crushed. She thought him hearing she was pregnant would make him act different, even if he did know about that mall bullshit. *I can't wait to get outta here. I'm gonna hurt this nigga.* She didn't say anything else. She walked off and had the deputy take her back to her cell. She had murder on her mind and felt betrayed. But at the same time, she was still in love. When she got back to her area she washed her face and cried a little into her towel. *All right, I'm done crying. Let me leave no trace of tears. Can't let them see me sweat.*

"Sanders, another visit!" the same deputy said to J-Rite before she got a chance to lie down. When she got to the visiting room, she saw Leesa. Seeing her after all the stuff that had just happened made her feel better.

"Damn, I'm glad to see you."

"Sis, you'll be out of here in a few. I had to put one of my houses I own back in Detroit up for your bond. You just waiting on your paperwork."

"Leesa, I'm pregnant." Her eyes started to water.

"Girl, that's good news, ain't it? But why you look so sad?" Leesa assumed she knew the answer but wanted to hear it outta Jessica's mouth just the same.

"Dino doesn't want me anymore. And he knows about Mario and Raven jumping his friends. I think he gonna try to hurt them."

"Girl, chill. He ain't that stupid or that tough. I ain't trying to be mean or nothing, but his soft ass ain't ready to go to war wit' Tone or Mario right know, so don't even worry 'bout it. We'll deal with him later. First, let your feet hit the bricks."

"I just hope you right." J-Rite knew Dino better than anyone. She knew that it wasn't about to be over that easy. His pride was at risk.

Shortly after she'd returned to her cell, her name was called to be released. After she changed back into her street clothes, they put her in a room and told her to wait. Abruptly, the door swung opened and a black female cop and her partner, a white cop, walked in.

"I'm Officer Edwards. How you doing, Sanders?"

"What y'all want?" J-Rite frowned, not beating around the bush.

"Oh, she's a tough ass," the white officer grinned, throwing a folder on the table.

J-Rite looked at the photos of her and her crew and seemed unbothered. "Okay and? Contact my attorney!"

"So you think you got it figured all out. I see you a smart ass; probably took after that dead brother of yours, huh? He thought he was above the law just like you do. And we know how that turned out. Yeah, don't look surprised. See, we did our homework on your foster-raised rejected ass."

J-Rite wanted to get up and swing on the smart-mouthed cop, but refrained. She knew that would be letting them win the game. *I gotta keep my composure, or they gon' bury my ass.* "Look, like I said, anything you got to say me, you can say it to my attorney."

"You ain't cute," the female officer added her two cents. "We trying to give you some help, you dummy."

"Help? I don't need y'all fucking help! I'm good! Look, I ain't trying to hear shit! Tell it to my lawyer!"

"Fuck you and your lawyer! You can go, Sanders, but we'll be in touch *real* soon, so you better watch your step!"

"Yeah, yeah, that shit sounds real good; you better watch—" She paused when she saw the look on their faces. *Shut up, girl! It's against the law to threaten cops.* She turned and walked out, shaking her head.

Finally free, J-Rite flagged a cab down and had him take her to the old apartment. She was going to call Leesa to pick her up but figured no need to give the cops what they wanted. Heated about all the smack the officer was talking, she went in the apartment and started planning her next move. She knew that she needed to get her stuff from the house because it wouldn't be safe to stay there with her and Dino beefing. *Dino done burned me, played me 'bout our baby, and talking 'bout getting at my fam. I gotta get to Raven and Mario and let them know what's good.* She called Leesa and told her to meet her at Starbucks in twenty minutes.

"All right, J-Rite, what's up?" Leesa asked after arriving.

"We hot. The cops just tried to question me when I was at the station."

"I had a feeling something was up. A deputy I'm cool with told me that I might wanna leave the building and let you catch a cab. What they was talking about?"

"Sis, they know all about us."

"How?"

"I don't know, but they know all the shit we been doing and whatnot. You think somebody talking?"

"Yeah, but who?" Leesa puzzled.

"I don't know, but it's time to make a move real quick," J-Rite said, looking around and checking her surrounds.

Leesa was already prepared to leave the game. She had never planned on getting this big. She knew how the game went. "Yeah, it's time to go," she agreed, thinking about living a simple life with Q.

"Well, look, of course, the ho-ass police ain't find my car yet, so I gotta get a rental car. We gotta get new phones and go under the radar. I'm going to go holla at everybody and let them know what's up. Then I'll go take care of Meka."

"What you gonna do about Dino?"

J-Rite didn't know what she was going to do. Her mind was saying strike first, but her heart was saying love. "I don't know, but I'm going to make sure that I think it through before I do anything. He is the father of my child."

After Leesa dropped J-Rite off at the rental car place, J-Rite went to see Tone and his brother. She walked to the door and knocked.

"Who is it?" Tone asked.

"It's that bitch!" J-Rite yelled through the closed door.

"Girl, I couldn't wait to see you get out. I hate to see a nigga caged up like an animal."

"You ain't lying. But I got some bad news for y'all. Where your brother at?"

"What up, girl? You out, I see," Mario said, walking from the back room.

J-Rite explained what was going on, and the look the brothers had on their faces said what they were thinking. "Do Leesa know?" Tone asked.

"Yeah, she know."

"This shit don't make sense. We don't fuck with too many people. You think it's Leesa's connect?"

"Hell, naw, Tone! Leesa been fucking with him for years. He was supplying Hutch."

"Well, somebody ass talking."

"Maybe it's Raven's wannabe husband! Maybe he the snitch!" Mario interjected. His brother gave him a hard look, and Mario knew what it meant. He knew better than to throw dirt on someone's name; after all, that's why the undercover cop was dead now.

"You remember Pops said that if a nigga ratting, stay clear; if you go trying to handle shit that don't involve you, then you gon' get fucked! So watch the shit that come out your mouth!"

"I don't think it's him anyway. Raven ain't gonna be running her mouth like that," J-Rite insisted.

"Well, we gotta find out who the fuck it is!" Tone was confused.

"All right, so what we gonna do now?" Mario asked.

"I ain't made it that far yet, but lie low for a while. I still gotta take care of Meka. After I handle that, take care of Rhonda and Sean. They can't be running around with dirt on us either."

"That ain't a problem. Let us know when." Mario smiled, ready to put in more work. "And, oh yeah, we been trying to find out who the fuck carjacked you and set you up on that bullshit charge!"

"Cool, good looking." J-Rite wasn't going to tell them about Dino. She wanted to handle that on her own but didn't want Mario and Raven running around blind, so she had to say something. "Look y'all, shit done got real thick! Dino came to see me when I was locked up. Somehow he know y'all who murked his people. He claim not the type that turns the other cheek. He wanna handle shit, but we'll see."

"Well, what he talking 'bout?" Tone asked, concerned for his little brother's safety.

"He didn't say much; he's not much of a talker. But I know that he can be a real problem and he—"

"I can be a real problem too! That nigga don't want to fuck with me on this war shit!" Mario cut in and said, not caring it was J-Rite's man.

"Where the nigga at?" Tone asked, ready to back up Mario when the time came. J-Rite didn't say anything. *What the fuck's wrong with her?* Tone thought.

Mario also noticed her not responding and figured something was wrong. "All right, what's up? Why you so damn quiet?"

"Y'all, I'm pregnant by his ass!"

CHAPTER TWENTY-TWO

Dino's feelings for J-Rite were up and down. After visiting her, he thought about the baby she was having. He wanted to be a father, and he loved her very much, but his jealousy got in the way of his judgment.

"Nigga, you getting soft! You need to kill that bitch and be done with it. She can't be trusted no more!" Marlon fumed.

"Watch your fucking mouth. She's carrying my baby."

"Man, is the baby even yours? I thought you said—"

"Hey, why the fuck wouldn't it be?" he said giving Marlon a *"nigga, what?"* stare after cutting him off.

"Well, Dre said you thought she was fucking around on you."

"Fuck Dre! And if you riding with him, then, nigga, fuck you too!" Dino said with murder in his eyes.

This nigga really tripping over this bitch. Most times he didn't even wanna be with the bitch. Now he wanna beef about the bird. Clown-ass nigga, Marlon thought.

"Look, man, all the fuck I know is my girl dead. I don't know how you feel about it, but I'm ready to make somebody pay," Rell said.

"So I'm supposed to kill the woman that's carrying my child? How the fuck that sounds?"

"Would you do it if it was you?" he asked, looking at Rell.

"Nigga, whatever has to be done has to be done! With or without you." Rell felt that Dino already took sides, and he had chosen the wrong one. *This nigga gonna put this bitch and a baby that probably ain't even his over us—his family. Well, nigga, you can get it too.*

"Well, I'll see her soon enough. I called the county lockup. She was released a li'l while ago. I'll be back later. Call me if you see her."

"Yeah, nigga, I will," Marlon promised as Dino pulled off.

As Dino drove away he saw a person he thought resembled Dre, so he turned around and parked. *Look at this nigga. He so damn fucked up it doesn't make sense.* This was the first time he had seen Dre since he took the money out of the account. He didn't know what he was going to say or do. Dino hopped out of the car and started walking toward Dre, who was as high as a kite.

"Yeah, what up, nigga? Why you looking so damn dusty?" he said, staring at Dre.

"I need a hit, nigga. You told me when you seen me again you'd give me a hit. You told me if I sucked your dick you would give me a hit. Well, I sucked your dick; now I want my hit," Dre begged, not knowing it was his best friend he was talking to.

Dino was furious. His face turned red, muscles tightened, and he heard ringing in his ears. He pulled out his gun. *I'ma kill this nigga my damn self.* Dino lifted up his hand and was about to pull the trigger. He didn't need to take the gun off safety because he didn't use it. As he put his finger on the trigger, the fiend that Dre was running around with came out of nowhere.

"Wait, stop! What are you doing?" the female screamed, jumping in front of Dre, ready to take the bullet. "I love him! Don't hurt him, please."

Dre was too high to know what was going on. Dino put his gun in his pants and got back in his car. He kept thinking about what had just happened. *She was willing to die for this nigga. He got somebody that loves him for him. I fucked over the perfect woman. I got my boy's girl killed, and I'm too deep in the game to leave. I don't know what to do.* For the first time in his life, he was lost. He didn't know where to go or what to do next.

J-Rite walked in Rhonda's building and had Sean, who was waiting for her in the lobby, take her to the apartment. When she got inside, Raven was sitting on the couch smoking a blunt with a Mac-11 in her lap, Mario was standing by the window holding a pistol grip pump, and Tone was walking back and forth with twin Glock .40s in his hand. They were ready for war. "What up, girl? Leesa told me what's up. So you better catch up with Dino before I do," Raven said after blowing weed smoke out her nose.

"Y'all know the cops watching us, so just chill out."

"I wanna know who talking," Tone hissed.

"Probably Tyrus. We should kill him and all his peeps," Mario said angry.

He had been waiting for the green light since he found out it was beef. Hearing this made Raven's stomach tighten; she knew that if J-Rite and them went at Tyrus, then Benji would get involved.

"Hey, y'all, we just can't murder niggas without proof," Raven immediately stated.

"So what if we do?" Tone joked. "You did it once before, didn't you?"

"Look, proof or not, I'm thinking hit the nigga anyway. One less crab-ass buster to worry 'bout!" Mario threw in his two cents.

"Yeah, he got a point," J-Rite conceded.

"Yeah, I'm down," Tone cosigned.

This made Raven nervous. *I gotta think of something.*
"Look, y'all, the cops watching us, right?" They nodded
their heads in agreement. "Then it would be dumb to go
to war right now."

"Why you acting like that? That ain't even like you. That
nigga you messing with got you soft or what?" Mario
looked at her amazed.

"Acting like *what?*" Raven barked, twisting her face up.

"Naw, it's just that we gotta be smarter than what
we've been. That includes me too. I mean, think
about it like this. If we would have gotten and got the
fuck on, we wouldn't be in this shit now. And if we
wouldn't have been so gung ho, then this shit with
Dino wouldn't have happened. Now, am I right or
what? Besides, girl, you out on bail." She was looking
directly at J-Rite. Raven was hoping they fell for it.

"Yeah, that's true, so now we should try to find out who
got us hot," J-Rite said as she sat back on the couch.

Raven smiled. *Good. That gives me time to figure out
how to fix this shit.*

"All right, so what the fuck we gon' do?" Mario asked.

"I'll holla at my attorney and see if he can find out anything on this bull and my other case."

Rhonda knocked on the door, then walked in the room.
Even though it was her apartment, they made her go out
into the hall. They knew she'd probably been listening,
but they would take care of that soon enough.

"Look, Rhonda, I'm going to give you and Sean some
cash to get Meka over here. Is that cool?"

"Hell, yeah! When you want her over here?"

"Just stay here for a li'l bit. I'm gonna get y'all something to have while y'all posted."

"Tone and Mario, I want y'all two to go back to the
apartment and get some clothes and come back to

my house. That way, if Dino comes home, I won't be alone."

"What about me?" Raven asked.

"Go get us some phones."

Each left ready to put their plan in motion.

"I can't believe my nigga going out like this. How the fuck I let this shit happen?" Dino said, talking to himself while sitting in Monique's den drinking Rémy straight out of the bottle. *I should've just kill that nigga and put him out of his misery. I gotta piss. This shit running through a nigga.* As he started using the bathroom he felt his dick itching and burning. "What the fuck? Monique! Monique," he shouted as she came running.

"What the hell is wrong with you?"

"I got something to ask, and I'm only going to ask once. Did you burn me?"

"Hell, naw!"

"Bitch, you lying!"

"Nigga, I ain't gave you shit, and you gon' stop talking to me like you crazy. I know you be out fucking them nasty hoes at them clubs, so go check *them*."

"I ain't trying to hear that. I know you fucking with one of them broke, dirty niggas and you supposed to be my woman!"

"First off, how the fuck am I your woman when you *got* a woman? That's so stupid! You think I'm supposed to just sit around and be by myself? Nigga, you crazy!"

"Bitch, you better stop talking right fucking now before I have to fuck you up."

Most people would have taken this as a warning and let things go. But not Monique. She didn't think that way. She geeked things up. "You ain't gonna do shit to me, you stupid nigga! I'll get you fucked up! So you best get right and take your ass home to *your* bitch!"

"This shit wild. You gonna talk to me crazy after you done burned me?" Dino couldn't control himself any longer, so he reached out, slapping blood out of Monique's mouth. She was shocked. She balled up her fists.

"What you think you gonna do? Bitch, you swing on me, I—" Before Dino could finish his statement she'd already attacked him, throwing everything she could put her hands on.

"I'ma kill you, nigga. You put your fucking hands on me. I'ma kill you," she belted out as she punched him.

Dino threw her off of him. He wanted to jump on her for burning him, but truth be told, he couldn't really be sure if it was her. He cheated on J-Rite with Monique and cheated on Monique with other women. *I need to try to fix things with J-Rite, even if it ain't my baby. Every time she think of me she gonna think about how I fucked her life up. I gotta live with that shit the rest of my fucking life. I hope she forgive me for this shit.* Dino stormed out of Monique's home and headed to the house hoping to make things right with J-Rite. He was confused. On the way, he tried her cell, but it just rang. He tried the house phone but got no answer. *I gotta catch up with her before it's too late, I can't let shit happen to her.* Deep down, Dino was madder at himself more than at J-Rite. He knew this was his entire fault. He also knew with or without him, Rell's out-of-control ass was gonna try to make a move. *This nigga might kill my girl and baby.*

CHAPTER TWENTY-THREE

"Hey, bro, my Desert E still under your bed?" Mario asked his brother as they were packing up some things to go stay at J-Rite's place for a little while.

"Yeah, where else would it be?"

Mario went in the room and started looking under the bed. "What the fuck? How this get under here?" he wondered, picking up an earring from off the floor. He looked at the gold hoop that he'd bought Raven for her birthday. "Hey, Tone! Tone!"

"Damn, what the fuck is it now, nigga?"

"Yo, how the hell this get under your bed?" Mario held the earring up for his brother to clearly see.

Here we go with this shit, Tone thought.

This nigga better not lie. Mario's heart was racing, waiting on an answer.

"Come on, dawg. How you think? You smarter than all that." Tone braced himself for the fallout that was sure to follow.

"I know she better not lost it like I think she lost it, *that's* for sure."

"Man, you better stop acting like some love-sprung pussy! She ain't your girl and never was. So what the hell does it really matter?" Tone was the only person that could talk slick to his brother and not expect to be killed.

"So you telling me that you been fucking Raven? *Really,* my nigga?"

"Come on, bro, it don't take a map to figure that shit out! But it was only once or twice when we was high."

"That's messed up! How could you play me like that?"

"Play you like what? She ain't even feeling you like that, so get off that bullshit! And I know we ain't 'bout to beef over no pussy, is we?"

Mario was heated. To him, it was more than some pussy. It was the point and principle. He felt betrayed by not only his brother but by Raven also. "You think I'm one of these ho niggas in these streets or something?" he said, squaring up on his brother.

"Nigga, I know you ain't trying to throw them—"

Before Tone could finish what he was saying, Mario sucker punched him dead in the jaw and rushed him into the wall. Mario hadn't fought his brother in a long time. He tried to swing, but Tone ducked and caught him right in the eye.

"This what you want, nigga? Is it? You stopped being smart because of some pussy?" Tone raged before he caught his little brother with a left to the jaw, resulting in Mario falling to the floor.

Fuck this shit! He jumped up, grabbed his gun off the table, and pointed it at Tone.

"What you plan on doing? I know you ain't gonna shoot me! Don't be stupid!" He started to wonder if his brother would actually pull the trigger.

"Fuck you, nigga! You're nothing to me." Mario started walking toward the door.

"Mario, damn, hold up. It ain't even that serious."

"Naw, nigga, you dead to me!" Mario yelled before walking out the door and slamming it shut. *Him and that scandalous bitch Raven got me all the way fucked up! Family, my ass!*

J-Rite had absolutely no remorse for what she had just done. She was headed back from handling Meka. Instead of going out and ending the woman's existence with gunplay, J-Rite sent her home happy. She'd prepared a "special" hotshot mixture and watched as the eager-to-get-high Meka stuck the needle into her own veins, becoming her own executioner. She knew Rhonda and Sean still had to be taken care of because when word of Meka's death got out, no amount of product or cash they were blessed with for their silence could keep a drug addict from running off at the mouth for the next blast. J-Rite called Mario and had him deal with those two ASAP. She truly had come to like both of them; however, this was business, not personal. They had to go.

Having gotten all her ducks in order, J-Rite received a call from her attorney. He let her know that she needed to be in court the next day and that the case was getting thrown out. Leesa had given the guy that was shot in the still suspicious carjacking some cash to "forget" his story. He reached out wanting money to go dumb, so now he was dumb. When J-Rite got back in the house, Tone was there asleep on the couch. He had a gun on his lap that he held tightly, and another next to him. She smiled, then went up to her room. With him big and strong and armed, she felt safe. J-Rite knew that even though he was big, he couldn't stop a hail of bullets, but he'd still try his best to protect her. Knowing that she had somebody that was willing to go out in a blaze of glory, with or for her, put her mind at ease.

She called Leesa to inform her about court in the morning, along with the update that she hadn't seen or heard from Dino, but only got her voice mail. After hanging up the phone she went to sleep. The locks and alarm code had been changed so that brought her even more piece of mind. She knew she had to move on with her life for her baby's sake; that was, if she decided to keep it.

***

Ever since J-Rite had her encounter with the cops, it seemed like they were everywhere. As Leesa drove home, she could see them following her. She wasn't worried about being stopped, because she knew that the only thing she had on her was a registered gun. She knew that they wouldn't stop her and try to harass her, because they knew that she wouldn't have anything on her that could get her locked up. All the time that she and Hutch were selling drugs, the police never could catch them in the act. The one time the police thought they had something ended up costing the police a lawsuit and internal investigation. Sadly, she always thought that was the true reason Hutch was tragically murdered by the police.

Leesa walked in the house and was greeted by Q. She loved coming home and having him there.

"Hey, baby," he smirked, kissing her softly as he headed to the bedroom in his boxers.

"I couldn't wait to get home. Half the time I hate having to leave at all," she said, following behind him.

Leesa walked over to the bed and sat down on the edge. Q immediately got on his knees. He started kissing and teasing her. It turned him on to see his woman squirm. As he teased her, Leesa let her mind wander. She thought about spending the rest of her life with Q. She still hadn't told J-Rite and didn't know when she would. Leesa didn't know how J-Rite would take the news, and at this point, didn't care. She was grown and going to live for herself, no longer the memory of the past. Right now, at this moment in time, she was just going to close her eyes and enjoy what Q had in store for her.

After making love all night, the couple woke up for round two, not missing a beat, going right at it. Leesa put her legs up in the air as he slid inside of her. "Baby, it feels like it's about to come out my throat," her voice purred as Q rammed her deep and hard. She could feel herself on the verge of coming. "Oh my God, Hutch," she moaned out loud. She didn't know why she did it or if Q heard her.

Q gave her a hard stare, indicating he did. Crushed emotionally, he pulled out and sat on the side of the bed. "Wow, Leesa, why you do that? You think of him when we have sex?"

"No, baby, I swear I don't."

"So why you just say his name then? I'm confused."

"Baby, I don't know." She dropped her head looking down at the floor. Leesa felt bad and embarrassed. She knew she messed up and didn't know what to do to fix it.

"Look, I'm going to take a shower. Alone!" Q said, heading into the bathroom smelling a strange woman's scent as soon as he took a piss.

Leesa went and sat on the couch staring at the wall. *Why the fuck did I call him that?* Hutch had been on her mind more and more lately, and she didn't know why. She hadn't had a lot of experience with men. Hutch was her first, and up until she met Q, he was also her last. *I guess I'm going to have to just sit and talk about it with him.* Leesa got up to walk to the bathroom to beg his forgiveness. Walking past a calendar, she glanced at it, and the fifteenth jumped out at her. *Oh shit! I know why I been thinking about Hutch. His birthday was the other day, and I forgot. Damn, but that's still not an excuse for calling Q by the next nigga's name; especially when I did.*

CHAPTER TWENTY-FOUR

J-Rite walked out of court feeling above the law. She had paid her way out of a prison sentence. Although J-Rite had never been in any real trouble before, she knew if she didn't have money she would have been possibly spending the rest of her life in jail. After talking to her attorney in front of the court building, she went to Asia's house and paid her for the phone calls. Of course, she was badgered into promising to finally putting her on, and since she and her team were pulling out of the dope game in Grand Rapids soon, Asia could have it and the entire headache that came along with what had proven to be a bad-luck city. On the way from Asia's house she thought about what her attorney said about the cops and the information that they had. Off the record, he suggested that her best bet was to maybe pay them off like Leesa had just done with the witness.

Overjoyed at the outcome, she decided to go to Leesa's house and tell her the good news in person. She pulled in the driveway, taking her spare key out of her purse just in case. *Maybe she parked in the garage or is still asleep.* J-Rite knocked on the door, then rang the bell but got no answer. She stuck her key in the door, letting herself in. *Damn, I gotta pee.* She went in the bathroom, used it, and then came out. As she stepped into the hallway, she heard sounds coming from Leesa's room. J-Rite slowly opened the door and couldn't believe her eyes. Leesa was naked, legs in the air, fucking some man.

J-Rite was at a loss for words. She couldn't even speak. She felt like somebody had punched her in the stomach. She closed the door and walked out of the house without saying a word. She drove off with tears running down her face. J-Rite was flying up the street not realizing how fast she was going as she thought about Leesa's betrayal to Hutch's memory.

A car was pulling out of the driveway. By the time J-Rite saw it, it was too late to stop. She swerved around the car—and hit a tree. On impact, the airbag deployed.

"Why didn't you do what I said to do?" Tyrus asked his nephew.

"The time wasn't right. I couldn't find a time when the place was empty."

"No sooner than I told you to take care of the place, the son of a bitch starts getting real busy, huh? Is that right?"

Benji wanted to tell his uncle to go fuck himself, but he knew that wouldn't be a wise decision.

"Well, it has to be taken care of, and I mean *soon*. And I don't give a fuck about how busy it is—*handle* it."

"But, Unk, I told you, it's always busy. I'm serious!"

"Listen, little nigga! I don't give a fuck if Jesus is inside passing out Bibles. You burn it down with him in it."

Benji couldn't take it any longer. "Fuck that shit! I ain't killing innocent people."

"Oh, you think you got the balls to disobey me?"

"Why is this so important, Unk?"

"Don't ask me questions! I done told you that before!"

"Look, Unk, I got love for you, but you better watch the way you talking to me."

"You think you can take me? I'll put you under the earth—and don't ever forget that! Now get the fuck outta my office before I put hands on you."

Benji was ready to explode, but he held it in. "All right, Unk. No problem."

"Hey, boy, what them niggas say about my money?"

"I'll be picking it up in a few hours if you still want me to."

"Yeah, and when you get it, take it to the safe house. The rest you keep. Remember, I love you, boy."

"I love you too, Unk." Benji walked out of his uncle's office low-key hurt. His old family wanted to hurt his new family.

He was ready to call Raven when ironically, she called and asked how things went. After he explained he had to pick up some money and would call her back, he pulled up to Dino's spot and hopped out. He was praying they had all the money.

"What up, guy?" Rell said when he saw Benji.

"Shit, the money ready or what?"

"One thing you ain't gotta worry 'bout when you fuck with me is your money."

"That's good to know." Benji nodded, hoping what he said was true.

Rell thought that maybe he should be hustling with Benji. Ever since he and Dino started having problems, he wanted to do his own thing. "Hey, dude, I need to holla at you over here on some shit. See, I been fucking with dawg and them for a while, and it's 'bout time I break and do my own thing. I was wondering if I could cop from you on the solo tip."

He trying to cut a side deal. "What, you need a plug?"

"Yeah, from you."

"How much?"

"Maybe a big eighth or so a week."

"Are you sure about that?"

Rell looked at him. "Yeah, that's all a nigga gonna need for now."

"Well, when you want it?"

"If you got it, I'll take it now."

"Well, let me think on it. I'll get back!"

Before Leesa could offer a heartfelt apology for her hurtful slipup, the phone rang.

"Hello, may I speak to Leesa Jones."

"This is her, who is this?"

"This is a nurse from Mercy Hospital, and we have you down as the emergency contact for Jessica Sanders."

"What about her?" Leesa panicked, concerned . . . knowing all that was going on with the drama from Tyrus and Dino.

"Ms. Sanders was in a terrible car accident earlier today."

"Is she all right?"

"She's still in surgery, and we'd like for you to come down to the hospital as soon as possible."

When Leesa hung up, she had tears streaming down her face.

"What's wrong, baby?" Q wondered, coming out of the bathroom still drying off from his shower.

"J-Rite was in a car accident!"

"Damn! Is she all right?"

"I don't know. I'm on my way down there now." Leesa was trembling as she started to get dressed.

"You want me to go?"

"Naw, baby, it's all right."

"Leesa, I can't let you leave here like this. I'd be worried to death about something happening to you, and you damn sure can't drive like this. I know we supposed to be doing the low-key thing, but fuck all that! I love you too much to let you leave here like that."

Leesa walked over and hugged him. She was glad that she had him in her life. *I swear to God if Dino had something to do with this, I'ma lay that nigga down!* Leesa sat quietly in the passenger side as Q drove her to the hospital. He dropped her off at the emergency door, then parked. She ran in the hospital and waited for an elevator. *Damn, I hope she all right. I can't lose my sister.*

After checking in at the front desk, she was led toward the area where her sister-in-law was. Leesa pulled the multicolored curtain back, and her eyes started watering. J-Rite was unconscious with tubes down her throat and IVs in her arm.

"Damn, girl, I hate to see you like this." Leesa walked over to sit down next to J-Rite's bed. As she sat down, Q stuck his head in the door.

"Baby, I'll be in the hall."

"All right." Leesa turned her attention back to Hutch's little sister. "J-Rite, you know I love you very much. I need you to pull through this."

Just then, a doctor walked in the room and put down his chart. "Hello, I'm Dr. Mead, and you must be Ms. Jones."

"Yeah, I am. How is she doing?" Leesa asked, wiping tears from her face.

"She's going to be okay. She's sleeping right now from the medication. The police said that she was going way over the speed limit. Luckily, she was wearing her seat belt. It saved her life."

"So she is going to be all right?"

"It's too early to say, but I think she's going to be fine."

Leesa had enough stuff on her mind to worry about, but this just made things a lot worse for her. "How's her baby?" she then asked, praying for the best.

"I'm sorry, but she lost the baby." Dr. Mead knew how Leesa felt from the look on her face; he had seen it many times before.

"Well, hopefully, she'll be all right."

"Yeah, I hope so. I'm going to give you some time alone. Don't stay too long. She really needs her rest."

Leesa sat silently, not knowing what to think or what to make out of the situation. *I hate I let shit get this far. We supposed to be on a beach right now. This shit's all my fault. I should have never let J-Rite get in the game. Hutch would be pissed. And damn, how do I tell her that her baby's gone?* Leesa had never second-guessed herself like she was doing right now. Even though she knew J-Rite was in the game anyway, she still felt that she added to the problem. She felt that she could have had J-Rite change her ways. At the thought of not knowing if her friend would live or not, she broke down and started crying. *I gotta get outta here.* "J-Rite, I love you. I'll be back." Leesa got up and walked out of the room.

"How is she, baby?" Q got up to comfort his woman.

"She's asleep. The doctor said that she should be okay, but you know how that goes. I'm about to call everybody and tell them to come down here."

After she called Raven and Tone they went in the cafeteria and got coffee, then headed back to check on J-Rite.

Leesa had her head on Q's shoulder, trying to calm her nerves when she heard voices. Slowly she opened her eyes and saw Tone, Raven, and Benji walking toward her. She felt a little better now that her family had arrived.

"Baby, you all right?" Raven asked, walking up and hugging her.

"Yeah, I'm good. The doctor said she gonna be all right."

"You shouldn't worry; you know she a trooper." Tone walked up putting his arms around Leesa.

"And who is this?" Raven asked, looking at Q.

"I'm Q. It's nice to meet you. Sorry it's under these circumstances."

Raven nodded her head and grinned.

"I'm Tone." He went over to shake Q's hand. Tone could tell from the way that Raven looked at Q she was wondering where Leesa had been hiding his handsome ass.

She better not get stupid. This ain't the time. Tone wasn't the only one that picked up on it. Benji noticed as well.

"Did one of y'all call Mario?" Leesa noticed he wasn't there.

"Yeah, I called him. He said he was on his way. But you know how that nigga is. He still mad about you know what."

I wonder what they talking about, Benji thought, remaining silent meeting Tone, Leesa and Q for the first time.

Raven didn't tell him that the two brothers had gotten into it. She felt she couldn't tell Benji that she had slept with Tone. Even though it was before they met, she knew how it sounded, and she knew how he would take it. *I wonder who this nigga is to Leesa. I should ask, but that shit gonna have to wait.* Raven had gotten suspicious of all new people that came around her team. She knew that Tyrus had long arms and could stretch out to touch, if need be. "I'm about to go see her," Raven said walking off toward J-Rite's room.

"Don't stay too long. The doctor said she needs a lot of rest."

"Yeah, I won't, I just want to check on her."

"Baby, I'm sorry. I didn't mean to do that to you, but you tried to flip the script on me, and that Detroit tramp you messing around with is the one out here burning niggas," Monique said to Dino after begging him to come back so that they could talk.

He didn't know why but he still had feelings for Monique, and it was more than just sex. Since he knew J-Rite couldn't be trusted, he was going back and forth in his mind regarding where his heart was. "Naw, baby, I'm the one that's sorry. I should have never put my hands on you. That's some shit that real niggas just don't do, and from now on, it's just gonna be me and you."

This made Monique happy. She had wanted Dino all to herself for a long time. "Bae, can I ask you something?"

"Yeah, what's up?"

I hope this nigga don't bug out. "What about J-Rite's baby?"

Dino didn't speak. He hadn't thought much more about it. He figured that J-Rite wouldn't want him to see the baby anyway. Plus, he still felt that it wasn't his. Instead of having a blood test done when the child was born, he was just going to wash his hands of the whole thing like it wasn't happening. Period. "What about it?"

This took Monique by surprise. She knew that Dino felt J-Rite was cheating on him and that the baby wasn't his, but she thought that by now he'd have come to his senses. *I wonder if that nigga would play me like that.* "Do you want kids?"

"Damn, what's with all the questions? A nigga not in the mood."

Monique didn't speak. After the fight they had she didn't want to fight again. She had heard that if a man hits you once he'll do it twice. But she loved Dino so much she didn't care if he hit her. She would do whatever it took to make him happy. *Here goes.*

"I'm pregnant."

Dino tightened his face as he sat up. "Oh yeah? When you find this out?"

"The other day I wasn't feeling good, so I went to the doctor, and she told me. Are you mad?"

"Why should I be? It's mine, right?"

"Yeah, of course, it's yours."

"Are you going to keep it?"

She started feeling sad. *He gonna tell me to get rid of it.* "I want to."

"Well, what we gonna name it?"

Even though Dino was burning and had some explaining to do, Monique felt like she had finally beat J-Rite at her own game.

CHAPTER TWENTY-FIVE

"Good morning, baby," Asia said as she rolled over seeing Hazel watching television.

Asia and Hazel had been spending so much time together that Hazel gave her a key to her place. "How did you sleep last night?"

"I slept good," Asia replied while stretching out her arms.

"You hungry or what, bae?" Hazel reached over kissing her on the neck.

"Yeah, just a li'l. You know I'm trying to watch what I eat."

"I told you that I like the way you look. You perfect." Hazel got naked and went to take a shower.

Hazel didn't mind that Asia was a big girl; she still liked her. Since they had started dating, Asia decided to work on her weight. She'd lost twenty pounds. Asia liked the way she looked but knew that it was unhealthy and slowed her down. As she started losing weight, she felt surer about herself and thought she'd be ready to hustle hard and go the distance in the streets when J-Rite dropped the package off to her as promised.

"Baby, your phone is ringing. You want me to get it?"

"Naw, I got it," Hazel panicked, jumping out of the shower soaking wet to answer it. She talked for a minute in a somewhat muffled conversation, then hung up. "I gotta go. That was my mom. She needs to see me."

Asia paused, "Your mom? I thought you told me your mother was dead."

"Naw, baby, she is deceased. That was my stepmother. She was the one that just called." Hazel fumbled over her words, trying to cover her story having just been caught in a lie.

Asia watched Hazel dry off, then dart out of the house without even fixing her breakfast. *Something ain't adding the hell up. This bitch better not be cheating on me, and if she is, fuck her. When I get this package I'm about to blow up anyway!*

Things had been going well for Rell, despite the fact that his girl was dead. He had started buying from Benji and was making a lot of moves. He still made money with Dino and Marlon, but he loved the solo hustle. Rell was all about money. Even though he was upset that his girl died, he was more upset that Dino didn't make J-Rite or her ruthless crew pay for it. "That nigga is over there with that old bitch with the good job, Monique, like fuck the world."

Dre and Rell had started hanging together on the low, and they didn't want Dino to know. They also made sure that Marlon didn't find out. Even though they all grew up together, they never really liked Marlon. To Rell and Dre, he was too high and mighty. They never told Dino or Marlon how they felt, but Dre believed that they both knew anyway. "Oh wow, yeah, he took me by her crib once before."

"Yeah, he ain't even fucking with J-Rite at all, so he claims. Dino like, fuck happened to my girl and me."

"That boy a damn green snake in the green grass, and he need his head chopped off!"

Rell laughed at the statement that his homeboy had made. Dre hadn't totally kicked his drug habit. He'd just slowed down a little bit. He knew in order to get money he would have to stay focused, so he was trying his best. "So what's up with this lick you talking about?"

"I told you, we should get that nigga Benji. I know he got major weight, and he seem soft as cotton."

"Yeah, that nigga gotta be holding. I wouldn't mind hitting him for that ride of his and that stash."

"So what the fuck we waiting for?"

"What Dino and Marlon think? Did you run it by them yet?"

"Fuck them niggas! We gonna do this one on our own, just me and you."

Dre didn't know if he should leave them out of the equation, especially Dino. "I don't know; we might need Dino." Dre worried, second-guessing himself. He never did any dirt without Dino since they had been hanging together.

"Man, why you keep talking this Dino shit? That nigga ain't thinking about your ass! He ain't been fucking with you for a while. I'm the one that's been bringing you and your girl food and money. That nigga don't give a fuck about you!"

"Yeah, you right. I'm tripping. I ain't got shit from that nigga Dino!"

"That fool told me and Marlon not to even fuck with you. He said as far as he concerned, you dead to him. How that nigga supposed to be your day one and he playing you like that?" Hearing how Dino was acting hurt Dre to the core, and his pain was easily visible. They had always been road dawgs. "If you ask me, we should rob both them niggas and leave 'em in the dirt," Rell suggested seeing Dre was on the verge of tears.

"Yeah, I'm down," Dre said, nodding his head. "So when you wanna handle this shit?" he asked, eager to get his revenge on Dino for leaving him high and dry.

"I gotta work out a few more kinks, then I'll be ready."

Hell, yeah! It's about time we handled this business. I gotta floss on all these niggas that thought I fell off. It never crossed Dre's mind that he might be getting played. He never thought that Rell might have the same feelings for him that he has for Dino and Marlon: pure hatred.

"I'm about to get outta here. You need anything?"

"Yeah, a few bucks if you have it to spare."

Rell went in his pocket and pulled out a bankroll. "This is all you, nigga," he said, tossing the money to Dre.

Dre looked at the money in his hand knowing it was enough for him and his girl to get high all night long. "Thanks, fam, good looking out!"

"It ain't shit. You my nigga. I gotta take care of you." Rell turned, walked off the porch, and got in his car. *I got Dre dumb ass riding with me, a new connect, and I'm about to hit a major lick. Shit might work out for ole Rell after all.*

Mario had gotten to the hospital as fast as he could. Even though he wasn't talking to his brother, he wasn't going to let that come between him and J-Rite. "Hey, how's she doing?" he said, running up to Leesa.

"She still knocked out, but the doctor said she gon' pull through. It's all good."

"What the fuck happened? Do y'all know?"

"They say she was speeding and hit a tree."

"How's the baby?"

Leesa didn't speak. Mario knew what it meant, and he didn't have to ask again. Q walked up and sat next to Leesa, handing her a coffee. "Oh, Mario, this is my friend, Q."

"What's up?" Mario half-assed spoke.

"You good?"

"Yeah, I'm good, baby."

"She woke up yet?" Q then asked.

"Naw," Leesa said, leaning her head back on his shoulder.

Who the fuck is this nigga? Mario thought just like the others had.

"Well, Raven downstairs and Tone and Benji went to take care of something. How long you staying?"

"I'll be here for a minute, but when two-face come back, I'm gone. But I—"

At first, Leesa wasn't going to say anything, but then she couldn't hold her tongue. "But I . . . *nothing*," Leesa raised her voice, cutting him off. "Our girl lying in the bed fucked up, and we don't know what really happened. But this beef you got with your brother over some pussy needs to stop! And it needs to stop right now. That's *her* pussy, she can give it to whoever the fuck she wants." Leesa had tears forming in her eyes. Q tried to get her to calm down, but she pushed him off her. "I know that you in love or was in love, but you gotta let that shit go. This ain't the time to be out here beefing with your family— blood or otherwise."

By this time, Raven was getting off the elevator. She saw Mario and braced herself for the fallout. *This nigga 'bout to act a damn fool.* She walked over to where they were and sat down in a chair. "Hey, Mario; you all right?" She hesitated to speak.

"Yeah, I'm good, and you?"

Raven was caught a little off guard. She didn't think he would even speak to her.

"Hey, can I hollar at you real quick?" Mario said, looking directly in her eyes.

"Yeah, sure." Raven got up. "You ain't gon' wild out, are you, boy?"

He smiled. "Naw, you're good. I just wanted to say that I was on some dumb shit. My bad."

"Naw, you ain't gotta apologize. You was acting on the way you felt, and ain't nothing wrong with that. Me and you just not meant to be."

"Yeah, I feel you, fam. I just gotta make my heart understand that. All bullshit aside, I'm glad you happy."

CHAPTER TWENTY-SIX

"So this why that boy wouldn't do what the fuck I told him to do," Tyrus shouted furiously to Tommy, his bodyguard, as he slammed his fist down on the desk. Tommy was no more than a loyal snake in training that would do anything to secure his spot at the right hand of Tyrus. He had gotten the boss pictures and detailed information on the girl Raven that Benji had been dating and was spending so much time with. He'd been with plenty of other women since working with his uncle, but this was the first that had his mind snatched away from business.

"Yeah, boss, her and them girls we've been having so many problems with are thick as thieves. That bitch and Benji, they been dating for a while. And if you ask me, seriously, that's some real disrespectful shit; ho shit."

Tyrus flipped through the pictures again and shook his head in disappointment. "That's what's wrong with things now in this world we live in and this game we play . . . Ain't nobody have loyalty anymore. Well, they kinda do, but it's always to the damn wrong people. How the hell could he switch on me like this? I been good to him, and now this turncoat done went straight renegade on me! It's a sin and a shame."

"You right, boss. So how you want me to handle this?" Rotten to the core, he was hoping that he would finally be able to kill Benji and be done with having to deal with him altogether. He hated Benji and always had since joining Tyrus's team. Tommy felt Benji was no more than a spoiled little nigga that had Tyrus's ear. He wanted to be the number two guy, and Benji was an obstacle in his way.

"I gotta think about it. I mean, that backstabbing motherfucker is family, even though he ain't showing me that consideration." Tyrus took a cigar out of the box on his desk and started prepping it to be smoked.

"Okay, then, I feel you on all that, but are you open to suggestions?" Tommy asked, hoping to give some input and manipulate the outcome.

"Yeah, dawg, go ahead. What you got for me?"

Tommy knew this might be his one and only time to accomplish what he'd been trying to do for years: make a permanent wedge between both parties. "Listen, like the old saying goes, why not take away the things Benji loves the most; show him that the same shit makes you laugh can damn showl make you cry. And if you don't be careful, kill your black ass!"

Tyrus didn't speak. He just sat back and thought as he lit his cigar, taking a few puffs to get it started. *Killing the girl would fuck him up and let him understand that when he signed up to be a part of this organization, it was serious. Not something that he thinks is a joke. It's about time he stepped up in case I have to ever step down. He needs to prove he's worthy. If the bitch is dead, then he'd have his mind on his business.*

"You know what, Tommy? I think you might be on to something. Go ahead and do what you do to that filthy three-baby-daddy-having whore. Just make sure it doesn't look like we did it. I don't want no connections to our camp. I want it done clean, simple, and quick."

"Gotcha, boss, I'm on it." Tommy was hyped as he headed toward the door to put his deadly plan into full motion. Anything he could do to hurt Benji was A-1 in his book.

"Hey, hold up, Tommy. What about the rest of the crew? Any thoughts on them as well since we talking?"

"Naw, right about now, I don't think they'll be a problem. I've put my ear to the streets and from what I'm hearing, they have enough shit on their plates to eat on for days on end." Tommy walked out of the office ready to rock and roll and get his murderous party started.

Damn, boy, how could you fuck over me like this? Tyrus thought to himself, looking over at a framed picture of him and Benji taken in Miami several years back. He was really hurt that Benji had made such a bad move choosing some ho over the family. Shaking his head in denial, Tyrus felt he should've known something was wrong when he had to tell his nephew the same bullshit over and over again. Benji usually did what he was told off rip without having to be told twice. *Now it's judgment time. Do I kill him? Or do I let him live? I wonder if he loves her enough to try to get back.* Tyrus hated to be in this unpredictable situation. He didn't know how things were going to play out, and at this point in time, was starting to care less. *It is what it is! If the boy comes at me wrong, I'm going to have to kill him.* Tyrus walked over to the bar and fixed a drink. He downed it, then had another. *Fuck it, I'll let Tommy handle it for now. That way, I can wipe my hands clean of the whole shit. Damn!*

"Hey, y'all, we gotta re-up," Rell said to Marlon and Dino as they sat around the living room of the spot counting up. "I'll call Benji and tell the kid to bring that through. We don't wanna miss none of this first-of-the-month money out here in these streets."

"Whoa, what the fuck you talking about? What you mean you gon' call him? Nigga, since when you start making decisions like that and calling shots? We don't re-up until I say so." Any other time, Dino wouldn't have cared, but as of lately, since the mall thing, he'd started catching bad vibes from Rell anytime they would be around each other.

I can't wait to get this bitch! When he least expect it, I'ma be all over his punk ass, then let's see who calling all the shots! Rell thought, trying to hold his hostile words for another time and keep the peace. "My bad, dawg. I just was trying to show that I can hold my weight too and step up. That you can count on me for whatever, whenever."

"Yeah, okay, then, no problem. My bad." *I don't know what's up with this nigga, but he gonna make me pop his fucking head. I'm starting to not trust this fool at all. He gonna mess around and make me send him on his way to see his girl Tiffany real soon,* Dino thought, smoking on a blunt.

I wonder what the fuck wrong with both of these clowns? If it ain't one thing, it's a damn other. Why can't they just stop bugging so we can get this bread before the next crew do? Marlon didn't know what was going on. He was slow to pick up on things.

"So, okay, real talk, my nigga, when we gon' take care of J-Rite's grimy-ass team that got down on me and mines, huh? That's what I'm waiting to hear."

"Damn, dude, what's the big rush? I mean, it ain't gonna bring your girl back one way or another. So just chill; be cool."

"Say what?" Rell got the dis on the sly and didn't appreciate it one bit.

"I mean, Rell, you got something up your sleeve, or you gonna just let me handle shit the way it should be done?" Dino asked, not really ready for what was to come next.

"Naw, ho-ass nigga, I ain't got shit up my sleeve, and what the fuck wrong with you to keep running off at the mouth at me like I'm one of them females you be dealing with?"

"Ain't shit wrong with me, faggot. It's just lately that you been on some real sneaky slimeball shit. Don't make me have to fuck you up! 'Cause if I have to fuck you up, I'm gonna kill you!" Dino knew that he shouldn't have said that last part but couldn't help himself. He was upset at everything that had been going on lately in his personal life and was letting it get the best of him.

Rell was in Dino's face violating his zone. With his fist balled up ready to go the distance if need be, he spoke his piece. "Look, boy, you better watch who the fuck you talking to! I ain't bitch made, and I ain't no damn Dre sitting around waiting for a handout! I'm a grown-ass man that calls his own shots."

"Whoa, whoa, man. Y'all niggas need to chill the fuck out! We family. This shit ain't called for. We just need to stop tripping and get this bread," Marlon said, getting between Rell and Dino, who were now nose to nose, about to swing.

"Pussy, go sit your punk ass down somewhere before you get handled too!" Rell swore, mean mugging Marlon.

"Hold up, Rell, this ain't what you want, dawg! You know that. I might not say much, but you already know I'm about that life when shit gets down to it. Bitch, I'll go," Marlon had tried his best to be the peacekeeper as always but had been pushed to the edge.

Rell stood silent. He didn't respond. Not a dummy by far, he knew right now he was in a lose-lose situation because if he hit Marlon, Dino more than likely was going to ride with him and jump in. Rell was pissed but far from being a fool. He knew he couldn't beat them both or take the certified ass whooping that would surely come with it.

"Look, man, we just all need to chill. You right, Marlon; we got too much shit going on to beef in the family. We need to keep getting this money and get out before the walls come down." Rell backed down still playing the game. *They think it's gonna be all good. Well, the fuck it ain't! Shit gonna get good real quick for me real soon!*

"Yeah, guy, you right, and we ain't gonna just hit J-Rite; we gonna get her whole li'l crew when they least expect it. I'm just waiting for the right time. I know you want some get back, Rell, and you gonna get it. Just be patient. I got you. Trust, I got you."

"Okay, now kiss and hug, you two pussy niggas!" Marlon said, laughing, glad the battle royal had been avoided.

"Fuck you!" Dino replied also glad things had calmed down, even though he set them in motion by going hard on Rell unnecessarily.

"Well, I'm about to get outta here. I'll get at y'all later," Rell said, walking to the door, then leaving.

Marlon got up and looked out the window. He wanted to make sure that Rell had indeed left and was not still on the porch possibly ear hustling. "Hey, man, something's up with that nigga. You ain't tripping." Dino didn't speak. He just sat and listened. Marlon walked over to the couch and sat down. "Look, I ain't wanna say shit when Rell was here and make shit crazy, but the other day I was out riding around and seen Rell and Benji together."

"What? When?"

"It was like two days ago, I think. I was riding around, and I seen them both over by White Castle, parked. And he's been fucking with Dre. Now, I ain't mad at him for that; but what's with keeping it a big secret if he a grown-ass man that calls his own shots like he just said?"

Hearing Dre's name, Dino got angry. "Oh, so his fake ass not only trying to back door the connect, he back fucking with Dre now too? He straight-up foul!"

"Yeah, fam, he's been taking the nigga money and food. But I'ma keep it real, Dre don't seem like he messing with that stuff as much as he used to."

Hearing this made Dino feel a little better. "You sure, or you just saying?"

"Yeah, I'm sure. I seen the nigga myself; face-to-face at the gas station around the way. He was buying milk and I think some toilet paper."

"Damn, I miss my homeboy!"

"Yeah, well, you need to go holla at that fool. Maybe he got his shit right. I mean, no matter what, he still part of this family. We can't just leave the nigga swinging in the wind long term. There gotta be a better way."

"Yeah, you probably right." Dino knew years ago he would have never thought twice about Dre, but now he had started getting high and shit changed. It had to, but now he wanted his man back in the car with him riding shotgun just as it had always been since they were teenagers.

"I am right, and look, Dino, we need Dre back on deck. I don't know what the fuck up with Rell, but I'm starting not to trust that nigga, just like you."

Dino sat and took it all in. He didn't know if Marlon really felt like this or if he was trying to shoot a move as well as Rell. He was suspicious of them both. *This nigga might be playing a game, trying to get me to go at Rell. But why have me fuck with Dre after I cut him off?* "So you think I should go get with Dre and see what's good, huh?"

"Yeah, man, that's what the fuck a real nigga would do; make amends with his people and not kick a nigga when they down; especially family."

Dino knew his boy was dropping that true science and that everything Marlon was saying was on point. "Yeah, man, you're right about everything, but the nigga was supposed to be stronger than that, you know! He disappointed me like a motherfucker!"

Marlon wasn't done giving it to Dino straight, no chaser. "Dre disappointed his damn self. I know this ain't what he really wanted. He ain't the first hustler that fell off and got caught up doing that dumb bullshit, and he showl ain't gonna be that last. Yeah, he is, or was, strung out, but deep down inside, he still Dre. He can make it back. And if we about to go to war, we need all the help we can get. Now, I ain't trying to be all in your business or in your head, but you gotta go get him and make shit right."

"Yeah, I am. You know where he at?" Dino finally gave in.

"Last time I seen him, he was over by the gas station, but one of the runners said they know where he lay his head at though."

"Cool, well, I'll go see if the nigga over there can find out what's up with Dre. And you should have told me when you first seen him with Benji. Don't ever keep shit like this from a nigga . . . Let me know soon as you know."

"Yeah, I got you. What we gonna do about Rell?"

"We gon' keep playing it cool, and if I have to kill him . . . then I'll kill him. We gonna hook up later."

Marlon was glad that Dino had finally decided to talk to Dre. They had been friends too long to stop talking. He was just hoping that Dino wasn't going to have to kill Rell, because he had love for Rell and Dre, even though he knew the feeling wasn't mutual.

Damn, my head killing me. Oh my God, what happened? I can barely remember. J-Rite felt weak. She was only able to open her eyes a little bit because the light from the room was hurting them. This was the second time that she had woken up since the awful accident the first time she was moved to recovery. The doctor had taken the tubes out of her throat. In extreme pain, she looked over and saw Leesa sitting in a chair asleep. She had no idea whatsoever that Leesa had stayed by her side the whole time she was unconscious since arriving at the hospital. *Oh my God, I hope my baby is all right.* J-Rite placed her hand on her stomach pressing slightly down. She felt way beyond a bit woozy from all the medication that she was under the influence of as well as the massive lump on the side of her head. Trying her best to put all the pieces together of the complicated puzzle she was now a part of, she didn't know how long she had actually been in the hospital. Glancing up at the IV that was dripping down into her battered and bruised arm, she grimaced. She tried to lift her other arm but couldn't quite find the strength. She still was very sore and softly moaned in anguish.

Leesa heard sounds of moving around coming from the other side of the room and looked in the direction of the bed. Elated, she saw J-Rite looking directly at her. Wasting no time, she leaped to her feet, rushing to her sister-in-law's bedside. "Jessica, baby, are you all right? How you feel? Oh my God, I'm glad you're awake."

"Yes . . ." J-Rite tried to speak but couldn't seem to be able to push the words out to form a response. Finally being able to raise her arm, she put her hand cupped around her neck signifying that something may have been stuck in her throat.

"Don't try to talk. Just wait. They just took the tubes out not too long ago," Leesa said, then pushed the call button to get the nurse to come to the room and render some much-needed aid.

"Oh great, I see you are awake, Ms. Sanders. How do you feel?" a nurse asked, walking in the room a few seconds later.

"My throat's really sore." J-Rite barely got the words out, feeling her voice getting a little stronger.

"So this is a good sign, right? I mean, this does mean that she's going to be okay, right?" Leesa had been on bed watch praying that everything was going to be okay.

"It's safe to say that she's going to be fine, but I have to go and get a doctor to give you an official update of what he believes the case to be." The nurse took her patient's vitals, then left the room to get the doctor on duty.

Leesa was ecstatic to know that she was going to be okay. "I'm glad you all right, li'l sis." Leesa rubbed J-Rite's arm. "Raven and them been down here too."

"How's my baby? Is my baby okay?" J-Rite anxiously asked the nurse who had returned with ice chips for her sore throat, ignoring anything else said or done.

The nurse looked at Leesa. She didn't know if Leesa was going to tell her the tragic news or if she had to. Leesa decided to take the lead. "Sis, now, you know I love you with all my heart, right?"

Not a fool by a long shot, J-Rite could easily sense that something was wrong when Leesa started the conversation off the way she did. "How's my baby?" She repeated as her throat got less sore.

The nurse had still yet to speak, but Leesa did. "Sis, did you hear me and what I said?"

This made J-Rite agitated. She wanted to scream. She wanted to cry. As Leesa and the nurse stood looking at her with pity, she wanted to hear the words. She knew the answer, but for some reason wanted to hear it spoken out loud. "How the fuck is my baby?" she asked for the third time, raising her voice.

"The baby didn't make it, sweetie. I'm so sorry." Leesa was hurt having been the bearer of bad news. Tears started pouring out of J-Rite's eyes. Seeing the amount of sheer emotion from her patient, the nurse took that as her cue, walking toward the door. She knew that the two girls needed to be alone and deal with what was just said. "Don't cry, it's going to be okay, I promise," Leesa swore, placing her hand on top of J-Rite's.

"Yeah, whatever. That's easy for you to say." She was infuriated, snatching her hand away from Leesa's touch.

"Sis, what the hell wrong with you?"

"Oh, now you wanna play dumb! It's your fault this shit happened to me off rip," she said, the moments and seconds before the car crash were now coming back to her.

"What the hell are you talking about? How is that?"

"Well, if you wouldn't have been in the house sucking and fucking some random-ass nigga like forgetting my brother, then I wouldn't have run up out of your damn place like that!" Hearing this, Leesa was speechless. "Yeah, you look real stupid right about now, you baby killer in heels!" J-Rite screamed looking at the blank expression Leesa was wearing on her face.

"Hey, sis, I'm sorry I didn't tell you about Q. I was going to, but I just couldn't find the right time."

"When? I bet you been fucking him for a long time. Like I said, forget Hutch, huh?"

Leesa didn't speak. She just sat there allowing a hurt-hearted J-Rite to have her say.

"Yup, that long pause tells me I'm right. That's all kinds of fucked up! Why is you even here? I'm confused! You don't care about me or Hutch. Just please go get Raven and leave me the fuck alone, please!"

"Look, Jessica—"

"I told you to get Raven! I *know* she's here," she yelled, turning her head the other way so she wouldn't have to look at Leesa any further.

"Fine then, I love you, sis; I really do. And I know you're hurt and confused right now, but you can make this your last time talking to me like I'm some stray bitch off the streets that ain't had your back since the day I met you and Hutch!" Leesa was done being J-Rite's verbal doormat as she stormed out of the hospital room and into the hallway.

How could she play me and Hutch like that? I done lost everything that matters to me. J-Rite didn't care how anybody else felt at this point. She had been through so much recently she wanted all the sympathy the world had to offer.

A few minutes later Raven walked in the room. "Why are you crying, girl?"

"I'm all right, I guess, but I lost my baby." She wiped her eyes with both hands.

"I don't know what to say. It's all right. Shit happens, but you're young." Raven was trying to seem hard knowing she was in pain for her friend.

"Yeah, I know, I'm just still glad I got you in my life."

"Girl, what are you talking about? I'm confused. You got *all* of us: me, Tone, Mario, and Leesa," Raven said confused by J-Rite's comment.

"Yeah, whelp, I ain't too sure about Leesa. She can't be trusted."

"Huh? What the fuck is you talking about? That girl been down here all night at your bedside crying, praying, and the whole nine," Raven stated, confused why J-Rite was saying what she had said.

"Naw, Leesa was on some real foul shit! That's why I got in an accident and why my damn baby is dead!"

"What the hell are you talking about? What she do? Please tell me!"

"Girl, she's fucking around on Hutch."

"Say what? Come on, J-Rite, Leesa ain't fucking around on Hutch. How could she?"

"Yeah, she is. I saw it with my own eyes. I seen her in bed with some nigga."

Raven knew that after all these years J-Rite still hadn't gotten over Hutch being dead. That was evident how she kept his memory elevated high on a pedestal. However, Raven didn't think that it was this bad. She had no idea whatsoever if J-Rite was delusional. "Girl, you know that I always keep it real with you, but you and I both know that he's gone, right? Hutch is not coming back."

J-Rite gave Raven a look that could freeze a polar bear. "So I guess you're on Leesa's side, huh? You think that whorish shit she did was okay?"

"Look, I'm on nobody's side. Y'all both my sisters, and I'm not gonna be in the middle of something that doesn't make any sense. You can't expect for Leesa not to have a life with anyone else until she'd dead. That's just crazy to think. I'm just being real."

"Yeah, I see what this is. You're on her side." J-Rite was about done talking and dealing with Raven as she was with Leesa. As far as she was concerned, the world was against her; all her friends included.

"Come on now, J, we can't be like this. There's too much shit going on right now that's life and death. You need to pull it together." Raven wanted to tell J-Rite that Benji and Tyrus were family. And that Tyrus was probably going to make a move soon. But she didn't know how. *I can't tell her this shit; she'll go crazier than she already is.*

How Raven gon' take Leesa's side? Leesa know she wrong for being with that dude. That's why she ain't say nothing all this time! "Hey, is Tone out there?" J-Rite asked not wanting to be bothered with Raven's judgmental ass any longer.

"Naw, girl, but Mario is. You want me to go get him?"

"Yeah, I do." She once again turned her face to the other side of the room showing that the visit was over.

Raven got up, turned, and walked to the door. When she got to the door she stopped and looked back over her shoulder. "You know we all love you, girl. That shit with Dino . . . know the baby and Leesa just got you off your square. But it's all good. I know you'll be back to your old self in no time."

J-Rite didn't respond, continuing to stare off into space.

A few seconds later, Mario walked in the room making all kinds of noise like this wasn't a hospital but a club on Friday night, "Hey, hey, now! What's good, baby girl?"

"Hey, Mario." Her face lit up knowing if anyone was going to be on her side no matter what it'd be Tone or Mario.

"Girl, you had all them busters worried."

"Oh, so you wasn't worried." She gave him a faint grin, grabbing a few more ice chips out of the white Styrofoam cup to ease her throat pain.

"Hell, naw! I know you a hood-raised trooper," Mario lied. When he got the call he was probably more worried than anybody. Without hesitation, he walked over to the bed and put his huge arms around J-Rite, almost bear-hugging the IV out of her arm.

"You know I'm always gonna be good. Where's your brother at?"

"He went on a run with that nigga Benji. Now all of a sudden they all cool. Maybe they forming an 'I fucked Raven Club' and a nigga like me ain't qualified to join," Mario sarcastically remarked.

"And what about y'all? Y'all all good yet or what?" J-Rite inquired, referring to Raven and his brother. "You and him got y'all shit back where the hell it's supposed to be instead of acting a fool?"

"Look, fam, after last night, I know life is too damn fucking short. So I'm gonna talk to Tone when they get back; me and Raven already kicked it. We a hundred with it."

"That's cool. That's what's gonna keep us strong as a team."

"Hey, J, I'm sorry about the baby. I heard."

"I appreciate you. I know I said I didn't know if I was gonna keep it or not. But I ain't gonna lie, I'm kinda fucked up over it, but what can I do? It is what it is."

Mario was happy to see she was as positive as could be expected. He was in the dark and didn't know not only about the way she felt Leesa had done her dead brother, but the way Raven seemed not to care. J-Rite felt that it was best to leave it alone for now and let things play out how they had to.

"So tell me this. Why you weren't tripping on me about being mad at Raven and Tone for that slimeball shit they did? I mean, you wasn't all on my head like *I* was the one that was out of order."

"Probably because I know what it's like to be in love, so I can understand how you feel. It's funny how you can want somebody so damn bad, and they don't want you in return."

"Yeah, I feel that. So what's our next move, boss?"

J-Rite smiled at his comment. She didn't know what the next move should be; if any at all. Part of her mind was saying go to war and let these Grand Rapids niggas know what's really good with the Detroit bloodline, while the other part was saying just leave and go back home where the love was real in the streets. "I don't know yet, soldier. You tell me what you think we should do next."

He sat down in a chair, leaned back, and rubbed his chin. "I ain't got a clue." He laughed, hunching his shoulders.

"Well, I'll be out of here soon, so we'll see then what should pop off."

After talking for a short while, Mario stood to his feet and stretched his arms high. "Well, I'm about to get outta here. You need anything?"

"Yeah, fool, a blunt."

"Okay, well that ain't 'bout to happen, but I'll blow a box for you."

"Yeah, that's gon' really help me."

Mario walked over to her bed and kissed her on the forehead. "I love you, J; to the moon and back. And, oh yeah, I took care of that R and S situation, so we good."

"I knew I could count on you, if no one else!"

Mario walked out of the room leaving her to her twisted mind thoughts. She didn't know what to make of the situation with Leesa. Deep down in her heart, she wanted Leesa to be happy, but she felt betrayed. *Maybe I am on some bullshit! I should want Leesa to be happy. I know I would want her to be happy for me.* Her mind then drifted off to Dino and all the heartache and pain he'd caused her. Not to mention he'd burned her fucking around with some other female that couldn't love him half as much as she did. *I can't believe that I lost the love of my life. I used to think that we would be together forever. Ain't no need to tell him 'bout this baby. He don't want it anyway. He probably somewhere laid up with the gut-bucket bitch that set his dick on fire in the first place.*

CHAPTER TWENTY-SEVEN

Dino pulled up in Monique's driveway and cut his car off. Since he'd left J-Rite he bought a struggle buggy and was driving that to be more low key. As he sat there thinking about how his life had changed so drastically in the past few months, part of him wanted to call J-Rite and wave the white flag. He was trying to lie to himself like he didn't want to do that, when truth be told, she was probably the best thing that ever happened to him in life. As he leaned back in the driver's seat caught up in his thoughts his cell phone rang. Dino looked at the caller ID, then answered it. "Marlon, what's up with you?"

"Hey, I got that address that you needed."

"All right, that's what's up. Give it to me real quick." After Dino was done getting the information that he requested, he pulled back out of the driveway and headed to his destination. Watching his surroundings, he pulled up to the address Marlon had given him. The fact that the small framed house was shabby came as no big shock. Dino had been around enough drug users in his life to know if they were high they would rest their spaced-out heads anywhere they could until their inner beast was once again awaken demanding another blast. Cutting the engine off, he got out of the car after seeing Dre sitting on the far side of the porch in a lawn chair.

Dre didn't move a muscle when the strange vehicle stopped in front of his temporary home away from home.

Thank God, since Rell had been swinging by blessing him with money here and there, he didn't have to get any credit from the dope man or beg, borrow, or steal. Dre didn't owe anyone anything, so there was no need to run, duck, or hide. Instead, he continued to sit back and enjoy the evening breeze and ponder on how to get back to his old self.

I swear before three or four gods this nigga better be clean, Dino thought, getting out of his car and walking up to the porch. "What's up, nigga? You good or what?"

"Dino! What up, baby boy? Damn, aww shit, it's good to see your ass; for real!" Dre jumped up rushing from the other side of the porch to the edge of the stairs smiling after realizing who it was. Not standing on formalities, Dre stuck his arms out to hug his old friend and show him some love. At first, Dino resisted, but gave in.

This dude look like he has been trying to stay clean. But who knows. I guess I gotta put him through the test and see what's really good with him. "So, fam, I ain't come here to bullshit with you or run some lame-ass game. The bottom line is we still at war every day with niggas who think they can relocate up here to Gun Ru and run our city better than us. I need you back in the car with me. You know, watching my back in the game like we used to do."

Dre was silent at first, caught off guard, not knowing how to respond. "I don't know, Dino; things a lot different now. I mean, I done changed since being on that shit. I have seen things and done things that I never thought I would have seen or done in two lifetimes."

"Look, guy, I know you clean. Well, you looking better." Dino looked his boy up and down. "But I ain't talking about what you done did fucked up in the name of getting high. I'm talking about you being my wingman again."

This nigga still trust me like that? He must still got love for me. So why was Rell over here talking that garbage about Dino? "You sure you want me back around like that, even after I done messed up and took the money from our joint account?"

"Yeah, fool, I wouldn't trust anybody but you for this next level we gonna try to reach after we tie up these loose ends out here in these streets. Look, Dre, I need you to watch my back like I said. Now, you gonna step back up and be all in, or you just out? What's the deal?"

"All right, Dino, I'm down, but I just need one favor."

"What is it?" Dino asked, hoping that it wasn't money.

"I need you to pay for me to go to rehab."

Dino looked at Dre with a surprised expression.

"Yeah, man, I need for you to pay for me to go to rehab. I need that in my life."

"But why if you clean now? I don't understand."

"Dino, my nigga, that boy is a bad drug. If you don't have it, you gon' get sick, and I'm trying to kick it without the meds. So I wanna to go there for the moral support. Like I said, I wanna be back down, no doubt. But I wanna be strong enough to stand tall and not fall back on my knees like some little bitch."

"Yeah, I can do that." *I'm glad my nigga trying to get his shit together.*

"Don't you wanna know how much before you start say yeah?"

Dino had been running amuck lately and would do just about anything to get someone back around him that he could trust. Sure, Marlon had proven himself time after time, but Dino and Dre were cut from a different cloth; well, they used to be anyway. "Dawg, I don't give a fuck what it cost! I'll take you tomorrow. Do you know a place?"

"Yeah, it's a place that I called. I like this place because I can't check myself out of it. Only the people on my papers can, which I figured would be you, Marlon, or Rell."

"How long is the program?"

"It's up to me. They say only I can determine when I'm ready. On another note, how is J-Rite? I ain't heard you mention her at all."

Dino's upbeat mood changed hearing his ex's name. "She's a closed chapter in the book of life. Me and her ain't got no more dealings. Matter of fact, to keep things real, we beefing strong out here; the streets gonna run red real soon."

"What that mean?" Dre asked, not understanding what Dino was talking about.

"It ain't nothing; it's just fuck her, that's all." Dino started walking off the porch and down the walkway. "Well, I'll be through tomorrow, and we can go do that."

"All right, fam, I'll be ready. And thanks for helping your manz out when he need you the most. I swear I appreciate you."

When Dino pulled off, he started thinking that for things to really get back to some kind of normal that he was going to have to take care of J-Rite. He'd been around her long enough to know how she gets down and how vindictive she could be when pushed. He'd seen her in action before, and the way she clown was nothing nice. Dino had a flashback of the last conversation they had at the county jail. Not only did he threaten to kill her and her people, but he had denied the baby she was carrying that deep down inside he knew was his. Not to mention he burnt her. Dino rehashed all of those things and knew that there was no turning back the hands of time. J-Rite was not going to let shit go, so neither was he. Snapping back to reality, he realized he had bigger fish to fry within his own camp before they were war ready. *I hope Marlon find out what's really up with Rell. I don't trust either one of them guys. But if I gotta trust one, it's Marlon. Rell always be on some money hungry type of shit. He stay too thirsty for his own good. Shit, let me make this call.* He reached for his cell.

"Yeah, what?" Marlon said answering on the fifth ring.

"Yo, so I just left our boy spot."

"What that nigga talking about? Y'all good or what?"

"You right, that guy look a way lot better."

"I told you. So we back fucking with him, right?"

"We gonna see. I gotta pick you up in the morning so we can check him in rehab. Only you, Rell, and me can check him out. You down or what?"

"Yeah, I'm with it, but considering, you think that letting Rell check him out is a good move?"

"I don't know, but that's what Dre wants. He came up with saying that."

"Speaking of Rell, I ain't found any dirt on him just yet, so I'm thinking we just ask the nigga and see what he say."

Dino thought for a minute. "Yeah, but if we do, the nigga might stop doing whatever the fuck he doing or planning. Whatever we gonna do, let's kick it in the morning before we meet up with Dre. I just pulled up back over at Monique's crib, and you know how nosy that old bitch can be. Peace."

"So what you think we should do about this crazy situation?" Raven asked Benji as they were driving home from the hospital.

"Baby, I don't know, but we gotta handle it for real—for real."

"Yeah, I know with J-Rite about to get out of the hospital she gonna want blood. Especially because she thinks your uncle has something to do with her getting car-jacked and catching that mysterious case." Raven didn't want to say anything about what she and Mario had done and how they were beefing with J-Rite's ex-man as well, so she let the weight fall totally on Tyrus. Raven also knew that if push came to shove, she would have to ride with a side and strange as it seemed, she was in love with Benji, so she still didn't know what side.

"Bae, you think you should just tell her?"

"You funny. And you tell me what in the hell I'm gonna say—the nigga that tried to get you killed is my man's un-cle? Let's all have dinner at my house."

"Come on now, baby, you ain't gotta act like that. I was just trying to figure shit out like you."

"Well, damn, it was some stupid shit to say!" Raven was on edge. Not only was she stressed out from all this beef-ing, she had been having nightmares about killing that undercover cop, and now J-Rite had flipped out on her. As far as she was concerned, shit couldn't get any worse.

"Hold the fuck up, Raven. You need to chill out and calm your nerves!" The anger was apparent in his voice as she drove.

Benji had never yelled at Raven, so she was caught to-tally off guard. *"Excuse me!* Who the hell you think you talking to?" She rolled her eyes with a savage attitude.

"Raven, chill out. And, yeah, I'm talking to you. The fuck you gonna come at me like that. I'm supposed to be your man. You gonna turn on me?"

"Boy, I ain't turned on you, and if I did, you would fuck-ing know it!"

"What's that's supposed to mean?" Benji got defensive.

"You heard me!"

"That shit sound good, but I ain't my uncle, remem-ber that."

Raven took this comment as an awful slap in the face. "What you mean by that? I'm confused. Please enlighten me."

"Look, I ain't about to argue over this bullshit! I got other things on my mind right now." Benji hated that he let things get this far. *I should have just shut the fuck up.* "Look, baby, I'm sorry."

Raven hated when she couldn't get her point across. *This punk think he just gonna say some shit and it's supposed to be over. Naw, it ain't like that.* She swerved, pulling her truck over to the side of the road. "You better get the fuck out now," she said, reaching for her purse.

Benji knew what was in her purse. He looked at her, then got out. Raven barely let him shut the door before she pulled off. A few seconds later, she was upset and wanted to go back, but her pride wouldn't let her.

CHAPTER TWENTY-EIGHT

Hazel had deep feelings for the street-oriented Asia. The odd couple was like night and day, and Hazel seemed to care less. Wanting to spend some special alone time from the norm, they drove to Chicago. Not used to doing things like this, Asia was overjoyed at all the new things her relationship with Hazel had brought into her life. After Buzzy had got knocked she felt lost, having no game plan or direction. Her first thought was to come up to Grand Rapids and hook up with J-Rite because Buzzy had always said that if there was anyone of his all-girl team of drug sellers that could survive without him it would be her. So, of course, Asia did what she thought was best, trying to hook herself up to a rising star. Since J-Rite had been playing her off about hooking her up with a package, she was more than ready to leave and go back home to Detroit until meeting Hazel. It was because of her and her alone that Asia was still in Gun Ru. Now, in Asia's eyes, life was perfect and everything was starting to fall in place. She was on a surprise minivacation getaway with her girl, and J-Rite finally promised to bless her with some product as soon as she got in a new shipment.

Asia turned over in bed in the lavish hotel suite looking for Hazel. After calling her name out and getting no reply, she got out of bed and took a shower. *Maybe she went to get us some breakfast or something.* Stepping out of the shower she called Hazel, who was still not back in the room. Her phone went to voice mail after the fourth ring, further annoying Asia. Glancing at the digital clock, it read one in the afternoon. Not realizing it was this late, she got dressed and headed downstairs to the restaurant. Getting seated in the far corner, she tried Hazel's cell once more; straight to voice mail again. Fed up and frustrated, Asia picked up a menu ready to eat and break her diet. When the waitress came to take the order, Asia looked up and saw the unimaginable. There was Hazel in the lobby area with some man . . . hand in hand.

Oh hell, naw! Who the fuck is that? Now back on her feet, Asia was pissed watching the man lean in and kiss Hazel on her lips. Throwing the menu down on the table, Asia stormed out of the restaurant heading into the lobby. "Bitch, have you lost your damn mind?"

Hazel was stunned. Caught red-handed, she didn't know what to say or do. Here she was having just been kissed on the lips by a man, and nine out of ten, her woman had seen it. "Oh, hey, Asia, I didn't see you standing there."

"What the fuck you mean 'hey, Asia'? Who in the fuck is this nigga? And why in the hell y'all kissing? You got me twisted!"

"I'm Maxi. It's nice to meet you." He extended his hand out to shake Asia's acting as if he hadn't just heard her turn up on Hazel.

Asia looked him up and down as if he was no more than filth. Besides the fact that she always dressed like a man, this day she wished she really was one so that she could sucker punch this joker directly in the face. She turned toward Hazel, not even speaking to Maxi. "Who in the fuck is he? And why the fuck was y'all kissing?" Hazel tried to give Asia a forced smile.

"It ain't what it look like, baby," Hazel tried explaining.

"Yo, this nigga had his tongue down your fucking throat!"

"Man, who the hell is this?" Maxi finally asked the million-dollar question, tired of being ignored.

Asia turned around to face her nemesis. "I'm her better half; now shut the fuck up talking to me and her!"

"Bitch, you got the wrong nigga! I don't let a ho wannabe a bro talk to me like that. You wanna act like a dude, I'ma treat you like one." Maxi walked up on Asia waiting for her to keep running off at the mouth.

Hazel jumped between the two of them seeing that things were getting way out of control. In between the noise that the three of them were making, other hotel guests and restaurant patrons were gathering around to see what was going on. Not wanting to have this type of thing go on in their establishment, security started walking over to intervene. "Excuse me, folks, but do we have a problem?" the security officer asked looking directly at Maxi.

"What in the fuck you asking me for? Ask that bitch. She the one that came up on me and my girl acting a fool."

"I ain't a bitch, and she ain't your girl."

"Just hold on a minute." The security officer took out his walkie-talkie asking for the front desk to call the police.

"Wait, sir, I can explain everything, Officer," Hazel vowed, opening the side of her purse. Not wanting the local authorities to come into play, she had to expose herself and the double life she'd been living with Asia.

"What the fuck!" Maxi frowned as he quickly turned to leave the hotel.

Before he got even a foot away, the hotel was flooded with DEA agents. As they swarmed Maxi, he was handcuffed and read his rights by Hazel who had her badge now clamped on her side.

This bitch ain't shit! She been playing me the whole time, and I fell for this bitch. Shortly after that, Hazel walked in the room she'd been sharing with her lover. Asia looked at her, then slapped her across the face. "Bitch, you ain't shit! How could you, and who the fuck is you?"

"Asia, I'm sorry. I never meant to hurt you."

"You didn't hurt me; I don't even feel you like that," Asia huffed, packing her things, ready to get back to her normal life before meeting Hazel in the first place.

Hazel knew that Asia was lying; she could see it in her face. *Damn, I fucked up. I gotta think of something.* Before Hazel could say anything else Asia walked over to her. *I don't care how mad she is, she better not slap me again.* Hazel knew that if it came down to it, even though Asia was much bigger than she, she'd been specially trained and could beat her in a physical battle. But that wasn't what she wanted to do.

"And the bad thing about all this shit is you made me think that you really liked me! You ain't about shit!" Asia pouted with tears in her eyes.

"Look, baby. I don't like you—I love you. I was on this case undercover dealing with Maxi even before we met. Now, I have to be honest. Sometimes cases cross and there's collateral damage, like your friend Jessica Sanders and her crew and Tyrus Collins."

Asia was lost and her expression showed just that. "Jessica Sanders? Who in the hell is that?"

Hazel forgot that she was back in personal mode and not police, "Oh, I'm sorry. You know her as J-Rite and Tyrus Collins owns the nightclub on Division Avenue."

"So, damn, the whole time I was telling you about my homegirl from Detroit you were building up a case against her?"

"Believe me when I tell you, I didn't mean for it to happen like this. I really didn't. Truth be told, we stumbled

up on her and her crew while we had Maxi and his organization under surveillance. He led us to begin watching
Tyrus and his nightclub, and J-Rite and her sister-in-law
Leesa just happened to pop up on our radar after Leesa
Jones shot a female that worked for Tyrus. Well, in reality, she was one of our DEA undercover agents that we'd
placed in his inner circle; so, yeah, we got a job to do."

"This shit is bizarre. I swear to God it's crazy!"

"Look, Asia, there was nothing that you told me that
I wouldn't have found out anyway. But I'm going to be
honest with you. I care a lot about you. Meeting you was
one of the best things that happened about me working
these cases; an extra added bonus."

"You must think I'm really fucking stupid! I ain't falling
for that bullshit again! You a liar!"

"Now hold the hell on! The only thing I lied about was
my job! You might have helped me put names to some of
these faces a lot sooner, but I would have found out over
time just the same."

"That's more than enough reason for me not to trust
you. I was just a pawn in your fucking li'l game!"

Hazel didn't know what else to say. She knew that if
the shoe was on the other foot she would be acting the
same way, if not worse. "What you want me to say, Asia?"

"I don't give a fuck what you say! I gotta go. You done
really fucked up my life," Asia said, grabbing her suitcase
and heading toward the door.

Hazel hated to do what was about to come next. As
much as she loved Asia, she'd revealed too much of the
undercover operations that she and her field squad was
involved in. "Look, baby, I'm sorry, but I can't let you go
just like that."

Asia stopped and looked at her. "What you mean? As
far as I'm concerned, we done; we over!"

Hazel was hurt, but this was a part of her job she hated; she'd taken an oath to uphold the law and was going to do just that. "I know you don't mean that, but even if you do, I have to have you detained until our other investigations are concluded."

"So now you fucking arresting me?"

"Naw, bae, we just detaining you, like I said. We have to get subpoenas together and warrants on deck. After all of that is in place, then it's on to the execution of the paperwork and arrests. Lucky enough, baby, your friend saved you from catching a case alongside the rest of them. See, every time she refused to give you a package, she was helping you dodge the bullet of being indicted as well; no crime, no foul."

Asia was heated and hurt as Hazel turned the doorknob allowing two male DEA officers to enter and escort her girlfriend to a secure location under federal jurisdiction until further notice.

"Tone, roll up a blunt," Benji urged as he and Tone were on their way to pick up Raven and go visit J-Rite. To Mario's dislike, the two of them had been hanging tough together ever since they met at the hospital. Benji had no idea whatsoever that Tone had hit Raven off a couple of times. He felt considering the way Benji felt about Raven it was best he didn't.

"Yeah, nigga, I got you." Tone grabbed a box of blunts out of his track suit pocket.

Benji and Raven still hadn't made up. He was making every attempt he could, but she was giving him the cold shoulder. "I need to get high before we pick up Raven, because she still giving me fever 'bout from some bullshit we argued about the other night."

"Dawg, you know females. Hey, stop at the store. I need something to drink real quick."

A few minutes later they pulled up in a parking lot next to a rust bucket with two guys sitting in it. "What you drinking on so early?" Benji asked as they hopped out going into the store.

"Nigga, something brown if we gotta deal with both Raven and J-Rite's crazy asses!"

"Yo, ain't that the nigga Dino and we beefing with hanging with Benji? What the fuck this bullshit about? Maybe that nigga Benji a rat," Marlon said to Dre as they sat in Dino's rust bucket parked in the store parking lot.

"That is that bitch nigga!" Dre agreed, getting hyped, knowing his main focus should have been getting dropped off at rehab like the plan was.

"Sit tight, fam, I'll be right back," Marlon said, jumping out of the passenger seat and putting his hood on.

When Tone and Benji entered the store Dino was walking from the back. He had a six-pack of Millers in one hand and a juice in the other. He slowed down his steps thinking that he'd just had a blessing from God. He was not expecting to run up on one of his enemies in the midst of dropping Dre off, but here the fuck he was—live and in living color. It was perfect timing. Tone was standing at the counter with his back turned seeing if the sand nigga cashier had a fifth of Hennessy that was chilled. He had yet to see Benji who had gone down the other aisle as he was creeping up the other one. Dino reached over, setting the beer and juice quietly down on a shelf next to some cans of soup and some instant grits. Ready to get revenge for Rell, even though he'd been acting funny lately, Dino reached under his shirt. Getting a mental rush, he pulled out his 9 mm that already had one up top. With the rear of Tone's head in his sight, he was a mere second away from pulling the trigger when Marlon walked in the thankfully empty store.

"Hey, Dino! Dino," he yelled out trying to make sure his homeboy wasn't getting stumped out on the humble.

Tone heard Dino's name being called out and instinctively spun around, whipping out his own pistol. Immediately seeing Dino duck behind the potato chip rack, he let loose a few rounds knowing it was going down.

Benji realized something was up when he heard someone's name he couldn't make out being called too. He had no idea what was jumping off. He just heard gunshots ring out and wisely took out his own gun to cover his ass.

"Awww fuck!" Marlon said, running out of the store not wanting to be caught in the reckless crossfire.

Benji assumed he was the one shooting at his homeboy Tone. On a mission, he gave chase, shooting as he was running behind Marlon, not recognizing him with his hood on. Meanwhile, Dino ran in the back of the store as Tone, a seasoned goon, seemed to be having better aim than he. As the barrage of bullets ricocheted off the metal racks and shelving, nearly taking his head off his body, he panicked. He felt trapped trying to figure out his next move. *I gotta get the fuck outta here! If this dumb nigga Marlon wouldn't have called my name I would have got his ass. And where in the fuck is Dre at?*

Tone wanted to go in the rear of the deserted store gangster style after Dino and settle up with him once and for all, but he could hear police sirens in the distance. *Shit! They done called the police. I gotta get the fuck outta Dodge.* "I'ma see you soon, pussy," he shouted out to Dino, knowing he was somewhere in the store being a coward.

With that being said, he darted out the door, smoking gun still in hand. Outside, he looked for Benji so they could bounce, seeing how he had the keys. He knew better than to call out his name in case it was possible witnesses were around listening. Tone crept to the side of the building to at least see if Benji was anywhere in that direction. Before Tone knew what hit him, he felt two bullets fly past his head. In an attempt to shoot back, he got hit with the third, knocking him damn near off his feet. With a gaping hole in the rear of his head shattering his skull Tone struggled to make it back to the front of the store where he collapsed.

Dre stepped over his motionless body calling out for Dino who had yet to come outside. Getting no answer, he fled the scene on foot hearing the sirens get closer. Rehab was the last thing on his mind now. He needed to get high after what he had done; and quick. A few seconds later, Benji ran back up discovering Tone's corpse. Knowing he couldn't run the risk of getting caught, he jumped in his car and peeled off. As Benji bent the corner in a rush, he failed to notice Dino who had run out of the back emergency door of the store and was hailing a cab.

Damn, what the fuck I'm gonna do now? Dino had the driver take him to Monique's house. Paranoid, he never stopped looking out the back window as the cab drove along. *I know they got me on camera. If this nigga wouldn't have called my fucking name I could've got Tone's ass!* Dino walked in the house and saw Monique lying on the couch.

"Hey, bae, I was thinking we should take a vacation." Dino knew the heat was about to get even hotter after what had just taken place.

CHAPTER TWENTY-NINE

Raven was just leaving the pharmacy when her cell phone rang. It was her grandmother.

"Hey, Granny, everything okay?"

"Jennifer, are you about to come home?" her old voice cracked as if something was wrong.

"Yeah, I have to meet Benji and my friend back there. We're going to visit Jessica. What's wrong?"

"Oh, it's just that the kids were running through the house and baby girl fell and cut her head. It's not bad though."

"All right, I'm on my way." *Damn, I'ma have to start getting a sitter. Granny getting too old.*

Raven got in her truck and headed home. When she stepped inside the house she felt a strange vibe. For it to be so early in the day and one of the kids was supposedly hurt, it was much too quiet. She took a few steps back, reaching in her purse for her gun. Before she knew what was taking place, her purse was knocked to the floor. After being socked in the jaw, somebody shoved a gun in her face as she slid down the wall. She was dazed, still trying to recover from the roughhouse blow. The mysterious man then snatched her by the collar of her shirt, dragging her into the living room. Once there, Raven was kicked in the side of her ribs.

After catching her breath, she saw that there were two other men she'd never seen before as well, standing off to one side of the room. As she cut her eyes to the other side, the usually calm, coldhearted female started to get hysterical. Her three children and grandmother were tied up in chairs and gagged. Raven tried her best to get off the floor and come to their aid but was once again kicked, then ordered to settle down. The two guys lifted her injured body off the floor and tied her up also. Minutes later, the strong overwhelming smell of gasoline filled her flared nostrils. It became painfully clear what was about to take place *Where the fuck is Benji and Tone at? Oh my God, let them pull up!* "Please, let my family go," she pleaded with blood trickling down out of the corner of her mouth. "I have some money put up. I'll pay you! Please!"

The apparent murder-intended arsonist paid her and her desperate attempt to bargain no attention. One of the three lit a match, tossing it in the hallway. Content with his actions, he stood smirking as the flames engulfed the area. Moments later, Raven could see them no more, assuming they had fled to safety. With the heat from the flames becoming more intense, she knew she and her family were in serious trouble. Not ready to die, her small son decided to try his best to get free. Wiggling his arms and feet around, he tipped the chair over he was tied to and got unloose. Next, he untied his mother.

"Thanks, baby, now go untie Granny and your sisters."

The dense smoke that had filled the house made her youngest daughter fall out. Granny was fighting to catch her breath. Raven had to think quickly seeing how the path to the front door was ablaze. Reaching for one of the chairs that were now scattered throughout on the living room floor, Raven took one, throwing it through the picture window. As the chair smashed the glass landing on the front grass, she and her family followed. "Help Granny out the window" she ordered her brave, heroic son who'd saved their lives.

After everybody was safely out of the house, Raven looked around to see if she saw anyone that could help. Thank God she noticed a car sitting in front of her neighbor's house. Although her eyes were watery and swollen from all the smoke, she could see people sitting in it. *Why the fuck ain't they trying to help us?* Seeing them getting out of the car Raven felt something was wrong as they seemed too calm.

"Help! Help us!" With his eyes just as impaired, her son took it upon himself running toward the people for assistance.

Before Raven could stop him, one of the occupants opened fire with an AK-47, cutting not only the small boy's life short, but massacring the entire family. Clinging to life, Raven started to choke on her own blood as she looked up to a man towering over her, smiling with the barrel of his pistol shoved in her face. "You ain't half as cute as that little punk Benji made you out to be!"

Benji didn't know where to go or what to do next. Not only had Tone just been killed in what he thought to be a botched robbery, he'd chased one of the would-be accomplices down, shooting him in the back. Not realizing there was a third person, he could only assume that it was the guy from inside the store that sent Tone home. *What in the fuck just happened?*

Fuck, I'm gon' tell this nigga's brother that he dead! He already don't like me. How Raven gonna take this? As he drove in the direction they were headed in the first place, Benji was still numb about how things had gone from sugar to shit so quickly. Now, he had to tell Raven Tone had just gotten killed. Benji had been trying to call her, but she wasn't answering her phone. He figured maybe she had her phone in her purse or on the charger and was just waiting for him and Tone to pull up. Benji had grown to love Raven and her kids, and he didn't know what he would do without them.

Turning on their street, he saw what looked like sheer chaos: multiple police cars, fire trucks, and several ambulances. *What the fuck going on?* He couldn't get any closer in his vehicle, so he parked. Now on foot, as he made his way through the mournful crowd, his heart started racing. Benji knew something was wrong; he felt it deep in his soul.

Standing in front of Raven's house from behind the yellow tape that was everywhere, he instantly wanted to throw up. The house was burned up, and there were five white sheets covering what had to be bodies sprawled on the ground with blood still leaking through. Benji's mind started going crazy. He tried to make his way over to the bodies but was stopped by two officers.

"Hold on, you can't go any farther."

"That's my family! Get your fucking hands off me!" he screamed, attempting to break through the yellow tape.

The two cops looked at each other, then sympathetically let Benji pass so he could see his family one last time. He ran over to the smallest sheet and pulled it back. "Damn, Brittany, bunny! I'm sorry." Through his tears he could see that one bullet had torn through her chest. Hysterical, he then went over and started looking for Raven's body. He found it. He paused for a second before he slowly took the sheet off her face. Benji had heavy tears coming down his face by this time. *How could you be gone? The kids and granny didn't deserve this. I'm sorry about the fight from the other day. I didn't mean it! I love y'all so much!* He was madder than he had ever been in his entire life. He hated himself at this moment. He knew that more than likely if he would have been with them, whatever happened would have not popped off. Benji knew that Raven was in the street, but he felt she wasn't supposed to go out like she did. He pulled the sheet back, covering her face, knowing that he had to get the ultimate revenge. Benji knew by the house being torched this had to be a deed ordered by the hand of his uncle. Arson was his style.

Benji pulled up in his uncle's driveway and got out. "Hurry the fuck up!" Benji demanded as he stood on the porch waiting for someone to open his uncle's door.

Tommy finally opened the door with a devilish smirk on his face. "What up, li'l nigga?" he said, moving out of the way to let Benji in, who looked visibly shaken.

"Yo, where the fuck my unk at?" His cracked voice echoed off the walls not responding to Tommy's greeting.

"The boss in the back in the den. I'll let him know you here. You hold on for a minute." Tommy walked off, laughing under his breath.

What the fuck he talking about "wait here"? Benji felt that something was going on. He never once had to wait to talk to his uncle. He usually just walked in the room.

A few seconds later Tommy came back in the room. "Yeah, youngster, you can go back now."

"Yeah, whatever." Benji had his gun tucked in the lower spine of his back, and it was itching to get put to use. He walked past Tommy, never taking his eyes off him. When he got in the den, his uncle was watching the news.

"It's a shame what happened to that entire family, but shit happens for a reason, doesn't it?" Tyrus eyeballed Benji as if he'd really receive an answer.

Benji looked over at the television and saw that they were talking about Raven . . . his woman. "I know it was you! That shit wasn't right, Unk! You didn't have to kill them like that. That was real bitch shit!"

"That's the way the game goes," Tyrus casually remarked with a crooked grin on his face. "I told you business always comes first, not pussy. I got a lot of irons in the fire and no time for no pole-swinging tramp from Detroit to interfere. Did you think I was playing with you or what?"

"Fuck you talking about? Old man, that was my family that you killed!"

Tyrus never looked Benji in the eyes. He acted like he didn't hear what was just said.

"Did you hear what the fuck I just said? That was my fucking *family* you murdered!"

"Yeah, I heard you, and like I said, that's the way shit goes, so man up. All this could have been avoided if you would have just handled my business and kept my money straight, but naw, you wanted to be your own boss making decisions and going against my word; so now it is what the hell it is. And FYI, I haven't been outta this house all evening, so stop saying that I killed anybody. We wouldn't want that nasty rumor to get started."

Benji felt the room getting hot and beginning to spin. His blood started boiling. This was one of the worst days in his life. He'd committed cold-blooded murder earlier and tragically lost five people himself that meant the world to him.

Tommy walked back in the den as if on cue. "Sometimes things have to get done to get people to understand that they have to follow rules. Ain't that right, Tommy?"

"Yeah, that's right. I hope you don't take it personal. I mean, it ain't like they was your real kids," Tommy said with a smile on his face as if he'd done no wrong or wanted a reward for eluding to what he'd done.

"Yeah, nephew, it was business; just business. They were becoming too much of a distraction for you. I told you, it's business first and always. Now when you take over for me, then you'll understand what I mean."

Hearing that Benji was going to take over didn't sit well with Tommy.

This nigga played me. "I thought I was going to be taking over," Tommy said with a mug on his face.

"Come on now, Tommy, we both know that you don't have what it takes to be a leader; you're more of a follower," Tyrus remarked.

"Look, old man, I've been watching your back for years and you gonna leave everything to this li'l fuck?" Tommy was heated. He got ready to pull out a gun but was stopped by Benji whipping out his own gun, placing it to Tommy's temple.

"I don't give a fuck what you two going through. Fuck both y'all! Somebody gonna pay for what happened to my family!" Benji vowed, holding the gun steady.

"Now, just hold up, li'l homie! Your uncle made me do it." Tommy was bitching up, but Benji didn't care as he pulled the trigger, letting one single round off into Tommy's head, killing him instantly.

Stepping over Tommy's body it was time to settle up with his uncle. "This piece of shit nigga was right. You *was* the one giving the orders, calling the shots. You knew that me and her was going to get married; that I loved her; and you took all that away from me!" Benji was emotional now, pointing his gun at his uncle.

"Listen, boy, I did what the fuck I had to do to protect this family—our family. Those girls were probably plotting to kill your ass, then me! You think it was just by chance she wanted you so bad?" Tyrus was trying his best to justify what had to happen to Raven, even in the face of his own death.

"All you had to do was let the shit go! If you would have let it go, none of this would have happened!"

"So you gonna choose her, that slut, over me? I'm your flesh and blood! You gotta be fucking kidding me!"

Benji was done listening to his uncle. At this point, it didn't matter what Tyrus said, because none of it would bring Raven, Granny, or the kids back. Benji felt life was meaningless. He lowered his arm slightly from aiming at Tryus's head and shot once, hitting the man that raised him to be the next king of the family business, directly through the heart. As his uncle's body slumped over to the side, Benji heard a loud crash in the front of the house and multiple voices. As he stood there, gun in hand and two dead bodies in the room, the army of footsteps got closer. When the door of the den was kicked damn near off the hinges, Benji raised his gun to defend himself but had no win against the highly trained DEA Task Force that had raided the place to apprehend and arrest Tryus Collins and his entire organization . . . Benji included. As they dragged him out in handcuffs, Benji didn't care about his fate because he no longer had anything or anyone to live for.

CHAPTER THIRTY

Leesa felt like she had one helluva run in the dope game. She had been running the streets since back in the day when she and Hutch first met. When he got killed, her original mind-set told her to just back away from the unforgiving streets and get a regular nine-to-five job. But she could not bring herself to live like that. She was spoiled to getting fast money no matter who got hurt or got in the way. Leesa had effectively cut herself off from feeling any type of emotion or having any sort of real true attachment to anything or anyone . . . with the exception of Jessica. She truly loved her like a sister; yet, now that relationship was strained because of Q. Not thinking Jessica was being reasonable in dealing with the reality that Hutch was gone out of their physical lives forever, Leesa was prepared to just give her a small bit of time to come to grips with it. She herself was behaving the same way . . . until Q. Now he had asked her to marry him and leave the streets behind, and, of course, she'd agreed. For the past few days since their big blowout at the hospital, Leesa had her cell powered off and was trying to get accustomed to the quiet life; damn beefing and damn drama.

"Baby, we've been in this bed all day." Q smiled, elated that he was about to have Leesa as his queen. "Get up and get dressed. I wanna take you to the jewelry store to pick out your own ring so it can be official. You can have whatever you want! I love you that much!"

Leesa could only smile as she got up and headed into the bathroom. After turning the shower on and allowing it to get hot, she stepped inside. As the water flowed down on her body, she made a mental list of all the things she had to do; the first being put her house up on the market, and then get in touch with the plug she'd been rocking with for years and inform him that she was retiring and out of the game. *I just hope Jessica can be happy for me and my new life. I wish she could be one of my brides-maids, but I now it might be too much for her to handle; especially after she just lost the baby. But fuck it, I'ma call her anyway and just clear the air.*

Never being so happy since being with Hutch, Leesa stepped out of the shower with a gigantic smile on her face.

"Put your hands up!" Hazel ordered, standing in the steamy bathroom with her firearm pointed directly at Leesa's chest. "DEA officer. Are you Leesa Jones?" she asked following the proper procedure. As she waited for the answer, she heard her fellow officers on the task force yell out "all clear" from the front of the dwelling. "Well, are you Leesa Jones, thirty-two, of Detroit, Michigan; daughter of Samuel and Patrice Jones?"

There was nothing to say; nothing to do but be honest. "Yes, I'm Leesa Jones." She then tried covering her naked body with her hands.

Hazel was there to do a job, but could not help but to lust after her soon-to-be-arrested three-county drug sting target's perfect body. After allowing Ms. Jones to slip on a track suit, she handcuffed her, then led her out to the living room. With Q, whose only crime was loving a girl from the hood, laid out on the floor, also handcuffed, the two of them never got a chance to say their good-byes when Leesa was paraded out onto the front lawn, then tossed in the rear of an undercover vehicle.

Once he was allowed to get up and the handcuffs were removed, Q found the nerve to ask the last officer on the scene what Leesa was being charged with.

"Attempted murder of a federal officer, for one! So get your pen and paper ready; she gonna be gone a long damn time!"

I can't believe my nigga gone. He was just here. It seems like we were just little young niggas running around getting into all kinda dumb bullshit. Mario had spent what seemed like hours reminiscing on his and Tone's childhood. That's all he had left—just memories. Mario took all the things that had happened to him in life with a positive attitude, but he couldn't do it this time. He was down for the count. Having received a call from some of the young guys they had out in the streets hustling that there had been a shoot-out up at the liquor store around the way involving Tone, he rushed up there. In denial, he saw his brother's arm sticking out from underneath a white sheet. He wanted nothing more than to run over to him, snatch the sheet back, and ask him who was the dirty rotten motherfucker that had stolen his life away from the land of the living. However, Mario knew that if he did that, he'd run the risk of police contact. He wanted to avoid any light being shined on him so he could hunt down Tone's killer without fear of being arrested.

"Gimme another shot," he yelled at the bartender, slurring his words. The bartender walked over with a bottle of Jack Daniel and started pouring. "Just gimme the damn bottle." Mario snatched the bottle out of the man's hand. He then went in his pocket and threw a knot full of money on the bar. "Keep the bottles coming! I don't care how much it cost!"

He keep this up and he gonna drink his self to death,
the bartender thought looking at Mario as he guzzled
down the brown devil potion. He had seen this a lot from
customers over the years. At other establishments, the
bartender would try to get a person that they saw blatantly overindulging like this to slow down. Not at this
bar. He didn't care. Long as you had money you could
keep the pity party going full speed. He grabbed the
money, counted it, then walked off. *Damn fool gave me a
thousand dollars. I love this job.*

*Why the fuck was Tone and Benji bitch ass hanging
together in the first place? I told that nigga to stay away
from him.* Just then, Mario's cell phone rang. It was
J-Rite. "Yeah, what's up, girl? What it do?"

"Mario, where are you at?" she somberly asked, feeling
close to the exact same way that Mario was feeling after
finding out about Tone.

"I'm at the bar, why? What you want, J?"

"Baby, I know you're hurt. I'm fucked up in the head
now too. But I need for you to come to my place, please. I
need you here with me. Shit is even crazier."

"Why, J, why? You know these niggas out here in
these streets gonna pay for what the fuck they did to my
blood. I swear on everything I love I'ma be all on every
nigga head I even *think* had something to do with the
bullshit . . . starting with that faggot Benji whenever I
find him, not to mention Dino."

J-Rite knew Mario was all up in his feelings and rightly
so. "Baby, please just come over here as soon as possible.
That's what I wanna talk to you about."

Mario put the bottle he had been taking to the head
down on top of the bar. "Hold tight, J. Have you heard
from that nigga Benji? Please tell me you have! What the
fuck he say happened? My little homies say Benji was
there. They say he was the one that was supposed to have

shot that nigga that run with your grimy-ass boyfriend, Marlon, in his back. I keep calling Raven cell, and that bitch sending me straight to voice mail. I know she know where that nigga Benji at. They probably somewhere together hiding out."

J-Rite was weak; not only in mind and spirit, but physically as well. She had got straight out of her hospital bed, pulled out her own IV from her arm, and got dressed after receiving Mario's frantic heartbreaking news about Tone's demise. Without bothering to officially check herself out of the facility, J-Rite walked to the elevator, out to the lobby, and in the front of the building hailing a cab. She wanted to tell Mario even more tragic news, but thought it would be in his best interest, along with any unfortunate person that could possibly be in his drunken destructive path, that it was delivered in person.

"Naw, I haven't heard from him, and yeah, you right; fuck Dino. But there's more to what's going on. Plus, we still got beef with Tyrus."

"Like what? What the fuck else could it be? Tone gone and ain't never coming back, and believe me when I tell you, the streets of Gun Ru ain't gonna be safe."

"It's Raven, she . . ." J-Rite couldn't even bring herself to finish her sentence. "Mario, please just come over now! Please, I'm begging you!"

"She what? Raven what? Fuck it, I'm on my way!" Mario hung up. "I wonder what the hell happened." Even though he couldn't have Raven like he wanted her, he was still on her side up until finding out that her man, Benji, was with Tone just moments before his death.

Mario stumbled out of the bar, got in his truck, and pulled off. Swerving up into J-Rite's driveway, he took a deep breath before he hopped down out of the truck. He ran up to the door, which was hard because he could barely stand. As his heart raced, the dark liquor flowing through his bloodstream seemed like it was starting to boil. He wanted to throw up and tried to fight it. Seconds later, he was doubled over, gagging into her flower pot that sat right on the edge of the porch. Using his wrist and hand to wipe his mouth, he grew dizzy wanting to pass out. Mario lifted his arm. Before he could knock, J-Rite opened her front door. Definitely not under the influence of liquor, she was drained. She fell straight into Mario's arms. Sobering up with the quickness, he caught her. Carrying J-Rite into the house, he noticed she had tears running down her face.

"Mario, Mario, oh my God! I'm so glad you're here."

"Sis, what the fuck is going on? Tell me," he demanded, setting her down on the couch.

"It's so messed up I can't hardly breathe."

Mario loved J-Rite like family, but she was pushing it asking him to drop everything he was doing and come to her side. But now, she was taking a year and a day to spit out what she wanted and what was so damn awful that couldn't wait until he finished drinking. "Look, I ain't trying to be on no bullshit with you. Right about now, my damn brother is dead and gone and truth be told, your people that you was fucking with before me and Tone even got up here is at fault! So if you got something to tell me about where Dino, Benji, or Raven's ho ass is at, then tell me. Otherwise, let me go back to doing what I was doing and I'll get up with all three of them hoes on my own!"

J-Rite managed to find the strength to lift her body off the couch. Knowing that if Mario was this angry and distraught now, she braced herself the best she possibly could for the fallout that was seconds away from taking place. She walked over to the television and turned it on. Using the remote, she turned on the DVR. Going through the menu, she pulled up the recently recorded show; the local news. Although hyped, Mario sat down on the couch and watched. When it was over, it was like he was in shock. He looked over at J-Rite who was about to pass out again, then back to the television screen. After repeating those motions a few times, he managed to speak.

"How in the fuck? What the fuck? I can't—I can't—" He didn't even finish his sentence before tears started coming out of his eyes. "Raven gone too? Her and them babies and that old woman? Naw, that's fucked up! I mean, it's one thing to try to get at niggas that's off into the game, but kids and somebody's grandmother? That's straight foul! I'm telling you, girl, that nigga Dino gotsta go!"

J-Rite had lost not only Tone but Raven as well. She didn't know how much more she could take. "Look, Mario, that's why I wanted you to come over here. Right about now, it's just me and you. Leesa acting like she don't give a damn because she ain't even called me back. I know we was beefing and all, but I done left over seven messages and blew her cell up. Plus, just like I seen this bullshit plastered all over news and the report of Tone's murder at the store, I know her wannabe white ass watches the news every night. So either she preoccupied somewhere with that nigga she fucking around with dick up in her mouth or she just like fuck me altogether. Whatever the case is, like I said, me and you out here on our own."

Mario took in all J-Rite was saying. He knew since Raven was gone, Benji and Dino were the missing pieces to his puzzle. "Look, baby girl, all this shit is too damn much. But I ain't gonna sleep until I get some answers," he bitterly guaranteed as he stormed out the door in search for two people that he planned to murder in revenge.

CHAPTER THIRTY-ONE

Monique had been watching Dino toss and turn all night. She knew since he'd come to her house talking about they need to go on some all-of-a-sudden-out-of-the-blue vacation, there had to be some shit in the game. She might have been desperately in love with him at one point, but that graveyard love had slowly dwindled away when he kept putting her on the back burner for J-Rite and any other piece of trash whore he'd come across. For months on end, she knew his game, all his moves, and what he was truly saying about her out in the streets to his homeboys. Monique knew he felt she was nothing more than his sugar momma and meal ticket. Some of his conversations she had even heard were recorded without him knowing. Thanks to Rell, she was not in the dark, but played the role.

"Hey, boo-boo, how's my baby momma doing?" Rell asked, knowing Monique loved when he would call her that. He knew that she'd told Dino that she was carrying his child. But what else could she do to cover her and Rell's secret affair? When they first hooked up, it was right after Dino had meet J-Rite and was playing her to the left. Like a mack, he saw the potential to get some of the money and gifts she was showering on Dino for himself. Rell felt Dino didn't need two females caking on him; that wasn't the way life oughta be.

"I'm good, bae. I didn't get much sleep, though. Your friend came over here last night bugging. I don't know if he done messed around and got burned again or what, but he was acting real strange."

Rell hated that his plan to rob Dino was starting to unravel. He'd been spinning his web of deception, and in the next few days, he had planned to make his move. Now, the streets were talking and not in a good way. Their team that used to be so tight was not only torn apart—they were done. Marlon had been gunned down, along with a nigga that was running with J-Rite; Tone. Rell didn't give two hot shits about the asshole who was rumored to be the brother of the guy who had stepped him and Tiffany out at the mall. He couldn't wait for them to bury the dead gorilla so that he could go and piss on his grave. Now, as for Marlon, Rell never really cared for him and would have had no problem killing him his damn self if he got in the way of the caper he was gonna perpetrate against Dino. But to have Benji, of all people who he thought could be trusted, pull the trigger, had him confused. Neither Rell nor Dino knew that Benji and J-Rite's crew had anything to do with the other. He didn't know the true connection, and since Benji was locked up on suicide watch, he never would.

"Yeah, baby, he did fuck up with his dumb ass. He was supposed to be getting at the guy from that mall bullshit and ended up being a coward, leaving our boys out to dry."

Monique couldn't believe she ever loved or cared about Dino in the first place. "Are you serious?"

"Yeah. You know Marlon? Well, he got shot in the back, and he's dead. And Dre, well, that nigga had got his shit almost together and was going into rehab. That ho-ass nigga you got over there in your bed left Dre to do what he obviously couldn't; kill somebody from J-Rite's crew.

"You bullshitting! Are you for real?"

"Yeah, bae." Rell had yet to deliver to her the icing on the triple-layer cake. "My manz Dre was so mentally fucked up behind the shit, having to kill that lame or risk being killed, his weak ass messed around and overdosed. His girl found him dead on the front porch this morning with the damn needle still sticking in his arm. And where the fuck is Dino while the streets is going crazy? Curled up in your bed like some little pussy!"

"Him and his loyalty to that bitch is so tired," Monique pouted, rubbing her stomach. "That's why I had my cousin and them carjack that bitch in the first place. Then her dumb ass wanna be all shoot-out at the OK Corral. That shit was perfect. I almost had her away from my damn life for good, but my cousin boy that she shot wanted to be greedy and take a payoff. Man, I hate that bitch probably more than I'm starting to hate Dino!"

Monique wanted to go to the kitchen and get a knife to stab Dino half to death with while he was sleeping. After she and Rell discussed more "hood news" and possible baby names, he ended the conversation telling her that his car alarm was going off and he'd hit her back later. Ready to get back to playing the game with Dino, she crept back toward the closed bedroom door. Turning the knob as quietly as possible, she was surprised when he unexpectedly snatched the door open, holding the other cordless phone in his hands.

"So, damn, Monique, it's like that, huh? You been rocking out with my boy, and y'all two motherfuckers been plotting against me! You a real bird for that shit! You done showed your true colors!"

She didn't know what to say or do. She was like a small mouse stuck in a trap. She was cornered and saw the rage in his eyes. She wanted to scream out for help, but before she could manage to get the words out, Dino's hands were wrapped around her throat and squeezing. Each second that passed she fought to stay alert. "Please, Dino, the baby."

"Rusty-faced bitch, please! Get the fuck all the way on. You mean you and that slimeball bastard Rell's seed? You mean *that* baby? Is *that* the one you talking about you want me to care about?" His grip tightened as his mind raced on how he was going to get Rell in the same situation that he now had Monique—cornered, scared, and begging for his life. Only seconds away from most definitely killing Monique, he let her go. As she dropped to her knees gasping for air, her now-blue lips quivering, Dino gathered some of his belongings throwing them in an oversized duffle bag. Still in his feelings, he stomped Monique in the stomach before leaving in search of Rell; apparently her baby daddy.

Who in the hell messing with my ride? Now ain't the time for trying to get down or over on a brother. Niggas better leave me be. Running to the window with his gun clutched in his hand, he was prepared to let loose, if need be. Seeing no one near his car, he clicked the alarm off, then reset it. *It must have been one of them damn stray cats around this son of a bitch apartment complex.* He wasn't going to allow no one to violate him or what belonged to him ever again. He'd been second best to Dino for years, but now, that was done. He was his own boss and was going to carry himself like one, even if that meant death or jail. That was the act that he put on for the outside world. In reality, Rell was trying to be hard. But after all the drama that had taken place over the last couple of months, especially Tiffany's death, he was drained. The plotting, the scheming, and just the game in general had him ready to give up.

Minutes later, Rell was sitting back in his favorite chair watching the news report about the tragic house fire and senseless assassination of five people, three being children. Ironically, he had no clue that one of the victims in this crime was the very female that started the fight that ultimately resulted in Tiffany's death. Rell had satisfaction and would never know it. Exhausted, he'd almost fallen asleep when his car alarm went off yet again. He jumped to his feet, this time swinging his front door wide open and darted outside. He was ready to put two in the head of any stray cat that he'd catch within five feet of his vehicle. Much to his dismay, it was not a stray cat that he found, but more than twenty-five guns aimed at him perched down behind various cars and pillars throughout the complex he called home.

"DEA Task Force! Drop your weapon and put your hands up," a voice rang out.

Rell was frozen in his tracks. His eyes darted from side to side, trying to peep out every single officer that was locked and loaded, prepared to do him harm. "Yeah? What the fuck if I don't?" he barked back while trying to convince himself he had a slim chance to come out of this alive and free.

"Look, no one has to get hurt! Just do as you're told! Drop your weapon and put your hands up! It's simple!"

Rell was done being anything other than a boss. He knew he'd done so much dirt; there was no telling exactly what they had on him. But whatever it was, he knew nine outta ten times he'd never see the light of day again once he was in handcuffs. Being in charge of his own destiny, Rell raised his gun.

Instead of handcuffs, he was taken away in a body bag headed to the morgue.

CHAPTER THIRTY-TWO

Mario drove over to Raven's house and saw what was left of the frame. Seeing several small shrines of flowers and teddy bears piled up on what was once the porch, he turned the bottle that he was drinking all the way up. After sitting there for close to an hour, he started his engine and drove over to the parking lot of the store where his brother Tone died. Going into the store, he grilled the clerk as if he was the police wanting to know what his brother's last minutes on earth were like. He wanted to view the security tape, but they swore to him that the homicide detectives investigating the case had confiscated it. Purchasing another bottle, Mario practically swallowed the fifth in three gulps. He'd been drunk since the moment he knew for sure Tone was gone. He was going to find his brother and Raven's killers if it was the last thing he was going to do. *These raggedy niggas up here is fucked up. Grand Rapids can't hold a real Detroit goon down!* Staggering, his eyes were barely open when he fell off the curb and into oncoming traffic. Thank God for Mario, his pain was brief.

Dino had been driving around for hours trying to figure out his next move. All his friends were either dead or had double-crossed him. He wanted to go and find Rell and split his shit to the white meat, but he was still trying to cope and process everything that he'd ear hustled up on earlier. He never knew what happened with Marlon and Dre. He assumed that Marlon had jumped in the driver's seat after he left the store and peeled off. Dino went to sleep believing that Marlon and Dre were somewhere tripping out about what popped off and how he'd pulled a disappearing act on all their asses. Dino was stressed out that Marlon was gone and Dre was gone also. He'd never talk shit with them again or clown the other one about this or that. He knew that they all chose to be in the streets and make money and with that decision came the threat of jail or death. Yet, like most people out doing what they do, neither one of those things they thought would be their fate. Now as Dino drove around in Monique's car unaware that the DEA Task Force was making its rounds and he was next on the list, all he could do was try his hardest to just say good-bye to the city he was born and raised in and jump on the freeway, destination unknown.

Sitting in the far rear side parking lot of Bob Evan's watching families go inside, he took stock about who he really was as a man. There it was; all the dirt he'd done and about the one person that never betrayed him or turned their back on him until he drew first blood: J-Rite. He wanted to call her or maybe just take his chances and go to the house that they once shared; after all, she was carrying his baby. But considering there was a war going on between them, he knew they were history. He pulled out of the parking lot and hit the road.

J-Rite wanted nothing more than to turn back the hands of time but knew she could not. She had been through hell and back and just wanted to get some rest. After trying to call Leesa a few more times and getting her voice mail, J-Rite popped two valiums and lay across the couch to take a nap. Shortly into her much-needed nap she thought she thought she heard a knock at her front door but was not totally sure. Praying to God it was Leesa who had come to her senses after listening to her messages or Mario coming back by to chill out, she opened the door without first asking who it was. Groggy, she was speechless as her jaw dropped open.

"Hey, Jessica, I missed you!"

Before she knew what was happening next, she was being shoved back inside the living room, knocked upside the head, and pushed down on the couch. J-Rite knew she'd taken two pills and that was one more than her small frame could ever take without being down for the count for days. When she took them, she had all intentions of just hibernating under the blanket until better days, no matter how long it would take. Now, here she was totally caught off guard and not in her right mind having to deal with this.

"Oh my God, what do you want? What are you doing here?" She held the side of her head not believing she'd been hit.

"I came to see you; to be with you. Wasn't that always the game plan? Wasn't that what we always said?" His words were deliberate, and his questions needed no answers. The expression on his face showed that he was here to claim what and who he felt was his one true love.

J-Rite tried to focus her eyes on her uninvited guest. She tried to think of what would make him think it was okay to just show up on her doorstep, but could not. So much time had gone by since they were together, his presence made no sense to her. In between Raven's and Tone's death, she had no time to deal in matters of the heart. She just wanted to mourn in peace. "Hey, listen, what was popping off then with us ain't popping now.

You know that. I told you a million times, but I guess you thought I was playing."

Word of Raven and her family's dreadful murder had traveled. It was being reported on just about every news station in the country, and Detroit was not the exception. Mike Mike had stolen one of his friend's cars and hit I-96. He had been off his meds for a few months and with J-Rite abruptly cutting him off from sending cash, he had been living life like a crazed man. He'd lost the house, sold all his video games for food, and oftentimes slept on the street if he had to. Mike Mike felt his life was perfect when he and J-Rite were together. It was torture for him to hear from the grapevine that she was up in Grand Rapids living life like it was golden; making money, driving good, eating good, and messing around with some new nigga, spending all her bread on him. Mike Mike was devastated his girl had just got up and thrown him and their love away like garbage. In his mentally deranged mind, the two of them had made a pact years ago that no one or nothing could ever truly break them apart. He never cared about her dancing or selling a little pussy here and there. Their bond was still their bond; at least in his eyes.

"I know you didn't mean what you were saying. I know that ho-ass nigga they said you was fucking with put you up to not talking to me anymore." Mike Mike hadn't had a haircut in what appeared to be several weeks, or even a bath. Jessica had never seen him look so bad and quickly realized he was having one of his infamous episodes when he was off his meds.

She sat back and let him rant and hopefully get it out of his system.

"Baby, look, I didn't mean to hit you like that. It's just that when I saw you I kinda had a flashback of how you been playing me far off to the left since you bailed. I know things weren't perfect, and I was gonna get a job. You just didn't give me time!"

"Crazy-ass nigga." She could hold her tongue no longer. "I did everything I could for you; for us. And all you wanted to do was play video games and smoke weed. Get the fuck on! Of course, I was gonna find me a real man and leave your ass alone!"

Jessica's words angered him even more. As he stood over her with his fist balled ready to attack, Mike Mike calmed himself down and smiled.

"What the fuck you smiling at like that?" Jessica hissed, wishing she had strength to get up on her feet and fight him toe to toe.

"A real man? Are you serious right about now? You mean, a man that was cheating on you with some other bitch he got pregnant? A man that was taking all your money spending it at the strip clubs and treating you like shit? A dude that couldn't come see you at court or give a damn that you lost his damn baby—that you should've never been thinking about having from jump! Or you mean that would beef with you and probably was the one that killed Raven and them kids?"

Jessica was stunned. She was speechless that Mike Mike was standing in her living room reading her like he had. "How . . ."

"What, you dumb bitch? How did I know? Because unlike your greedy out-for-self-opportunist ass, Raven didn't come up here, start making money, and turning her back on her friends back home. She told Wild Child what was going down up here, and she told me."

"Really?" J-Rite wanted to call Raven and chin check her for running off at the mouth and telling Wild Child all of her business, but she couldn't.

Mike Mike wasn't done with his tirade. "You was so busy saying I wasn't about nothing, but I ain't never did half the shit that lame Dino did to you, and you was just like, fuck me. Truth be told, it's your fault Raven and them kids dead, and everybody back home know it. They all talking about if you never came up here in the first place dealing with Buzzy's good snitching in the fed joint ass, Raven would've never followed!"

J-Rite's spirit was crumbling. She knew half, if not all, of what Mike Mike was saying was true, as harsh as he'd delivered it and as painful as it was to hear. Lately, her life had been turned upside down and full of regret. Ready to just give up, she had no more fight left in her. "Look, you probably right. I know I been leaving foul, and, yeah, that was wrong for me to stop looking out for you because of some nigga; especially one that got something to do with Tone and Raven getting killed."

On bended knee, Mike Mike perched on the side of the couch. Using the backside of his hand, he softly caressed the side of Jessica's face where he'd struck her. When she didn't flinch, part of him prayed that he had a chance to make things right between them. "Okay, baby, I know I look fucked up, and I know I ain't got jack shit to offer like before, but can you at least just come back to Detroit with me and chill? Maybe we can go somewhere and watch movies all night like we used to. Maybe that's what you need to do to get your mind right; get out of this bad-luck city. What you think? All this bullshit will be here when you get back."

Jessica still wasn't thinking straight, but had been missing her old life. Although Mike Mike was talking out of the side of his neck, for the most part, he was right. He'd never fucked her over or did her wrong like Dino had on so many occasions. Maybe a trip back home was what she needed. Besides, then she could get him some help to get back on his meds and make sure he got back on his feet. "You know what? You right. That's what the fuck I'm gonna do."

Mike Mike didn't expect things to really go his way. In reality, he'd come there to kill himself and Jessica, having nothing else to live for. Now, she was flipping the script, letting him feel they had another chance at a new life. "Are you for real?"

After having Mike Mike help her gather a few of her things to toss in a suitcase, she tried to call Leesa and Mario once more before leaving and received their voice mails. Still weak, she leaned on her ex's arm as they walked to the rental she was still driving.

As Mike Mike went toward the rear of the vehicle to put her bag in the trunk, he noticed a flat tire. Reassuring her that he was good to drive, she got in the stolen car he'd come in and settled into the passenger seat slumped over, wanting to sleep. Now totally high as a kite off the pills, Jessica didn't care that the steering wheel column was broken and that he'd started the engine with a screwdriver. All she knew that she was on her way home. Mike Mike was turning left off her block at the exact same time the DEA Task Force was turning onto it. Not paying attention to the car that was not on their description of vehicles Jessica Sanders was known to drive, they kept the federal convoy moving, ready to raid and execute yet another person on their indictment list.

CHAPTER THIRTY-THREE

Hazel and her people were livid. After months of investigations, surveillances, and losing sleep, some of their raids had definitely not gone as planned. Coming up empty-handed at J-Rite's residence was one of them. They'd searched every single inch of her home, and there was no sign of the small-in-size wannabe drug queen. She had vanished, but Hazel was confident she'd catch up with her sooner or later. Her years in law enforcement taught her that females like J-Rite couldn't stay out of the limelight for long; they had to be seen and heard.

Receiving a call from the captain in charge of the raid of Dino's home, Hazel's spirits were once again dampened hearing that their target Dino, like J-Rite, had somehow eluded capture. After kicking the door off the hinges, the team discovered his girl Monique, pregnant on the floor, throwing up blood. The only thing she was interested in was hopefully saving the life of her unborn child. As the ambulance took her away, she was more than eager to tell them that Dino had not only tried to kill her, but he was in her car. Monique provided them with all the information so they could track the GPS and locate the vehicle and Dino.

Mike Mike hated to wake Jessica up, but he looked at the dashboard and saw that the gas light had just popped on. Taking it upon himself, he unzipped her purse and took a twenty-dollar bill out of the many rubber banded rolls of cash she had stuffed in there. *Same old Jessica, always about her money,* Mike Mike smiled as he pulled off the freeway and into a gas station. Pulling up at pump number seven, he reached under the seat retrieving his screwdriver to turn the car off. Watching her curled up in the front seat with her jacket serving as a blanket, he got out to pay for the gas admiring the pearl-white sports car on the other side; pump eight. Looking back over his shoulder at the car, he grabbed the handle of the door, not watching where he was going. "Damn, my bad." Mike Mike immediately took a cop apologizing to the guy he'd accidentally bumped into coming out of the gas station.

"Yo, you dirty, stinking-ass nigga! Watch where the fuck you going! And, damn, nigga, get a haircut or some shit!"

Mike Mike was unbothered by what the guy had said. First, because it was true he did smell badly and knew it, but second, he was on cloud nine because he had Jessica back on his side; what he'd been praying for since the morning she walked in with the plan to leave.

After giving the cashier the money, he pumped his gas, then pulled over to the far side of the station to put some air in all of the bald tires. Mike Mike didn't want to take any chances on him and Jessica getting back to Detroit where they both belonged. Putting air in the last of the four, he dropped the hose to the ground as over ten police cars, some unmarked, roared up into the gas station. He didn't know what to do. This wasn't who he was, a car thief. He just wanted to find J-Rite, maybe find the courage to kill her and himself, then rest in peace. Now, he was about to go to jail for stealing a car.

Frozen, he took a deep breath, then exhaled as all the cars whizzed by him and surrounded the pearl-white sports car and the rude guy that was sitting behind the wheel rolling up a blunt. As the cops jumped out of their cars, guns in hand yelling "DEA Task Force, put your hands up!" Mike Mike looked up to sky thanking God for sparing him from that bullshit. Seeing that they were all preoccupied snatching the man out of the car, slamming him down onto the ground, Mike Mike started the engine and eased out of the back way of the gas station. J-Rite never once woke up to see Dino getting arrested. In bliss, she was deep in a dream that she was back home in Detroit living her old life.

And soon she would be.

THE END

ORDER FORM
URBAN BOOKS, LLC
97 N. 18th Street
Wyandanch, NY 11798

Name: (please print):_____

Address: _____

City/State: _____

Zip: _____

QTY	TITLES	PRICE
	16 On The Block	$14.95
	A Girl From Flint	$14.95
	A Pimp's Life	$14.95
	Baltimore Chronicles	$14.95
	Baltimore Chronicles 2	$14.95
	Betrayal	$14.95
	Black Diamond	$14.95
	Black Diamond 2	$14.95
	Black Friday	$14.95
	Both Sides Of The Fence	$14.95
	Both Sides Of The Fence 2	$14.95
	California Connection	$14.95

Shipping and handling-add $3.50 for 1st book, then $1.75 for each additional book.

Please send a check payable to:
Urban Books, LLC
Please allow 4–6 weeks for delivery